City of

City of Birds

Elisha Reids

Elisha Reids

City of Birds

Elisha Reids

ISBN: 978-1-3999-4179-2

Authors Note

City of Birds is a New Adult, Dystopian, Romance.
If you need to read the Trigger Warnings, they are as followed:
Mental and physical abuse, descriptions of violence, self-harm, strong language, anxiety, and depressive thoughts.

City of Birds

Grandma, you always knew I'd be a writer, even before I knew it myself.

To all the people who suffer in silence, this is for you...

Elisha Reids

The Unity Building, Citadel, Altaras

Elyria Nightingale

Fire dances across the sky, the embers rising like shooting stars. Thick, black smoke clouds above like a blanket. If I close my eyes, I can almost hear the screams, but the roar of the flames engulfs the sound.
All I can do is watch the city I despise crash and burn because of me...

Chapter One

Before

My mother always told me I was born a fighter, kicking and screaming as soon as I came into this world. It was probably because some part of my brain already knew I was being brought into a cruel place, dictated by monsters. The only reason I did not become a cynical and atrocious girl is because of the love and devotion my parents give me and my siblings, bringing us up to be empathetic and kind. Despite this love from my parents, tonight I'm deceiving them.

Holding my breath, I pause as the floorboard creaks against my foot. Silently, I curse this old house for nearly exposing my movements. The sound of my heartbeat thumps in my ear as if it's the loudest thing under this roof. My family are long asleep, but I still fear the slightest noise will wake them. Testing the board with my toe again, to my luck it stays quiet, signaling that I can walk on.

Slowly I open my twin sisters' door to retrieve one of Lila's gowns; she loves to play dress up, even at sixteen — she owns the most beautiful ones out of all of us, using them merely to perform , showing off and prancing around like she's better than all of us. If any of us were to be an elite, it would be her. We're always clashing heads. She's so caught up in the luxury of Altaras: an air head with no concern for anything that doesn't directly affect her. Gia is the softer sister; her empathy and selflessness is the water to Lila's fire – and one does not exist without the other. The twins are inseparable, even if they are nothing alike.

It is the first of the month — a ball night. The first ball I'll ever attend.
Our government, the Consulate, hosts balls at Centralis. They last all night long. So, to conceal my actions from my family, I'm attending later than most. My parents have always been invited to go; however, in recent years, they have been firm in their decision not to - making that choice for all of us.

Without hesitation, I pull her dress from the wardrobe as quietly as I can and soundlessly leave the room, careful not to wake the sleeping girls. Passing the fraying wallpaper and broken floorboard — that will never be fixed — I creep back along the hallway that leads to my room. This house is even older than my grandparents were, and it shows. I step into the gown; it's a pretty sage green with pearls woven into the bodice and sleeves only just concealing the tops of my shoulders. A perfect dress to blend in with the other fancy gowns soon to litter the rooms of Centralis.

Slowly moving down the stairs so as not to wake anyone, I grab my boots and cloak, heels in hand. Walking to the mansion requires suitable footwear and I will never get far in heels high enough to break my ankle. The air is fresher tonight — a sign that winter is coming — so I pull my cloak tight around my body as I make my way through the dimly lit maze of houses. The houses here are as old as the trees, some of them crumbling, tiles missing and windows thin as paper. But the houses change as I take the shortcut_through the elite estate — the homes are too big, too grand, in a bid to show off their wealth in competition with the other families.

It doesn't take long before Centralis can be seen as I round the corner; it sits above on the hill as soon as you exit the estate. No one occupies the grand mansion: built solely for the purpose of socialite events like this ball, held during the first day of every month in the heart of Altaras. It's where the richest people of the city come to exploit their wealth — amongst other things. The elites will be on show: gossiping, drinking, and dancing with everyone, reveling in each other's presence after hiding away in their mansions.

The elites are the wealthiest in the whole of Altaras; their families from the lineage of the first founders of our homeland. They built this city to protect us, to keep our people safe, so we could prosper and live in harmony, free from the outside world and the people that live there. Elite families mostly work in the Unity building, situated inside the Citadel, alongside the board of Commanders — the select few elites that have the authority to run Altaras. Then, there are those elites that just don't work at all, their family name worth more than any job could offer. The elites perceive themselves vastly superior to the rest of us *lower folk*.

But still, at these events, everyone gets to wear their finest dresses and suits, no expense spared for the extravagant decor and the banquets of food on display. Men talk politics and women talk matches. A match would grant me status, safety, and some power within the elites. Aligning myself with one of them would change my family's lives.

I turned eighteen three weeks ago, my birthday in the peak of the summer sun when it shines the brightest and emits the hottest rays. With that comes new responsibility. Now comes the time to start thinking of my family's future —

whether that be working for the Consulate or marrying into the world of elites — I will make these choices myself. With or without the blessing of my family.

Nightingale is my mother's name; our family took it to honor her lineage, my father is a merchant who trades for the Consulate, for Altaras. My parents stopped attending the balls after my brother was born. They both felt their family was complete and grew tired of the façade, for the socialites were draining and pointless to them. Drinking and dancing throughout the entire night was no longer appealing, nor did they care to listen to the rich talking of their riches, or the gossiping rumours spread by the mothers. My father did not need to listen again to the men discussing politics or trade having already attended the many meetings which briefed him well enough.

Carriages of white and black file up the road, pulled by stallions. No one who attends ever walks, always driven to the front gates to make an entrance. I count twenty-five carriages, pulled by horses of all colours, as I make my way up. More have already entered or will arrive later as the balls always last until the early hours of the morning. It's the most exciting time of the month for most of Altaras. My breathing hitches, palms becoming sweaty as the realisation sets in. I'm going to the ball. I have never even been inside Centralis, yet I'm about to walk straight in. Brushing my hands off my cloak and tracing my fingers through my hair — *this is real,* I think. I can do this. This is what I want to do.

Before I enter, I scope out the area, concealing myself within the tree line leading up towards the mansion. I want to be as discreet as I can in case my parents catch wind of my attendance here. I'll slip in without anyone noticing. I wait, looking to find the best entry point. If I walk through the front entrance, I will be asked for my family name to gain access and, without fail, the knowledge of me being here will instantly return to my parents.

The back of Centralis has several doors and paths for the wagons to pull up, mostly used for the transportation of food. Finally, after waiting several more moments, a door opens. A girl dressed as a waiter steps out and lights a cigarette. She exhales the smoke and sighs, leaning against the brick wall. She must be one of the staff working tonight. Once she's finished, she crushes the embers with her foot and heads back inside, slamming the door behind her. Emerging from beneath the cover of trees and the darkness, I dart to the door. Checking my surroundings with each step taken, I release a breath I didn't realise I was holding, until my hand is reaching to pull it open.

Inside, there's a long corridor with four metal doors either side, and one situated at the end. It looks like a kitchen basement, illuminated by horrid florescent lighting. No one seems to be here and there's no sign of the waiter as I hesitantly walk in. All I hear is the sound of my boots upon the floor, clacking with each step. Behind the door, at the end of the corridor, voices, and metal crash together, accompanied by the sound of water bubbling and people shouting. *The kitchen.* I lower the hood of my cloak. If I step through the door looking like this, they will soon become suspicious. Word travels fast around here.

I take off the cloak and put on my heels. If anyone asks, I'm simply lost and heading for the ball. No one of importance knows my face; Altaras is huge — it is unlikely anyone will know who I am, so it's not hard to go unnoticed. Straightening my back and holding my head high, I psych myself up, ready for my performance. Turning the handle, I'm met with a flurry of people rushing about with pots and vegetables, trays of champagne flutes and canapes. Not one person looks up from their task: heads down, busy, and preoccupied. I quickly waltz past a waiter holding a tray overflowing with canapes; he doesn't look twice at me.

Glancing around, I'm not sure where to go...

I spot a door where the waiters, carrying their full platters of food, head through and I know that's my exit. Hurrying, I pass the busy collection of waiters and chefs at work. The waiters file out to a long red carpeted corridor, high chandeliers casting light on the grand oil portraits of the elders — the men who saved and built Altaras so long ago. This is a place fit for royalty. Spotting a cabinet beneath one of the paintings, I quickly open it to find nothing inside. I place my cloak and boots inside, so as not to draw attention upon entering the main hall. Wearing a ball gown whilst carrying a pair of dirty boots would not fit in with this crowd.

The last of the waiters round the corner, so after closing the cabinet, I stand, ears following the noise of music and drunken laughter growing louder with each minute. Before I proceed, I notice a large regal mirror perched on a table, there to flatter the invited guests.

My cheeks are flushed from the mixture of the cold air and the tension of the past minutes; adrenaline and curiosity rushes through me, I'm completely out of my comfort zone in this place. But I must channel this tension into confidence, I must put on an act in front of these people, not to seem unsettled or anxious.

Straightening out the front of my dress, I shake out my dark curls, so they fall against my back.
Two men in suits hold open the doors to the hall and they stare straight ahead as I pass. A lump forms in the back of my throat as I survey the sea of people: men grab onto their wives — or women not their wives — laughing and shouting to one another. Other older women and girls stand alone at the sidelines, assessing the prey in the middle of the dance floor like vultures. All draped in jewels, with dresses crafted in every colour and fabric you could think of. The room emulates an artist's pallet: rich deep reds, to violets, to emerald greens. Silks to velvets. Groups gather and huddle, darting looks at one another, and casting the occasional glare of hatred or jealousy to those around them.

Glasses are constantly topped up by blank faced waiters, weaving in and out of the guests like ants — or rodents, which elites openly call them. I walk along the outskirts of the room, matching some names to faces, recalling those from Consulate press briefings; always held inside the Unity building and broadcast into our homes. Homes abruptly invaded; our screens automatically consumed by the alert, signaling that the briefing was about to commence before streaming to our live feed. On rare occasions, if father's presence was demanded, we would all go to the square inside the Citadel and watch the briefing on a huge projector. A show of absolute control, and usually brutal. I shudder at the recollection and tell myself to regain my focus.

There is a corner of the hall where no one is standing – the perfect spot for me to gather myself. Huge floor to ceiling windows tower behind me, the crowd at my front.

Anyone looking will think I'm just another carnivorous girl, waiting for the perfect boy to prey on.

Picking up a glass of champagne from the passing waiter, I note he too has the same blank expression. I take a sip; the bubbles and sharpness are a foreign taste for my tongue, but I can get used to this.

No one seems to notice me, not one glare or whisper or head turn in my direction. Am I invisible to them? If Lila were here, she would be in the centre of the hall, making everyone laugh, shining with her biggest smile, and twirling across the dance floor with some unlucky boy. Whereas I, I am the type to stand on the sidelines, carefully watching, circling a little, and seeing what I can learn by keeping my mouth shut and ears open. A hawk watching its prey.

Chapter Two

By the time the clock strikes three, I am tired and irritable from an unsuccessful night, learning nothing of importance. I decide to go home. Placing my empty glass on a table, I walk towards the doors to leave. At least this has been an eye opener for the socialite balls, knowing what to expect for when I next return. I push the thoughts of failure away, instead thinking of how to act at the next ball. I must talk to these people if I plan to ever find a match or work here.

"Leaving so soon?" a deep voice asks. I spin to face the man behind me, greeted by an impeccably smart, black suit. Tilting my head, I look to his face and almost gasp.

Handsome is a light way to describe this boy. Overwhelmingly *striking*, seems more fitting. His height towers above me, his body muscular and broad. He seems a little older than I with a sharp jawline, high cheek bones, and big brown, almost black, eyes complimented by his shaggy blond hair. Long at the top with a shorter length on the sides, it makes him look more unique than most Altaras rich boys with their clean perfect look.

How did I not spot him in the crowd? He must have been talking amongst the girls because I have never seen this boy before —an elite hidden away from the rest of us, perhaps.

"Umm, I —" I'm stammering, unsure how to respond. The way he's peering down at me, unnerves me, studying me like I'm an animal in a cage. His eyes rake over me with raised eyebrows, as though expecting me to smile or blush.

He laughs, a grin creeping upon his lips, "Have I taken your breath away?" His quick response catches me off guard, but he continues before I can reply, "Surely not. You were the one doing that to me all night."

He straightens his jacket and holds out his hand for me to shake; I grasp it then he pulls me closer, leaning in to whisper, "I was enjoying watching you watch everyone else. But I couldn't let you walk out of here without getting your name first."

Confidence radiates off him, directing our conversation without letting me get a word in. Even though his demeanour is cocky and self-righteous, there is an air of serenity about him.

Looking directly into his eyes, I have the oddest sense of butterflies flitting in my stomach as my cheeks flush a furious pink.

How does this stranger have this effect on me already? I shouldn't be shocked when someone comes to say hello... it's not like I hid my face or went unseen.

"I've not seen you here before, is this your first time attending a ball? A medi perhaps?"

I laugh at his slight abruptness, but also at the sour intent behind *medi,* as though it was an insult. At a station below elites, medis have always been seen as less than, but his tone told me he knew I was not an elite just by looking at me.

"Well, if you let me get a word in, I'll be able to answer at least one of your questions," I say with slight annoyance to my voice.

"My name is Lila, and I've just moved from the outskirts of the city. My Father just secured a new job in the Citadel, and no, I have never been to one of these before."

He smiles, exposing a glimpse of his perfectly white teeth, somehow making his handsome face that bit more handsome.

"That's what I thought. There has never been a girl as pretty as you attend this ball. I would have known about it," he smirks. "The girls here bore me, but you have sparked my interest."

His dark eyes glimmer as he looks into mine and I'm suddenly trapped in his gaze. Conviction oozes from him, knowing that right now he has me just where he wants me. "Well, I'm flattered..." I trail off. I don't even know his name.

And as if he read my mind, "It's Jude, by the way. Jude Lightfall."

The feelings from before: the butterflies, my rosy cheeks, that sense of enrapture, sours by that one word.

Lightfall.

The family whom I know to be the enemy.

I don't want him to see my look of complete disdain, so I cover it with a mask of surprise, hoping my face does not reflect my thoughts.

The Lightfall family — well at least his father, Marik — works for the Consulate: one of the Commanders, overseeing tactical military and weaponry for Altaras. A family firmly belonging to the elite heritage that has been in place for as long as the Consulate has been established.

The board of Commanders are ruthless, power-hungry men that dictate our city. No one dares break the sacred laws of the Consulate for fear of disappearing like those before who grew too curious. Being executed in front of a crowd for treason is a common occurrence in Altaras, a violent tactic employed to keep order amongst our people. Countless lives have been killed by his word: the Altaras people tortured and executed by his guards for any act of defiance.

Hatred is bred from his power, with followers demanding and reveling in the suffering dealt by his cruel hand. The Consulate demand mandatory viewings of executions, regularly broadcast for the people of Altaras to watch — showcasing their power and forcing their people to obey.

My parents had always tried to hide us from the screens, shutting us in our rooms as soon as the alert for the viewings flashed upon the screens in our home. Fear was always there, clear in their eyes as they rushed us out, protecting us from the horrors about to be shown. But that very first time... they had not been quick enough, unable to usher me from sight as I witnessed the execution of a man on their bloodied public stage; the loud bang as his body crumpled to the floor. Red dark liquid seeped from his body. I knew he was dead. My mother looked to me in dismay, her features softening as she brought me in for a hug, whispering repeatedly that it was going to be okay. My father decided that day to tell me of the corrupt nature of Altaras and the fear ingrained into its people.

I was ten years old. The nightmares never stop.

The constant showings of their executions and beatings instilled that fear among us, to warn us: do not step out of line.

His family name is always spoken of with a hint of distaste but with an even greater hint of fear.

I just didn't know he had a *son.*

And I have told him a lie, pretending that my father works in the very same place as his does. Even if this is a big city, he is sure to catch me out.

"Yes, Lightfall is my family name. I have a lot to live up to." Still gripping tightly to my hand, I want to retch and pull away, to get away from him and everything his family stands for. The feeling of giddiness has quickly turned to distrust and loathing.

"That's some act to follow. I never knew the Lightfalls had a son?" I say, hiding my disgust as I watch his face. His eyes darken.

I wonder how often he comes to the balls if no one really knows much about him?

"I'm the family secret," he jibes. "My mother likes to keep me hidden, doesn't want me swept up in all of this." He motions behind him, gesturing to the other guests. "She's quite protective, and for good reason. In fact, I have only been to the ball a handful of times. But I'm finding it's a good place to unwind," he says with a crack of his neck. "Enough about me, I want to know more about you... Lila." A wry smile creeps across his lips as he says my sister's name. His eyes never leave mine. They almost make me melt. Almost.

I feel stupid for giving him her name now that I've learnt his. I can't chance word getting out that I was here, but if it did my parents would never believe that little Lila came to the ball.

"Ah, there's not much to know Jude," I reply, holding his stare. "But it's getting late now, and I need to be getting home. Maybe I'll see you around sometime?"

Smiling one final time — a forced grin, or is it a grimace? — I finally remove my hand from his.

"Oh, there is so much more to know about you, sweet Lila. And I can't wait to find out," he answers, his lips curling into a devilish smile. "And I will definitely be seeing you soon," he finishes with a wink.

I turn and head towards the doors. "What is your last name, Lila?" he calls after me, his deep voice sending shivers down my spine. I spin to face him, whilst retreating backwards towards the exit.

His hands are now stuffed into his pockets, so incredibly tall amongst those dancing and standing near him. Effortlessly attractive — a thought I wish I did not have about a *Lightfall.*

"That's way too much information for me to disclose just yet," I say. "I'm sure I'll see you around though." I take one last look at him.

Behind, I see the girls watching our encounter beginning to whisper, shooting me looks of hatred and jealousy. Barely gone from his side, they make a beeline for Jude. Maybe they already know who he is, or maybe they just can't wait to find out.

My smile fades as I turn back towards the door. *It's fine.* Jude may be a pretentious *ass,* but he could help me in my plans. If I play this right, he could be my ticket into the Consulate. He could help me to provide for my family. For now, I will have to bury my feelings of hatred for his father and their corrupt ideology of violence and suffering, and play them at their own game of manipulation.

It's all about the chase, I think, as I try to convince myself that this is a good idea. I will just have to endure him for the sake of getting my family a higher rank in Altaras' societal standing.

Swiftly, I make my way down the hall, towards my boots, the kitchen, and home. Back into the cold night. Jude Lightfall might just be what I've been searching for.

Let the games begin.

Chapter Three

By the time I return home, it is nearly dawn. The streetlights are still on, and the air has become dewy, the morning sun about to peak above the trees, waking Altaras with its glow.

Mother normally wakes up when the sun starts shining, so I am good for time. I open the door and quietly travel upstairs to my room, hoping for a few hours' sleep before the day begins. I do not forget to place Lila's exquisite dress back in her wardrobe before slipping under my covers and letting sleep consume me. I surrender to exhaustion as the thoughts of the Lightfall family slip from my mind.

The smell of eucalyptus and lavender oils floods my senses and, as my eyes open, I see mother standing over my bed. People often say I am the spitting image of her.

"Elyria, you and your mother look like twins!" my professors would say — always the male ones, that is. We have the same slight frame, the olive skin, the dark raven hair, and the distinct blood red eyes. The beautiful crimson eyes that bore into your soul, always making passersby do a double take. The identifier of a Nightingale: the eyes. Each of us have them: a family trait passed down, a gene from my grandmother on my mother's side. But my mother and I are the only ones with raven hair — she and I are so alike in that regard: same full lips, same high cheekbones, and sharp jawline. Lila and Gia bear father's height, just an inch off me

already, with heart shaped faces and bright blond hair; Alec has his mop of darker blond, a mix of us all.

But features aside, mother has always been my opposite. Whilst she is quiet in her demeanour, careful not to hurt a fly, I can be stubborn, never backing down from what I know is right, even if it makes a scene. Mother makes herself small to forever keep the peace. I can't fault her for that: the tiny bird that everyone loves.

"Good morning, Elyria," she sings pulling back my curtains. Beams of light suddenly flood the room making me wince and groan and I pull the blanket high above my head. I have not had enough sleep!

"You're going to be late for class if you don't get up," she says, ushering me out of bed. She tugs at the bottom of the blanket as the light from the window blinds my eyes.

"Yes mother." I groan again. I have never been a morning person. Mother used to wake us up early when we were children, making us recite passages from our textbooks, make our minds sharp with completing puzzles or telling us a riddle we needed to solve before breakfast. *Our minds must be sharp,* she would say. But now we have gotten older, and much more resistant to our morning mind tasks, the riddles and puzzles are left for Alec.

Once I'm changed, I can hear the squabbling from my sisters in the kitchen, typical of most mornings.

"But Gia you can't have your hair in a braid today... I'm having *mine* in a braid! People will think you're copying me!" Lila whines.

"Oh, of course I'm copying you," Gia responds, rolling her eyes, "You're so fashionable and pretty and popular, Lila. Why wouldn't I want to have my hair exactly like you?" Her sarcastic tone drifts over Lila's head which, in turn, has us all quietly laughing. Lila shoots her a glare when she hears our chuckles and, without fuss, Gia starts to un-braid her long blond hair, letting it flow loose around her face. Gia — the water to Lila's fire.

"Morning everyone," I say as I sit down at the table. Mother passes me a coffee. It's hot and bland but does the trick. Our kitchen is a warren: small ceilings and laden shelves crammed with pots and plates. Every surface is covered — things we might need for the hot summers, things we might need for the cold winters — with no free space to put it all away. The mornings are chaotic, with Lila always finding something to moan about.

"I can't wait around after lessons today and I must run some errands. Lila and Gia, you'll have to walk Alec home," I continue between sips of boiling coffee.

"I can walk alone!" Alec interrupts. Even at eleven, he acts like an adult, raising his voice when he doesn't get his own way.

But everyone knows it is too dangerous to be walking the streets on your own, especially when you are so young. It's better not to risk getting into trouble with no-one else around. Too many people have gone missing to chance it.

"Alec, you will not walk those streets without your sisters with you! You know this and I don't like it when you fuss." Mother says nothing more and turns her attention back to the worries arising from the latest Consulate briefing.

Another attempt of treason last night. Someone from Penury had tried to gain entry to Altaras by scaling the city wall! Yet how can this happen? A one-hundred-foot fortress wall encloses the city, built by our ancient hands to keep the Penurians out.

Penury — past the wall that circles Altaras, the poorest part of our country, Ceraea. The place where no one wants to live, home to the people we desperately want to keep out of our city.

Our fortress wall would take someone half a day to reach one side to the other, the terrain beyond stretching for miles. The Consulate keep the tightest control on our borders. We have grown up with stories of Penury and their savages that try to steal from us, break into our homes, and take what is ours. Penurian children cry at night because their bellies are empty. Screaming in hunger, the only food they can get is from their failing crops. Crops their families *try* to grow in the wasteland that is their home. Their adults are left illiterate, for what need is there for education when your life leads to nothing? We are fearful of Penury — for them to come to us or for us to be sent there. Life there is not living. It's barely *surviving.*

I've never laid eyes on the people that live there. It's forbidden to step foot near the gates of the wall, let alone past it. The tree line that surrounds the wall is under constant watch. We do not mix with Penurians. Ever.

Seclusion and prosperity are our way of life — ideology drummed into us by the Consulate. The wall maintains our seclusion, but even at a hundred feet high, people *still* attempt to scale it. The last man who did was apparently shot on sight.

This is not an unusual report. Consulate briefings always tell us of the numerous attempts to breach our walls; they say the people of Penury grow restless and vengeful, wanting to harm and steal from us. For us to survive we need to live inside these walls. Altaras can only prosper and grow from our seclusion.

But the next report is what suddenly grabs my attention. Idris Amal, Commander of communications in

Altaras — the director of all briefings — announces a murder at the ball. The body of an Altaras guard was found in the bushes near Centralis in the early hours of the morning.

My blood runs cold. A guard? Killed? Could it be Penurians? Did they breach the wall without being detected? I never saw a thing. The questions rattle in my mind.

My eyes search the board of Commanders for Marik Lightfall. Without a shadow of doubt, he would have ordered the brutal execution at the wall. Marik's there, sat in a grand chair amongst the other men on the platform. He's easy to spot with his stark white hair and piercing blue eyes: the image of icy death. Jude doesn't have his eyes, but nevertheless, he could still be hiding the same evil within his.

Marik doesn't say anything at first, his expression hard and set in silence, only nodding to Idris Amal's words. Finally, after Idris confirms Altaras is safe and that the situation is under control, Marik Lightfall speaks.

"We all know how imperative it is to keep our borders secure - to keep our families safe from these *savages.*" His blue eyes fill with inhumane rage as he speaks. "As long as I stand, I will uphold the duty of protecting this great city at whatever cost."

The only thought I now have is that Marik Lightfall is pure evil.

My mind flashes back to when I was thirteen. The Consulate ordered a power outage on our housing estates in the darkest and coldest winter we had had for years — a punishment for the people of Altaras over something trivial... I now can't even remember the reason. The power and hot water didn't turn on for fourteen days, the Consulate oblivious to the pain and suffering it caused. Finally, everything was switched back on,

but no one dared to question what had happened. The elite's power, however, was not cut off.
Our Consulate have authority to do whatever they want, whenever they like, and often just to prove their point.
Once Marik Lightfall finishes his speech, Idris Amal thanks him and the other Commanders for their briefings and the screen switches off.
I glance at my siblings; Lila and Gia have already turned their attention away from the briefing to talk between themselves. Alec was too busy eating his food to pay attention, but my mother's brows furrow as she returns to washing up. I don't question her. News of an executed Penurian is common but news of a guard being killed is rare. Mother never wants to talk about what we hear, her solemn silence now clouding the earlier buoyant mood in the kitchen. Lila and Gia gather their things and Alec quickly finishes his breakfast. Soon we're out the door and heading towards the school building.

Here in Altaras, there are three schools: lower, middle, and upper. The Consulate work tirelessly to select the brightest and the best from the earliest years. In the lower years, all children study the same comprehensive curriculum. Failure to thrive is looked upon with great dissatisfaction, even from the youngest students. Middle school is a punishing barrage of constant assessments, with the professors informing the Consulate of pupils' successes and failures. Selection of the brightest is what every parent hopes for, deselection a cruel blow to future prospects. The brightest move to upper school where their talents are honed. Finally, those with the highest academic awards — or often the wealthiest — will be chosen for specialist schooling and attend a graduate programme. I will never make that class; I am not an academic and my family are not wealthy. Some elites never join the city system and have the privilege of private schooling, never mixing with the likes of us. Out of sight, like Jude Lightfall, I wonder?

The board of Commanders enforce mandatory scripts for all professors. No deviation, and no student questions to be answered. Our historical scripts are read to us when we enter middle year – when the Consulate feel we are old enough to appreciate our city's history...

Hundreds of years ago, a group of town elders, the founding fathers of Altaras, gathered to discuss their failing crops; the ground had become desolate, and nothing would grow. Children started to become sick, mothers too weak to care for them. With winter approaching, the families would starve if they did not act quickly. They decided to travel north – something the town had not done for many years. Young and old died on the journey but, after the long expedition, they finally found salvation: ground so lush that seedlings took right away. Homes were built, families recovered and grew in number. By the following winter, they had more food than they knew what to do with. But news travelled and stories of their salvation were heard in neighbouring lands. Desperate for what the elders had built, others wanted to take it for themselves, even if in doing so, it destroyed the crops and left the townspeople with nothing. With the prospect of wars ahead, the elders decided to protect their people to preserve life and prosper amongst only themselves. So, they built the wall, choosing solitude within their sanctuary: Altaras.

Children listen to the story in awe, yet I always wondered why the elders did not choose to help everyone. To keep the gates open for everyone to use the land. Land that didn't belong to just them.

The professors never speak of other lands in Ceraea; they answer no questions — only repeating the scripts. Only ever telling us of the sacrifices the elders made to build our empire. Details of Altaras' trades are still unknown to us; how it worked then and how it works now, all cloaked in mystery. My father knows, but he never divulges.

The little we do know of Ceraea, is that there are other lands out there. Those beyond Penury are desolate, savage, and unimportant to Altaras. There is no reason for us to know more. The Consulate is certain of our city's power, and that our lives here are incomparable to anything outside. Why would we be curious when our land is lush with promises of more? The ground we walk on is rich; we can grow as many crops as we desire; our water is clear; our air is pure, and our knowledge and scientific advancements are unlike anything outside of these walls. We ask no questions — questions are not tolerated.

Yet, I often ask myself, if these other lands are so unimportant to us — why do the Commanders need merchants? What trades are happening across the city? What happens beyond the gates? The lands *must* have some value; they just aren't telling us.

Someone is shouting as I walk down the hall after lessons, the last hour spent learning how to cross stitch to perfection.

"Elyria, Elyria!"

I spin to face the embarrassingly loud shouting, already knowing it's Clover by the sound of her shrill voice. Beloved Clover, my closest friend. Joined to my hip ever since lower year when we sat next to each other in class. Constantly punished by our professor for talking too much but always loving the time spent together in detention.

Clover Lacewood is an elite, but never shows it. Her father works for the Consulate as one of the many advisers to the board of Commanders. Much like the Commanders' lineage, most of the advisers can trace their ancestry back to the first elders that built Altaras.

I had once thought that Clover's father would be best placed to advise me on working for the Consulate, but even after all these years, I've never met him. Clover's father is never around, always in meetings in the Unity building, cooped up within the Citadel walls. Knowing that he is absent from her life most of the time, I never ask Clover about him. As my only friend, I never want her to assume I'm taking advantage of her wealth or her position. Her friendship means more to me than that. Clover is one of the good ones. One of the few.

"I've been looking for you!" she sings, her voice airy as she comes to a halt in front of me. "Are we still going?" Her long auburn hair is tied with a ribbon in a low bun at the nape of her neck, framing her pretty face, showing off her small nose, high arching brows and heart shaped mouth. Her rosy cheeks are slightly more flushed than usual from the brisk walk over.

Elites question our friendship as she lowers her rank merely by being with me. What does she get from our friendship? Others are confused at how her charisma and charm aligns with my blunt demeanour. The other girls in class turn away from me, as I do to them. I've never cared for them. Why would I want to gossip or talk about potential matches with them? That's all they *ever* seem to talk about.

But Clover and I work well together, like Lila and Gia. *Fire and water.* We share the same passions and, for the past couple of weeks since we both turned eighteen, we have been walking to the edge of the borders. To the wall.

Chapter Four

Curiosity gets the better of both of us. We're more alike than my sisters and I in that sense.

"Of course, we are Clovey… but do you want to draw any more attention to us and what we're doing, especially after what happened last night at the ball?" I say sternly, but with a hushed voice.

She laughs as she responds, holding her hands up in defense. "I forgot! Totally my bad!"

Shaking my head in defeat, we link arms and walk out of the class building towards the back paths of Altaras.

"Let's only stay for a few minutes this time Elyria, I was getting worried last time. I really don't want to get caught by anyone." Clover keeps her voice low as we make our way, careful not to make eye contact with any passers-by. A tip given to the Commanders about suspicious activity could earn a heavy penalty, something that has happened on more than one occasion.

"I promise we'll only stay for five minutes. I just want to see if they open the gates this time." I say this, yet in my gut, I know it's unlikely.

Cameras are placed in the streets for Altaras' security, but there are no cameras on the path we take. Our route has been studied to perfection to reduce the worry of getting there without incident. Nevertheless, the odd guard walking past still rattles us with fear, fear we could be perceived as doing something wrong — to offend them, to not do as they ask. *Even when we are doing just that.*

"I swear, if we see these gates finally open, I'll never doubt you again." Clover laughs. "Maybe we might even see someone from Penury trying to get in! Or even try to scale the wall," she continues. Clover often makes light of the situation, without realising the full extent of what she's saying. But this makes me like her more. She can't help who her parents are, and she's nothing like them.

It's so unlikely for us to see someone from Penury. They wouldn't be stupid enough to come out during the day.

"You shouldn't tease Clover. Those people out there live in sickness and fear; it's no wonder they try to come here. We have all the luxuries they don't, so you shouldn't laugh at their expense."

"Someone's cranky today! I know, I know, I was just trying to lighten the mood." Clover says as she turns to look behind us. I glance back as well but see no one on the path behind. After walking through the maze of buildings and weaving through the courtyards, for what feels like hours, we nearly reach the edge of the city. A place where no one dares venture to.

"I know what will lighten the mood for the rest of the way," I exclaim with a grin. "I may have met someone last night." My tone is coy and I lift my chin.

"You did what!" her voice is almost a shout as she swivels to face me, squeezing my arm with a tight grip of excitement. "That should've been the first thing you told me! How could you keep this from me? I'm too offended to talk to you!" She pretends to walk off, crossing her arms in a huff.

"To be honest, I completely forgot until now," I say as I catch up, linking our arms again.

"Details please and don't leave a thing out," she says, still pretending to be annoyed; she refuses to look in my direction, chin upright.

"So, I was at the ball last night..." I rush to get my words out, before she shames me for not telling her sooner, "Yes, I know... I should have told you — I was going to! But anyway, I was leaving, and this boy came over and asked for my name." I study her face for any sign of annoyance for withholding this information, but I'm greeted by waiting eyes. I continue, "He was quite abrupt, rude and cocky."

"Go on," she probes, facing ahead as we walk.

"I told him my name was Lila and —"

"You gave him your sisters name!" she shrieks, whipping her head towards me. "Elyria, I can't believe you just met some cute guy at an elite filled ball — which you didn't invite me to, by the way — and then gave him your *sister's name*! But what if he tries to find you?" her voice whines now.

I shake my head at her, "Firstly, I never said he was cute. Secondly, it was my only choice. I couldn't give him the chance to find out mine just yet; what happens if mother and father discover that I went to the ball on my own? I'll never be allowed to leave my house again!"

Clover doesn't reply at first, only looks at me with eyes of a wounded animal. Finally, her pretense breaks as she shakes her head.

"I guess you're right, but I knew he was cute, you would have mentioned otherwise if he wasn't... you're so coy, Elyria," she laughs. "Are you going to try to find him next month? I must join you when you go, I could start trying to find a match! It's the full moon event — the ball no one wants to miss! I'll sneak out too, no one will even know!"

Many matches are made at the full moon ball, with everyone of importance in the city attending. It's the place to be, to meet people outside of our day to day lives. Mothers flaunt their children, hoping they will be matched with another son or daughter. A match with someone of an elite heritage, would be their greatest hope — to then marry, their lives changing forever.

Matching at the ball was one way of securing a future, and the easiest. Much easier than my plan to one day work in the Consulate.

Clover's parents haven't let her go to the balls yet either; she will probably attend in a couple of months, or they will just find a match for her without the preening. It's not like she doesn't have options lined up. Girls already pine at her feet; if they knew she was open and looking, she would have the pick of anyone in our class. She is just *that* desirable.

I laugh and hug her arm tighter. "Of course, but if your parents find out we went alone, they will blame me and never let us see each other again — or worse, I'll be sent to Penury!"

"They could never keep me from you." she finishes, returning the squeeze.

I sense something strange behind me; I quickly spin, only to face an empty pathway. Maybe the wind is playing tricks on me, I convince myself, as I hug my cloak tighter around me, my skirts blowing in the breeze. We are now at the edge of the city, where the houses stand in a curved line, creating the perfect circle. The Citadel stands in the middle of the city, flanked by the elites' housing, and the regular Altaras housing estates built to the edge of the city line.

The poorest people of Altaras live on the outskirts of the city circle, nicknamed the *rooks,* a term given to them over the

generations. Regarded with bad fortune and branded as the lowest, they are deemed unworthy by the elites. They are the workers completing the jobs that the rich would never do: cleaning, fetching, carrying, and clearing the rubbish. Servants to the wealthiest of the city: not respected or paid what they deserve, further dividing us all. All of us have our place, the lower ranks having to work so hard to survive and thrive. Never stopping, like bees urging to get closer to the queen in her nest at the centre of the hive.
My family are *medis* — not rooks, but not elites, just somewhere in the middle. Never really accepted by either and always trying to avoid falling for a rook or grappling at the chance of matching with an elite.

Past these houses, a stretch of grass meets the trees that stand so tall they reach beyond the top of the wall. Even if you climb onto one of the roofs, you can see nothing except the treetops stretching to meet the sky above. Even now, I think this is why they are there: to conceal the wall. Using nature to pretend it's not there. The trees were planted hundreds of years ago, showing how long the wall has stood.
The gates are situated on the south-east of Altaras, gates which only open for the few people permitted by the Consulate; advisers, officials, guards, and merchants — only allowed access by the Commanders' word. Gates opening only for those that serve an economic purpose in Altaras.
To get to the gate, you must go past the border of trees, through a tiny opening I had found in the undergrowth. I had stumbled upon its location one day whilst exploring, and I couldn't keep this secret discovery from Clover. We must hide ourselves amongst the tree line, so as not to be caught by the guards, or anyone peering from their windows. It's always a

risk, but we haven't been caught yet. This is the only part of the tree line where we have not detected a single security camera. Once we're in the trees, we then head south following the curve to reach the location of the gate.

"Quickly, we'll run on my mark," I say, assessing for any movement or noise, or even the flicker of a curtain. One last check and it's clear. Clover looks around too, tightly gripping my hand. Her palm is slick with sweat, and she shoots me her best fake smile, pretending she isn't scared.

"Run! Now!" I order, pulling her toward the tree line. Tugging up our skirts, so as not to fall, we run fast. Whilst it only takes a few moments to hide amongst the trees, in that briefest of time, someone can see us. Better to run than to get caught.

"I hate that part," she exclaims, breathing heavier than before as her hand rests over her chest, smoothing her red hair down with the other. Even my heart rate is up, but not from the run, I can run for miles without tiring.

"Don't worry, me too," I reply, for her reassurance and my own...

The tree line is thick with the growth of many plants; thick ferns and huge rubbery leaves, creating a perfect mass of green. Vicious grasses growing just as tall as us make it hard to venture through the tiny opening. Twenty minutes later we are nearly through to the other side. Brambles catch and prick through our skirts as we navigate through the leaves and branches, careful not to make too much noise, or to tear our cloaks. Climbing through the undergrowth, we finally reach our goal. We can finally see the light of the wall.

Most people that live in Altaras won't know that the huge wall surrounding our city is made in the brightest shade of gold.

Or, if they do, no one speaks of it. Everyone is too scared of the Consulate and the consequences of asking questions; imprisonment, public beatings — or worse — execution. Otherwise, there would be more faces alongside us in the trees, trying to peek at such an extravagance. Word would spread fast.

The wall is covered in the most intricate designs of spiraling vines crawling their way to the top. If you squint, you can make out the beautiful engravings of flowers and birds flying towards the sky. It's the most beautiful thing I have ever seen. I remember when we both saw it for the first time. We shrieked so loud, I was sure someone heard us, and I covered Clover's mouth with my hands to muffle her noise.

It's puzzling why the elders would build a wall like this to keep people out. The most intricate artwork ever to be seen, only to shield it with a blanket of trees? A façade. An extravagant symbol that everything is perfect and beautiful yet concealing it with trickery. Keep the horrors out but disguise it with beauty. The biggest mask, and no one knows why. It's presence making me wonder why people can't ask questions.

Clover stares at the wall again, wide eyed and opened mouthed. We have seen this same section of the wall before, never daring to venture a different route. We already know this is where the gate is, we always take the same path, passing the same trees. We're too frightened of the consequences of getting too close, *especially* when more guards protect the gates. But there is always the possibility that we may *finally* see the two giant golden gates open, to show us a glimpse of what's hidden beyond.

Chapter Five

My heart drums against my chest as I attempt to quiet my breathing. *Slow steady breaths Elyria,* I say to myself, *just as mother taught you...*

"I think we've seen enough for today. Can we go back now?" Clover whispers in my ear, careful to keep her voice low to avoid alerting the two guards positioned either side of the giant doors. Staring straight ahead, dressed in Ceraea's armour of red, they are heavily armed, guns hanging at their sides. Their breastplates are heavy with metal, silver and red — like a blood red wine. Colours that stand out against the forest green of the trees and the glimmering light of the gold behind them. If we're to ever be attacked and the walls breeched, the enemy will know exactly who to aim for first.

I take one last look at the two guards, draped in red, and fix my eyes to Clover's.

"Maybe next time." I mouth.

We silently nod our heads, agreeing to turn back and make our way home.

~

Scanning the windows for any sign of movement, I see nothing. Still clasping Clover's hand, I tug her in quiet encouragement, signaling that its clear for us to move; she obeys and follows me in a quick run to the closest house for cover.

"What are you thinking?" she questions after we get our breath back. The adrenaline still courses through me, my breathing fast, my head pounding.

"I have too many questions, Clover. I never know where to start, but *why* does no one go there, or why does the wall shine gold?"

Every time we leave, I am more frustrated than before.

"That's what makes this thrilling, Elyria!" She pulls me into a side hug, clinging to me as we set off down the path towards home. I laugh at her excitement. One moment, she's scared for her life, the next she's like an excited child entranced by the world. "I was scared this time though. I totally thought the guards could hear us breathe!" she giggles, her hand covering her mouth to muffle the sound.

"And they've not caught us yet, so all the more reason to keep going," I say with a grin. "I wish we could ask our parents about this." I wonder aloud. "I can't believe my father doesn't tell me all about the wall when he travels?"

"Maybe he's sworn to secrecy?" Clover replies. "It doesn't surprise me that everyone is told never to repeat what they see or hear. This can be a scary place."

She's right, I think to myself. I don't know enough about the Consulate to make assumptions. *Especially* because my father would have a good reason not to tell us.

For whatever reason my father keeps the wall a secret, he does it to protect us.

The sun's rays have stopped beaming, the sky now darker. Pulling my cloak tightly around my shoulders, the evening breeze whips through my hair, and I shiver, prickles down my spine. We make sure to keep to the cobblestone path, passing the same houses as we always do. Past the houses closest to the borders, occupied by the workers of Altaras. Dilapidated homes that I am thankful I do not reside in. We make our way back to where I live, a short walk from our school building. Clover — as an elite — lives only a few minutes from the Citadel; she must walk on alone much further than me.

Loud footsteps pull Clover and I closer together; we recognise the sound instantly. *A patrol.* Blood red uniforms appear from around the corner, walking straight for us. We keep our eyes trained on the ground as they close the distance.

"Where are you girls going?" the lead guard says. His eyes are bulging, thick facial hair covering most of his face. I look up from my boots as Clover grips my hand tightly. Somehow fear has left my body and I'm able to speak.

"We're just coming back from class, we stayed behind to do some extra work, sir."

Side looks cast between the other guards make Clover and I cower our heads, but they stay silent, only waiting for their leader to respond.

The bearded guard looks us both up and down, then signals to the rest of the patrol to carry on. "Back home. Now. And I don't want to see either of your faces out this late again, understood?"

"Yes sir," we say in unison as the patrol lets us get on our way.

Once we're at a safe distance, Clover looks behind us and exhales, "That was close!"

"He was just trying to scare us; he never really suspected us of anything."

Clover, changing the subject to lighten the mood, takes me back to thoughts of the night before. "We still need to discuss your mystery boy."

I laugh. "There's nothing more to discuss about *mystery boy*."

"Just don't scare him away. You know you can be very abrupt and sour at times, Elyria."
She has a wonderful way of telling you how it is. Usually, she phrases it in the nicest way — a lot like my mother, but clearly not today.
"But I'm sure my father will know who he is? I could ask him once you learn his name?"
I contemplate her offer; the lie of not saying his name aloud — *Jude Lightfall* — burns my insides. I want to tell her the truth, but I think better of it. I will tell her soon, but not yet.

Her cloak hood is up so I can only see glimpses of her face in the darkening light. I grab her hand again and squeeze. "Thank you, Clover, but if I want to get to know him, I must do this on my own. I will take your charming comments of my shortcomings as constructive criticism." I roll my eyes playfully.
Clover is too innocent to know of my ulterior motives as to why I want to know Jude Lightfall. It's not real. I do not *fancy* him or wish to date him for any reason other than securing a future for my family: I loathe everything his family stands for. If I get to know Jude Lightfall, it will be a strategic move... if I get another chance to make it happen. But... maybe Clover can help in some way.

"If you lend me one of your dresses for the next ball, I will tell you every detail."

"Deal," she grins, squeezing my hand back in delight. Clover loves her dresses! "I'll bring the most beautiful dress I own, and you can charm the pants off mystery boy at that damn ball. And in return, you can tell me every detail about Anera — what she's wearing and who she's talking too," she grabs my shoulders in excitement. Clover, infatuated with

Anera for months, has been too scared to talk to the stunning blond.

"Of course, I will. Every detail. Thanks Clover, and thanks for investigating with me again. Hopefully the gates will open one of these days." I smile.

"We'll go everyday if we must." She crosses the road, swiveling in her step as she reaches the path, offering me a final wave before rounding the corner out of sight.

We will see the gates open. I wish for it every night.

Taking down the hood of my warm cloak, I step onto the porch now covered in leaves. It looks like every other home on our estate, but better, because it is mine, where my family and I live. But I would leave this place in a heartbeat if it meant giving them a better house, a better place to live. Each house is taller than it is wide, some with steps to reach the entrance or a porch front covered with vines. Flowerpots and lamps add to their charm. Our big blue door is hard to miss under a canopy of green vines. Many, but not all, have red somewhere around their doors, the colours of Altaras to signal their patriotism. We have a tiny red flag, almost as small as my hand just hanging by the window. Its weathered appearance shows just how much my parents care.

I take out my key and unlock the door, greeted by the warm heat from the fire and the beautiful smell from the kitchen. Whatever mother cooks is bound to be full of flavour. She loves to cook and can make any recipe from scratch without instructions, turning the most basic ingredients into the most delicious meals. Elite families don't cook for themselves — I'm sure Clover's mother has never lifted a finger in the kitchen. Mother always cooks our meals for us. My mouth waters.

"That smells good, when is dinner ready?" I kiss her on the cheek, not forgetting to say hello to Alec who's sat at the table colouring with bright wax pastels. I scruff his hair as he shakes me off begrudgingly. Taking one of the pastels, I hold it in my palm, only to make it disappear beneath my fist and reappear behind his ear. Alec looks at me with narrow eyes as I chuckle to myself at the trick. I had often done this when he was a boy, but he has grown too old to be amazed by magic.

"Ready in about ten minutes," she answers, wiping her brow with the back of her hand and pushing up her sleeve. "What errand did you run today?" She carries on with whatever is boiling in the pot, tipping a glass jar of deep red powder into the mixture, then stacking it back on the shelf packed with an array of herbs and spices.

"I just had to help Clover with her Mathematics, nothing major."

It's always easy to blame an errand on Clover as my parents think she's an elite air head, always needing my help and unable to do anything on her own. Mother seems to take that answer as a good one and asks no more of it.

"When is father back? He's been gone longer this time and I miss him."

Father, by his rank, has provided my younger brother, sisters, and I with a life better than some. For this, I am grateful. So many rooks suffer: suffering within the walls, as well as the suffering of those outside of them. Sometimes he goes for weeks at a time, dependent on when the gates open, and no one can predict that — except those working for the Consulate. I wish he could be around more, but we're used to his absence now; there's a familiarity to it, but it doesn't change the sadness of him not being here.

"He'll be back next week, I reckon. But I'm sure he sends his love and misses you so much more."

I pull out a chair and sit, stretching my weary legs underneath the table. Today has been a long day, and I crave sleep, my eyes close to the sound of bubbling from the cooker.

"Mother," I say, my eyes still shut. I brace my arms on the table so I can rest my head against them. "Can you tell me the story again... the one of the girl in the forest?"

I remember her telling me the story when I was little: Lila, Gia and I all tucked into one bed. We would ask for it every night, her voice soothing us to sleep.

Mother chuckles and turns to face me, her long ink-black hair flowing behind her; she really could pass for my sister, still so beautiful — not a wrinkle in sight.

"Gia, Lila!" she calls. "Dinner!"

I stand up and take a bowl from the countertop, spooning in the warm soup as hints of turmeric and basil waft in the air. We all take our seats, devouring the warm thick broth with haste.

"Go on then mother, I heard Elyria ask from upstairs," Gia grins, watching our mother with doe-like eyes. "Tell us the story."

Mother takes a breath between mouthfuls, for this bedtime story takes a while. My siblings settle into silence, smiles on our faces as she begins to recite the tale.

"Deep in the forest on a warm summer evening, a girl was running quickly through the trees, weaving between the tall trunks, and bounding over fallen branches. The warmth of the summer sun's rays pierced through the canopy, creating a trail of heat up her arms. Her face was already freckled by the countless days spent in the sun and she finally made it to the edge of the forest. Bending over to catch her breath, she paused for a moment. Recovered, she quickly carried on, to avoid missing the scene in front of her. Taking a few more steps, the girl emerged from the tree line and, as she did, her eyes lit up. For what she saw in front of her was something so beautiful, she had to blink twice to make sure it wasn't a dream."

Mother took a spoonful of soup, all of us listening intently to her words. Lila's eyes are closed, like she's picturing the tale in her mind.

"Vast land stretched as far as she could see, hills almost reaching the sky, and an expanse of green laid so far ahead it would take weeks to cross. Many rivers flowed down through the hills, gathering at the bottom into a crystal blue lake. She could see deer grazing in the lush grasses, and birds flying around her into the trees, swooping and singing their beautiful songs. The sky was so blue, the air so crisp, she was sure she was dreaming for no place could be this magical.

"The flowers carpeting the floor were so many different colours, she didn't even know there could be so many! Pinks and blues, oranges, and purple. So many different ones, she couldn't name them all. It was the best thing she had ever seen. She would come here every day if she could and explore. But to her sadness, she could not venture further into the dream land; she knew she could get lost, unable to find her way home and her parents would miss her too much. But all she wanted was to smell the flowers and walk through the grass, lying out in the sun, the warmth heating and browning her skin." Mother pauses, feeding herself some more. I look around at my siblings, all entranced by her words. Even Alec had stayed quiet.

"In the distance, she could hear voices and laughter; were there children in the forest? Did they live amongst the trees? Maybe they were merpeople that lived in the lake. Enchanted by what she saw, she longed to stay but knew she had to return home for her mother would worry. She wiped her tears, as she would likely never venture into the hills with the tree children, or swim in the lake. So, she took a final look at the dream land, taking in the colours and the smells one last time, before she turned around and headed towards home. She would never forget the beauty she saw in the nature before her, and how badly she wanted to see it again." Mother finishes her story with a gentle sigh.

Listening to her talk of this dream land again is the epitome of perfection; I wish more than anything for it to be real. I imagine I am that girl, running through the open forest: the warm sun on my cheeks, dipping my hands through the bubbling stream, hearing the birds and seeing the wildlife roam freely — just like me. I know the tale by heart now, but I know it's not real. The girl only dreams of this magical place, then her mother wakes her, which is why she cannot enter the world again.

After dinner, we settle in the living room, while Lila tells us of the latest boy in class she wishes to be matched with. My mother fusses around the record player, passing records between her fingers as she decides which one to play.

She finds the perfect one, winking at me over her shoulder as she places it in. I roll my eyes but smile as the tune starts to play. It's a happy, fast paced melody, one she rarely plays. It seems to be only played on the days when she wants to hear joy again. Gia and Lila stop their chatter to dance, spinning themselves round and round in the centre of the room. My brother stands, beginning to move to the music as the violins quicken their pace. My family dance with bare feet on the hardwood floors; Mother outstretches her hand with a grin on her face, encouraging me to uncurl myself from the sofa, and join them in this moment of madness. With a groan, I grasp her hand and she hauls me up. As the song gets faster, Gia throws back her head with outstretched arms, laughing as she spins. Everyone dances together in a circle, moving, jumping, twirling — smiles so bright, they light up the room. If anyone walks past our window, they will think us mad.

In this moment, I am happy, breaking down my wall of stubbornness for this silly dance with my family. I let myself go. Enjoying the madness. Tonight, when I go to sleep and my head hits the pillow, I will dream of the dream land just like the girl in the forest.

Wishing I was anywhere but this city of grey.

Chapter Six

After a month of waiting, the full moon ball arrives. Clover's dress sits concealed in my wardrobe under an old cloak, smuggled in after class without my family noticing. I wait until I hear the snores of my sleeping family before taking out the beautiful gown. It certainly is fitting for a full moon event. Its champagne colour reflects the light and shimmers with crystals strewn all over the fabric. The tiny straps hang delicately on my shoulders, its neckline low to expose the top of my cleavage. I run my hands along the length of the fabric, over the beads and jewels sewn over the dress like shining stars. It fits to my body, flowing effortlessly at the bottom. It's breath-taking. I wonder who made such a beautiful gown. It looks like starlight.

Grabbing my heels and walking down the stairs, I'm careful not to make a sound as I head out the door and into the night once more.

Going back to the mansion this time is less nerve-wracking; I know where to go and how to get in. This time it's easy. Hiding my boots and cloak in the same cupboard under the mirror, I once again peer at my reflection. My hair is striking against the colour of the dress, my eyes are glowing, my skin slightly browned by the afternoon sun and my cheeks rosy from the walk here in the cold. I place some hair over one shoulder, the rest falling down my back as it cascades down my spine in waves. Exhaling, I nod at my reflection to boost my confidence. It's time to make my mark.

I carry myself with a strut: head high, chin up and shoulders back, like I know exactly what I am doing. Looking around the room, my eyes go wide. Altaras has spared no expense for tonight's ball. The hall is submerged in a low blue hue, the ceiling covered in dark fabrics hanging in every direction, littered with tiny stars, shining silver and gold, forming constellations over every inch of space. A replication of the night sky. After a few more minutes of gazing at the masterpiece above me, I make a beeline for the refreshment table, halting in my steps as a strong large hand grabs my arm and stops me in my tracks.

I spin to face the rude culprit, ready to give him a piece of my mind about those things called *manners*. Until I see who the hand belongs too.

"Your name is definitely not Lila," he says, smirking down at me. His grip turns to a slight squeeze before he releases me, my breath taken from my lips. "I did some research… and I found out some interesting information about a blond sixteen-year-old named Lila with crimson eyes, and that is definitely not you."

My mouth turns dry. He *researched* me. This is a mistake, coming here. I should have known he would have access to civilian records considering who his father is. I internally curse myself.

"Stranger danger and all that," I say, smiling up at him and trying to conceal my shock.

"Danger? I thought we got on just fine… from what I remember," Jude bends down to trace my ear, his breath hot against my skin. A tingling sensation runs across my entire body, making me shudder. "It's nice to finally meet you, Elyria. I've been waiting a long time to see you again," his whisper is like a song to my ears, yet my name on his lips makes me startle.

I finally snap out of his trance. My name hot on his lips sends not only feelings of *whatever that was*, but alarm bells. If he knows my name, he will expose me, my parents will find out, and my plan will be ruined. My eyes dart to his, frustration pulsing through me. "Don't say my name out loud."

"But darling, I love how it sounds," he smiles, his perfect face so close to mine. Frustration courses through me at his teasing.

"I'm serious, I could get into trouble if my parents know I'm here!" I say, moving away from him.

Straightening up, he pulls down his jacket; it's the same midnight black, and the cuffs have tiny crescent links to match the theme of the hall.

"And that is why I whispered it," he smiles.

I back away, not sure how to take this revelation: my guard now higher than it has ever been before, barriers reinforced to protect me. His father is the military advisor for the Consulate, of course he can't be trusted. Jude and his family should be treated with caution.

"I give you my word, your secrets will always be safe with me," he says with a nod of his head. "Now we're properly introduced, let's get you a drink." Jude extends his arm. I'm not sure if I can trust him, but two can play at this game. With a deep breath, I take his arm and walk with him over to the refreshment table; a waiter comes to meet us with the bubbly liquid I liked so much before.

"Actually, we want the good stuff please," Jude abruptly tells the waiter, who quickly pulls a bottle from under the table. Jude stands there, leaning against the table with a proud look on his face. I watch him and how effortlessly he commands everyone around him. How he enraptures everyone around him. Is this really a boy I should hope to match myself with? An arrogant boy?

A smooth dark liquid is poured into two tumbler glasses and handed over by the now nervous waiter, avoiding all eye contact.

Jude holds up his glass, looking into my eyes, "To you, the girl dressed in *Starlight*."

Starlight — that's what I called my dress earlier. The coincidence makes my cheeks flush, but I quickly recover my cool.

Jude raises his hand, placing a finger under my chin, forcing me to look up. He raises an eyebrow with his usual smirk etched again across his lips. We clink our glasses, each taking a sip, refusing to break eye contact the entire time.

I don't know if it's the liquid that gives me the courage to ask such a thing, but the words come tumbling from my mouth, "It must be terrifying with a father so well respected." I lie. Respected, more like *hated.*

He takes another sip of the liquid and places down his glass, holding out his hand. I hesitate but accept the gesture as he guides me over to the dance floor. Everyone in the room's eyes lock on us.

"I don't want to talk of my father when I'm looking at you," he replies as we slowly move to the music. My cheeks redden as he circles me in a spin, pulling me closer once more as we dance beneath the stars. In the background, amongst the harmony of music, I hear murmurs of voices. *Everyone will be talking now.*

"Everyone is looking at us," I say, whilst not breaking the rhythm and pacing of our steps. The confidence in my tone surprises me.

He chuckles, "Let them look. I'm glad, no other suitors will try to pursue you now."

A laugh leaves my lips, already clocking his jealousy for potential competition, his need for control apparent. Maybe my plan of enticing Jude has started to take effect after all.

"I just don't want the girls to pull out my hair or spill drinks down my dress, that's all," I tease, as he spins me once more. In the breeze from the open doors, my skin shivers at the cool air brushing over my body. Jude pulls me towards him once more and bends close to my ear. The smell of mint mixed with rainwater floods my senses. The smell of Jude is a subtle aphrodisiac.

"Watching you fight over me would be a delight," he says with a wicked grin, his lips brushing my ear, "but I will gladly protect you. I have a whole army at my disposal to protect you."

The comment, however, makes me want to scowl. To have an army at his dispense! I remind myself that this is a boy born of a man with hate in his veins. Instead of grimacing, I only tilt my head and look to his face. The blue hue from the room cools his features, making him look as though he's trapped in ice. His hair falls above his eyes; I feel compelled to move closer, yet also to kick him in the shins for being so insensitive. I resist. Jude already makes me feel so many different things. Trapped in a dilemma of whether to kiss or kick him — I can't quite work it out yet.

"Let's walk outside, I would love to see the stars. It is the full moon ball, after all." I want to get him alone without prying eyes or ears.

He nods and leads me to the doors as I hold onto his arm, his jacket the softest material I've ever felt.

The courtyard is filled with giant white pots bordering the mansion; foliage and shrubs lavish the grounds in beautiful colours, lined up in their uniform rows. The lawns stretch far beyond, it's hard to see where they end. I gasp at its beauty.

"Have you been out here before?" he asks. I shake my head in response.

The moon is so bright and large, it makes sense to celebrate its magic on a night like this.

"I used to play in these grounds when I was small; there wasn't much to do as a Consulate kid when your parents drag you to a garden party full of old drunk people," he says, as we walk amongst the pillars that wrap around the side of the mansion.

"There weren't any other Consulate children to torment?" I ask.

Jude chuckles in response, "Who ever said I tormented anyone... do you really think so lowly of me, Elyria?"

Yes, I want to reply. But instead, I redirect the conversation. "Did you have a nice childhood then?" I ask, curious to know his response.

"It was better than some," he replies. "But enough about me, I want to know all about you Miss Nightingale." Jude smiles as he looks down at me. It still irks me that he knows exactly who I am, but after dancing with Jude inside, I'm sure the whole city will know about me by morning. Their gossiping will have already filled the room.

"There's not much to say really, my father is a merchant, so he's gone a lot, I have three siblings, I—"

"Those are just facts, I want to know what goes on in here," he interrupts as he touches my temple; I jolt, it's like a spark running through my entire body. Shrugging the feeling away and burying

it deep inside, I scold myself. I need to always be in control with Jude, I cannot ever let my guard down.
"I don't even know you; I'm not going to tell you all my secrets, Jude," I look out towards the grounds.
"I'll tell you mine, if you tell me yours?"
"You'll have to know me for longer than two balls for me to spill my secrets," I reply, my grip on his arm tightening from the cold.
His voice is low when he replies, "I count on it."
We lap round the entire grounds once more, and by then, it's nearing dawn. My mother will be awake soon; I need to get back.
"This has been lovely, but I must go, or my mother will worry."
We head inside to the growing noise of shrill drunks and music.
"Let me chaperone you home, it's the least I can do for your time tonight?" His eyebrows rise, but my face sours at the comment.
He laughs to himself, "You really are something, Elyria."
I consider his offer — it would be quicker than walking but having to retrieve my cloak and boots from the cupboard would be mortifying. What happens if mother sees the commotion of the carriage from her window? I decide against it.
"Thank you, but no. I enjoyed talking with you tonight," I head towards the grand doors. The crowd of people is still heavy, with drunken guests laughing and dancing with no care in the world.
"Okay, I will see you very soon, Miss Nightingale." He takes my hand and brings it to his lips, the gesture catching me off guard.
"Goodnight Jude,"
"Goodnight Starlight girl."
I remove my hand, the loss of warmth from his hitting me instantly. I leave him standing by himself, amongst the others who continue to dance and drink the night away. Alone in the hall, under the stars.
Jude is confusing. I should be enthralled that he wants me, that he is even looking in my direction. But I can't suppress this looming guilt, the fact his blood is the same as the man I so desperately

despise. Would I ever be able to sit in the same room as Marik Lightfall without thinking of every man and women murdered by his command, sometimes even by his hand?

Retrieving my cloak and boots, I walk briskly down the corridor towards the exit and try to rid my swirling thoughts. But, before I even have time to open the kitchen door, a hand grabs my shoulder. I jump, readying an explanation to Jude as to why I'm down here, but I set eyes on a small boy. He's a good few years younger than me, more like my brother's age. So small with his wiry frame. His eyes dart quickly towards mine — he's in a rush. He must be trying to get into the kitchen.

"Miss, you dropped this," he says; his tone is hushed whilst his amber eyes dart from mine to the piece of paper he holds by his side.

I look down at his hand, "No I think you have me mistaken..." I start, but he quickly places the folded paper in my palm in a hurry.

"It's yours, don't let anyone see it," he whispers, before darting down the corridor in the opposite direction. Out of sight before I can object.

What a strange encounter, I think, as I push the kitchen doors open and place the note into my cloak pocket.

I make my way out of the mansion covering my head beneath the hood of my cloak. That encounter was odd, and throughout the whole journey back, I feel as though someone is watching me. I don't look at the paper until I'm safely in my room.

It's only a few words, but it makes my stomach drop, nonetheless. This can't be right. I read it again to make sure my tired eyes aren't playing tricks on me.

Tomorrow, midnight. East tree edge.

At the bottom of the note, a little bird is embossed.

Chapter Seven

The few hours I have left until morning are filled with restlessness, tossing and turning under the covers, unable to sleep. Questions flash through my mind, questions I cannot answer myself. What does the note mean? Who is it from? Is this some sort of trick or a bait from the Consulate? Who was that boy back at the mansion, and what does he want from me?

I have so many questions I feel as though my brain will explode.

After a few more hours of struggling to sleep, mother enters my room with a soft knock.

"Good morning, did you sleep well?"

"Not really, I was up most of the night."

She sits at the edge of my bed; her smile instantly relaxes my mood. But now, the thought of my parents hearing of me at the ball last night sets my nerves running high again.

"Well, the news of your father's return may brighten your day?" she says with a knowing smile.

I return the smile like a mirror. I didn't even hear him come back! We all miss him so much — my mother most of all.

"Now get dressed, he's waiting for you downstairs," she gets up and plants a kiss on my forehead before she leaves the room.

Father's journeys never have a start or end date; he is summoned without good warning, and we're never told of how long we will be without him. We only know of his return when he shows up unexpectedly at any time of day or night. I remember one day the twins and I had begged to see him leave the gates, but he said it was strictly not allowed; we must stay at home in case the guards saw us. It was never safe when the gates opened — Penurians could be waiting outside ready to attack.

I quickly throw on a plain brown dress, cinched at the waist, with white sleeves capped at the elbows. A casual attire compared to the gown I wore last night, currently hidden in my closet.

My siblings are already up and present, all sitting round the table looking in adoration at our father, even Lila gazes at him with loving eyes. Big black boots sit by the door and father sits in his chair. He opens his arms when he sees me and I fall into him, hugging him tightly.

"I missed you," I say into his clothes. They smell worn, of earth and smoke. It makes me wonder where he has been. What he's seen.

"I missed you too, but probably more," father replies, releasing me from his embrace.

Mother stands by his side with a hand resting on his shoulder. We all miss him, but it's strange when he's home. We become so used to the house without him, that when he returns, we don't know how to fit in around him for a while. By everyone's expressions, no one has heard yet of my late-night escapade.

"Father what did you see this time?" Alec asks him, almost falling out of his seat with excitement. My father looks to him, glass of rum in hand. Despite the alcohol now dulling his mind, his thoughts, he looks to Alex with a soft expression on his face.

"You remember I can't tell you much," he furrows his brows. "It was a successful trip in the Consulate's eyes."
There has never been a time I haven't seen father without a drink by his side, his clothes smelling of whiskey or rum. But he's my father, and he endures a lot, seeing what he does outside the walls, being away from his family for so long just to provide for us. He has missed a lot, too, so copes the only way he can — with a drink.

Alec groans. "It's not fair, why can't you tell us?"
I look to my father, always interested to watch him never explain the ways of the Consulate to my brother, never revealing the truth.
Mother interjects before he can answer, "Because he is asked not to, sweet boy." She puts her arms around Alec. "Just appreciate that he's home."
She may hear of the stories later in private but will not divulge them to us.

We spend hours telling father what he has missed these past weeks, recalling stories of class, or funny things Alec has done to annoy us. It's a good day, only sharing happy memories with one another, drinking countless mugs of coffee, and eating chunks of bread with cheese. Father takes out a blue flower head, pressed between the fabric of his pocket and hands it to me, apologising for missing my birthday. On a rare occasion, like a birthday, he would try and smuggle something home for us to share, to look at and admire. I look at the once pretty flower head and smile: picked for a while and now crumpled, the petals squished from the journey home. The flowers are never the same — always different. Easily concealed in his cloak pocket when he enters the gates. Unchecked by the guards, but if found... my father would be punished... crimes against the Consulate. Most of the time, I pencil sketch the flower, finely replicating its beauty onto paper. Sometimes, I add watercolours to the drawing, so that even when it has shriveled and died, I can always remember what it used to look like. I feel lucky to be gifted something so secretive.

'There is nothing better than having and sharing knowledge. Knowledge is power,' he would say before venturing on another trip outside the walls. It was enough to light a spark within me. As my intrigue grows, I have a constant longing to question and learn, to see other people — maybe see the people of Penury one day.

After eating our meal together, Gia is fast asleep in father's lap whilst Alec drifts on mother's shoulder. It's time for bed.

I had almost shifted the nervousness from my mind, the whirlwind of father's return making me lose track of what happened last night.

The note.

Midnight.

I must go to the tree edge. Is this a mistake or will I finally find some answers? Is it a trap? I could get into trouble. Deep trouble.

The mental game goes back and forth in my head as I weigh all options before deciding. All my questions will go unanswered if I don't follow my gut. I need to go.

I check and hear two sets of snores from my parents' room; the rest of the house are fast asleep. I wear the same plain dress, pulling my cloak tightly around my body; the air is much harsher tonight. I pull my hood up to further disguise myself as I keep to the shadows, hiding from the streetlamps, walking alongside the wooden houses of the rooks' estate.

Tonight is not the night of a ball; it is suspicious to be alone outside just before midnight. I don't want to raise any questions, so sticking to the darkness will keep my cover.

I make it to houses at the trees' edge, leaning back against one of the walls. I look down at my wrist: 12:00. The nerves make my tummy somersault. Ten minutes later, and no one shows. A few more minutes and still no one.

I've been set up, I think to myself. Tricked into coming here. Anger and embarrassment rise in me and I round my shoulders, cracking my neck in a huff. What a waste of time. My fists tense and I turn to leave my hiding spot.

A ball of light flickers in the distance. Spinning on my heel, I move towards the tree line. The light was so quick. There, and then it's gone. Did I imagine it? Once more the flicker reappears, partially hidden amongst the foliage: is it a torch or a flame? Quickly, I check to see if there are any cameras nearby or pointed in my direction, then make a run for it. As fast as I've ever ran before. I make it into the safety of the tree edge, concealed by the darkness of the night. My heartbeat is the only thing I hear, hands trembling from the adrenaline.

"You only lasted thirteen minutes before you were about to give up," a voice said. It was strong — powerful, but I could not see the face to whom it belonged.

I swivel on my heels, looking towards the direction of the sound.

"Who's there?" I half whisper.

A rough chuckle comes from behind me. I turn again, panicked, searching in all directions, my heart rate even higher. It feels colder than before, my skin prickling with both the air and fright. As I open my mouth to question again, a figure emerges from behind a tree. The tallest man I've ever seen. His body, stocky and muscular, is draped in a black cloak, his hood blocks me from seeing his face.

"Who are you?" I ask, my voice a bit louder than before. Now that I can put a face and body to the voice, my panic has lessened.

"We've been watching you for a long time, Elyria." the voice says, still hidden in the shadows. His words send shivers down my spine, but I wait for him to continue.

"We saw you at your first ball. We saw you running through the trees with your little friend. You're daring and fearless and you have a curiosity that we do not see in others. I think you might be useful to us," he continues, his arms folded in front of him. "There's a fire within you."

"What are you talking about, why have you been watching me?"

"My birds tell me you're quite the little charmer," he says, his tone adopting a comedic edge. "We have a proposition for you."

"Who's 'we'? Answer my question!" I say, voice edged with anger.

The figure steps out from the shadows, his hidden face now illuminated by the moonlight seeping through the trees.

"We are the Sparrows, and you are going to help us."

Confusion rattles through me and I take a step back. The Sparrows? Then, I get it. The little bird embossed on the note: a Sparrow. Twigs and crispy leaves crunch under my boots as I almost trip. The man's face is harsh, his features strong and dark; big eyebrows and a square jaw concealed by a closely shaven beard. A long scar covers the left side of his cheek. His presence makes my whole body tense.

"The who?" I say again. I've never heard of them. Is this some type of Consulate group? Is this a joke Jude has played on me?

The man looks me dead in the eyes, his features hard as his face contorts into a sneer. "We're the rebellion."

Chapter Eight

The what? Shock takes over my body, paralysing my movements and, apparently, the ability to form a better sentence. "What are you talking about?"
The man keeps his distance, his stance one of power — a stance to incite fear.
"The rebellion has been active even before you were born, little one." He takes a step closer as I step back. "The recent panic from the Consulate is our doing. The death of that guard at the ball last month was down to us. And I want you to join this rebellion."
Confusion courses through me. A rebellion has been in action for *years?* Why has the Consulate never mentioned a rebellion in the briefings? And most of all, what do they want me for? What can I offer them? My body and mind are stunned.

"What would I have to do?"
The man's mouth contorts to what I can only describe as the most sinister smile I have ever seen. "First, you need to train. Fear radiates from you now but that will go with time. The fire will rise inside you and that thing — that curiosity that's killing you — will be channeled into something deadly. You can train to be one of our spies and we will teach you how to fight." He looks me up and down. "The dresses will have to go! When we're done, you will become a Sparrow: one of Altaras' most feared assassins."

My heart stops. *Assassin.* Killing people? This is too much for me to handle. My hands start shaking at the thought of ending someone's life.

"You want me to kill people for you? I've not even so much as got into a fight before — no!" I cross my arms over my chest. "No way. I'm out; I can't do that. Find someone else, I won't do it."

"The Sparrows will train you; I will personally see to it..." he starts, but I interrupt.

"No, I will not kill anyone."

"Elyria, you already know too much now, you don't have much of a choice." His words are harsh. I don't know if the adrenaline has turned my fear into anger, but it's bubbling inside of me now. "I will not kill."

My fists tighten and as he comes closer, the smell of him hits me: a mixture of dirt and metal.

"Why are you doing this? Why me?" My eyes cower to the floor at his closeness.

"You're the only one who can." His words are final and absolute. "You want to protect your family? You want to see the Consulate fall? They've taken so much from us, and they will continue to take more."

His words are not wrong; the Consulate has taken so much from many of us, without justification and without morality. But could I really be the one to help? What could I really do to benefit them? I look up to face him, his eyes illuminated by the moonlight: the darkest brown — almost black, fueled with fire.

"You have questions, we have answers. Join us. You can make a difference."

The magnitude of this choice is overwhelming. I could learn so much about the inner working of the city. I could help change the way this city is run… I could help my family. But at the cost of taking another's life? Being just as bad as the Commanders?

"I will be your spy, but no killing. I won't do it."

"You will train in the art of both; it will develop your physical strength, your drive, your mental stability." He uncrosses his arms and places a big hand on my small shoulder. The gesture makes me cower; this man is unlike anyone I've met, even the most terrifying Consulate guard. He is worse. "We have seen a spark in you. The rebellion needs you to help free the people in this cage."

I wait. Digest what he is telling me. After a few moments, I start to nod my head. Okay. I do want answers, I've always wanted answers, and now the answers are falling into my lap. He nods his head too: a mutual understanding, an unspoken agreement.

"Your training will start from tomorrow. Say quiet goodbyes to your family, you won't see them for a while."

What? How long? How long will it be till I see them again, how much time will we spend apart? No more dancing in the living room, listening to my mother's stories, not hearing my sisters' squabble at the table.

"Why do I have to go so soon? Where am I going?" I plead. My voice now a frantic cry.

"You will live with us in our base whilst you train; if we delay, we risk someone finding out. It could be detrimental to the rebellion. We need all the help we can get and now we need your help," he says, his grip on my shoulder firm. I try to shrug him off, but with no use.

"This is crazy, it's too much."

"Do you want to help, or do you want to live behind these walls forever? Be *controlled* by fear, forever?"

He accepts my silence as a no. "Tell your family nothing, only goodbye, then we will make you disappear."

"They won't believe that! They will have so many questions, my mother would *never* give me up."

"They will be fine. We will protect them." When I look up, his eyes have softened a fraction, the only glimpse of humanity I've seen from him tonight. "Do this for them."

My mind chants the same words over in my head as I try to deliberate this choice. "Your family, save your family."

"Give me your word you will protect my family and Clover Lacewood while I'm gone. Swear that you will keep them safe."

He nods his head once. "Done."

Slowly, I nod my head in response. For the greater good. To help change this place. Yes.

The entire walk home, I'm in a trance, not caring to stick to the shadows. All sense of awareness has dissipated within me. What just happened? What have I got myself into? In a way, this is what I wanted. To know everything, for all my questions to be answered, for this corrupt place to be changed. A whirlwind of emotions unravel in my brain, attempting to change my mind.

I wasn't given much of a choice, but I should want to do this. I should want to change this world. I've been handed an opportunity to make a difference.

But why does it feel like a betrayal to do this? Why do I have to leave my family? Is there no other way? All these internal questions pound my head and tug at my heart.

When I get home, I stand and take it all in. The leaves reaching up to the sky, vines and branches winding to the very top of our house, enveloping our home under a canopy of green: the blue of the door, the small Altaras flag hanging by the window.

This is madness, does that man really expect me to leave my home? My family? I can't do this.

~

Luckily, class is not on until tomorrow, and mother doesn't wake me until late in the afternoon. There's a series of soft knocks as she enters. I peek out from beneath the warm covers.

"Are you feeling ill? I came in earlier, but you were so deep in sleep, I thought it was better to let you rest." She sits at the end of the bed and brushes the hair out of my face, kissing the top of my head. "Come down for dinner, it's almost ready."

I look up at her, her soft features downcast and full of concern.

"I'm okay, I just couldn't sleep much last night," I reply, pulling the cover closer to my head. She comes closer and I watch her: is this the last time I'll see her for a while? Ever?

I sit up and wrap my arms around her, her frame as small as mine, but fragile, as though she will break at the slightest touch. She returns the embrace and strokes the back of my head.

"What's wrong Elyria?" she questions in the soothing way all mothers do.

"Nothing, I'm just tired."

She lets go and gets up, pulling me with her. "I love you, little flower," she smiles, "Get changed and we'll have some food, okay?"

Dinner is hard to be present for as I fight this internal battle — reflecting on the possibility of not seeing my family indefinitely, whilst trying to work out what the Sparrows' excuse will be for taking me away. *Maybe they will change their mind?*

I'm lost deep in thought when Lila says my name, "Elyria, are you listening?" she repeats impatiently.

"Yeah, sorry what is it?"

"I was telling everyone about this cute boy in class. I am trying to get him to ask me to go with him to the ball!" she exclaims, flicking her long blond hair over one shoulder.

"He is cute, but he talks to every girl in our class," says Gia. She's always looking out for her twin. "Don't get your hopes up." she finishes, plonking a spoonful of food into her mouth. Gia always knows how to talk to Lila, to get her to listen. The bond I'll never share with my sisters. Gia is so much like our mother, only talking in absolutes; when she says something, you know it to be true.

But father bursts her bubble, "Lila you are too young to go to a ball, even if an elite asks you to go. When the time is right, we can find you a match." He looks to my mother and then to me, "and besides, Elyria doesn't even have a match yet!" His attempt of making a joke at the expense of my feelings makes my hand clench under the table. Gia and mother chuckle with amusement but Alec is too busy eating to pay attention to what's being said. My cheeks redden but at least they still haven't heard any rumours from the moon ball, which relaxes me slightly. My fingers unfurl. Lila crosses her arms in a huff.

I glare at him. "I don't want a match yet; I'm perfectly fine."

"Okay, okay," Holding his hands up in surrender, the crinkles by his eyes grow deeper from smiling, "don't bite my head off."

The rest of the evening goes by painfully slowly and I'm lost in a daze, nervously awaiting a knock at the door, some indication that they're here. My leg bounces under the table and I steal glances to the door, but no one comes. My parents clear the kitchen, and everyone heads to their rooms; Alec and Lila are arguing as they go, whilst Gia trails silently behind.

"Father," I say, pausing on my way up the staircase.

"Yes dear?"

"How long do you think you'll be home for this time?"

He looks between mother and me. "You know, I never really know until nearer the time, but it could be a couple of weeks, maybe less."

I nod, "I was just wondering, that's all."

He smiles and carries on drying the dishes, chatting with mother whilst I go back to my room. I hope he is home for longer this time; my family needs to be together for as long as possible once I am gone.

Uncertainty keeps me pacing in my room, unable to stop the flood of thoughts. Why has no one come for me? They *must* have changed their minds; the Sparrows will leave me be. Wringing my hands, I decide to just lie and wait on my bed. I should rest, all these emotions make me sick to my stomach.

I must have drifted asleep, still fully clothed on top of my sheets. Scratching my eyes, I wonder what made me wake in the dead of night. But then I see it. A dark figure standing at the foot of my bed. I jolt upright and scramble back into the headboard. Before I can make a noise, the figure — a man — runs to the side of the bed and puts a gloved hand over my mouth. My eyes bulge. I thrash and kick, but the man is too strong, his grip around me firm.

"Stop kicking," he says in a sharp whisper.

I do not stop. I want to do more, to scream or bite his hand. But I can't, he's far too strong; he is prepared for this, and I am not.

The man lifts me off my bed, forcing me to stand. I feel like my knees will give way.

"Eris did not tell me you were going to be this difficult," he mutters to himself.

He takes a cloth and puts it in my mouth before I can do anything to stop him, tying it around my head like a muzzle: a gag stopping my scream. This can't be happening. The tears come then, hot and streaming down my face. This is it, I think. I'm being kidnapped.

The man pulls me forward towards my window, the curtains blowing in the wind. He's going to make us jump.

I was half right.

He's fast, pulling me to his side before leaping from the window. But instead of hitting the ground with a splat, like I thought, we're dangling; one arm wraps around me, the other holding onto the rope. He must have used it to gain entry to my room.

My arms cling tightly round him for fear of falling. The only safety net is his arm taking the full weight of me. We shoot to the ground so fast my head is spinning.

The tears stop, my only feelings now are adrenaline-fueled fear. And shock. I think I'm in shock.

"You're probably in shock," he confirms. With a flick of the rope, the spiked end falls from my window to the ground. *A grappling hook*. He binds it up and places it in his belt loop, his head concealed beneath the hood of his cloak.

"Come on, we don't have much time," he says, pulling me to walk with him. I try to plant my feet firmly to the ground, halting his movements.

He huffs and yanks me harder, pulling my arm so hard it will probably leave a mark. I'm being led in the dark, taken from my home; my family will be so worried when they awake to find an empty bed.

The tears start again, beginning to soak the fabric wrapped around my mouth.

After a few pulls, he leads me to an alcove, crouches down and retrieves a backpack. I want to sink to the floor and not move, but he shoves a cloak in my direction. "Put this on, its cold."

I don't realise I'm shaking until the fabric is tight against my body.

"Boss said you can't know where we're going so, I'm sorry for this." But before I can resist, a linen bag is shoved roughly over my head. I thrash and kick, trying to get away. But it's no use.

The last thing I remember is being thrown over his shoulder. The powder laced within the sack has me drifting into oblivion.
When I wake, my head pounds. That was the weirdest dream. Yet when I look at my surroundings and where I lie, I realise it's not a dream at all. It's real. I've been kidnapped. I'm sitting on an uncomfortable spring mattress on the floor, pushed up against the wall of what looks like a tiny cell. The gag has been untied from around my mouth. Light comes from under the door in front of the makeshift bed. I start to get up, but my legs are numb... a side effect of whatever it is that made me pass out.
I try again and I stand and walk towards the door; my feet are still bare, but the cloak remains around me. *Locked*, I think... but no, it opens. My eyes to adjust to the pool of dull fluorescent light; I squint and cover my eyes; I feel like throwing up, so I put a hand on the wall to steady myself. The feeling passes after a few deep breaths. Outside is a long corridor and there are doors everywhere, the same as mine. *Are these cells?* Stepping from the room, I look around, but no one is here. It's so quiet. Too quiet.
I walk down, constantly turning behind me to check if someone's there. I try each door. Locked. Frantic, I begin pulling on every handle, but none of them budge. I run to the end of the hall, but my legs slow me down and, finally, I make it to the last door.

It opens with a click.

Chapter Nine

I enter a dimly lit room, the walls are bare — there are no windows. The only thing occupying the room is the group of people sat surrounding the round table in the centre. They all turn to me.

"Elyria, you're awake!" the big man says as he rises at the head of the table. I recognise him instantly. Nausea erupts in my stomach and bile rises to my throat. The man from the woods. I don't say anything but scowl. Their faces are unmoved by my arrival: a mixture of men and women, young and old. I glower at each one of them.

"You look a fright girl, stop scaring everyone." he says with a laugh. Others join in with a chuckle.

"You need a bath, your hair is a mess," says an older woman, her grey hair braided down her back; her expression is vacant, despite my entrance.

"Everyone, this is Elyria. Elyria, this is your new home," he gestures to the people gathered around him. In this light, and the way he speaks, I know for certain this is the leader of the group.

"I want to go home," I rasp. The group look to the man in question, hesitant for his response.

"This is now your home."

I will not cry in front of these people; I will not shame myself more. He moves his chair back, and walks towards me; doing so, I back myself up until I feel the solidity of a closed door at my spine. His face is clearer now, no longer hidden by a cloak or the darkness of night. His skin is more wrinkled than I last thought with a jagged scar over his cheek.

He looks more terrifying here, right now. Power radiates from him. If it wasn't for his face or build, I would see him as an ordinary man, dressed in brown tunic and trousers. A leather cord necklace, attached with three brown feathers, hangs low against his chest, and catches my eye as it swings back and forth with his movements.

I cower back. His scent of metal and a slight undertone of bergamot hits me.

"I know that was frightening for you, but you'll have to toughen up if you want to make it out of this training alive," he says.

"Alive? What are you talking about?" I hiss, "My parents will come for me, they will ask questions; the Consulate will come for you!"

He does something I don't expect. Grabbing my chin with his calloused hand, he turns my face so his mouth reaches my ear. "No one is coming for you little bird... everyone thinks you're dead."

I gasp. He lied. This has been a trick — a deception to get me to agree when all along this man knew this was to be my fate. My family... they think I'm dead? I clutch at my heart as if it is about to explode, trying to turn my face from his grip. The others in the room can see I'm trapped, but I see no sympathy in their eyes. This can't be true. I look to him, confusion set all over my face.

"There was a disturbance at your home..." The satisfaction is clear in his menacing eyes, "I'm afraid there was an unfortunate fire in in the middle of the night. I think it was an ember from the hearth not put out. Everyone made it out safely, other than poor Elyria trapped in her room." He can't stop the smirk that forms at the side of his mouth.

They think I'm *dead. A fire.* But everyone got out? He answers my question without me even asking. "Yes, they're all safe. We were watching. It had to be believable."

My home. Burned to the ground. How could he do this? How will they survive with no home, no shelter? The back of my throat burns as if all my fears are trying to escape at once. This can't be happening. This is not what I wanted. I try again to turn my head, but his grip is now tighter on my face as he holds me to look at him.

"They think I'm dead," I say, the tears threatening to spill.

"We planted a corpse — a similar size to yours. The fire charred the body. No one will ever know."

"How will I go back home after this, if everyone thinks I'm dead?"

His grip on my jaw slackens, and he steps back, straightening up. "That's enough talk for today. I'm finished, and you need to rest. Training starts tomorrow."

I straighten up, stepping away from the door and towards him, "You've kidnapped me, drugged me, and faked my death. Why on earth do you think I would listen to you!" I shout, my voice louder than I expect.

I don't see it coming but only feel the pain that courses through my jaw and the ringing which begins in my ears. I fall to the floor, clutching my cheek. I've never been struck before. Someone at the table gasps, a few mutter to themselves. I wince as the pain in my head floods my senses.

"You will never talk back to me again. You will do as I say because I say so!" He towers over my slumped body, "Get her out of here."

I look up through tears in my eyes as he turns and walks back to his table, but I will not cry.

So, I stand before anyone can escort me and remove my hand from my stinging face. I will be brave, I tell myself. But I only half believe it. Turning to the door, I take one last look at the table. None look at me, only the man who struck me — the man who ripped me from my family and manipulated me into this place. This dungeon. Holding me against my will.
From the corner of my eye, I see a cloaked figure standing near the table, backed away into the shadows with his arms folded in front of him, his face masked by the dark. I don't need to see his features to know he is the one who brought me here. I glare in his direction right before I slam the door as hard as I can. After finding my way back to the room, I slam that door closed too, just in case they didn't hear me.

Tears don't come until I'm curled up on the mattress, hugging my knees close to my chest. But when they do, they're silent and hot, streaming down my cheeks.
My poor family... I wish I never met that man in the woods. Was this the only way to get answers? Why do they need me? Becoming a Sparrow and joining the rebels...
I guess I made the choice when I decided to go to the tree edge at midnight. My curiosity has killed me and led me here. I didn't even say goodbye. I can't remember the last time I told them I loved them. It's clear to me now that that *man* never intends for me to go home. His plan for erasing my former existence already set in motion, and I will stay here for the rest of my life.

~

Dreams of home come, painfully beautiful memories; Lila and Alec squabbling, Gia calmly trying to keep the peace... mother quietly watching on, making dinner but laughing to herself at the children she loves so much. Of father coming through the door and scrambling to bombard him with hugs, all at once repeating the same phrase: 'I miss you'. I do this most nights if my dreams don't morph into nightmares. I do this huddled on the worn mattress on the floor, its springs constantly shifting and stabbing with every move of my body.

In my dreams, I tell them I love them over and over. In my reality, it's been so long since I told them, I can't remember if they ever heard me say it at all. And I will never be allowed to tell them again in case of compromising the mission.

For one year and three months, I dream of them. For in the waking world, I cannot afford to think of them as the emotions that rise make me weak — I cannot afford weakness. The mission is my only priority now.

Chapter Ten

Now
1 year, three months later

I climb the side of the building, my brow slicked with sweat as I grab the last hold and pull myself up with ease. I brush the dust off my leather suit; it sticks to my skin like a glove. He was right, this is easier to run in than a dress. Concealed by the night, the only movement comes from the flags on the houses whipping in the cold breeze. All lights are switched off; it is too late for anyone but me to be awake. As I sit there, my legs dangling over the side of the building, I look out at the city. The turrets of the houses and the Citadel are visible in the distance, its walls surround the Consulate buildings — the place I've been trained to hate, the city I now despise so much. Every day, Eris informs us of new tragedies — the Consulate's actions against innocent civilians. He has revealed his plan to take Altaras for the rebellion. For the people.

Over the past year, I have endured more pain than any soldier in Altaras. I have been kicked, punched, my head smashed against the floor. I have been waterboarded and starved for weeks, just to prove that I could endure the torture techniques used by the Consulate. The Sparrows didn't speak to me for months. I was isolated with my fears, enabling me to overcome them myself. I was cast aside and shunned, prolonging the pain of being away from my family. But I survived. I pushed back. I hardened my emotions, forcing them deep within me to keep me strong. I learned to not care, to toughen up, to be a person the Sparrows could no longer ignore. I would raise my voice in meetings, to give my point of view, even if it meant Eris would crush my fingers for interrupting him.

Blade work every day... Eris had warned me that if I could not fight with my left hand to the same standard as my right, those fingers would suffer the same consequences. I shut them in a door myself as soon as I left his office.

I perfected my skill for throwing knives, my weapon of choice, practicing with fabric tied around my eyes until I could hear the swish of the blade and know exactly when it would hit its mark. Using ropes bolted to the ceiling, ariel work has perfected my balance, strength, and breath awareness. I can climb faster than anyone here. Target practice with any weapon we had, strategical planning and tactical manoeuvres for hours on end. My brain has evolved into a fighting machine. I can identify the plants that harbour the deadliest poisons and how much is needed to kill a man just by their smell. I progressed rapidly in training — pushing my body to extremes, rarely sleeping, practicing, and perfecting the art of combat. Finally, to earn my place among them.

I am no longer the clueless girl running through the trees to see the golden gates — no.

I am a cold, ruthless, deadly assassin.

My head whips round to the sound of movement and I rise to a crouch, my blade swiftly taken from the concealed compartment in my boot. Its sharp point glimmers in the moonlight.

"Relax Birdie, it's just me," a voice says, and I lower my blade. Axon. His head pops up from the side of the rooftop, swinging his body over with ease as he joins me.

Following me. *Typical.*

"Creeping on me again, Axon?" I say, my voice laced with amusement.

His head is cloaked but, even in the dark, I still know his every feature. Tanned skin, bright blue angular eyes, sharp cheekbones, stubble. He slaps me on the shoulder with a deep chuckle, but it doesn't shake me. He stands at six foot five, but I still like to push him around. We sit back down in my original spot, our legs dangling, bodies covered by darkness and shadows. If someone looks out their window, they will see nothing but the night. Yet we are aware of every movement, senses alerted before it ever gathers momentum. We both look out towards the horizon; we're high but not high enough, even at the height of the tree line, no one will ever glimpse the wall. It is fully concealed by centuries worth of tree growth and Consulate control. Axon takes a breath before he speaks, his body is so close to mine. I could rest my head against his shoulder if I wanted to. "Do you think you're ready?"

It takes me a moment before I answer, "Yes, this is what I've worked for." I look across the rooftops. There's so many, I can't count them all.

"You've trained well, better than most of us. You've lived—"

"Endured," I correct.

"Endured, yes..." he finally looks to me, his blue eyes bright — eyes which make you want to confess your deepest thoughts.

"Elyria, you did what none of us have done, you've trained harder than us all — give yourself credit."

"I do give myself credit," I snap, eyes turning back to the rooftops, "I have been through hell, more than once Axon. And don't make it sound like I chose this."

"Don't play that card, Birdie, I didn't say that. But you knew what you were doing the minute you answered that message."

I spin to face him, the frustration bubbling from me. "Don't tell me what I did or didn't know! I don't want to argue about this again and let's not forget it was *you* who ripped me out of bed that night! Drugged me so I wouldn't put up a fight!" My tone is laced with spite, and I stand and pace the roof top, unable to be near him anymore. Axon stands too, his movements sleek and swift. He grips my shoulders.

"That was his orders, we've had this argument a hundred times!"

His voice is harsh, but mine is harsher, "Then don't start it again!" I try to shake him off, yet my attempts are not genuine. We both know I can take him to the floor — if I really want to.

"I know you're only picking a fight as it's your last night," he says calmly. He tries to get me to look at him, but I won't budge, my eyes glued to the city.

"I wanted to come up here for peace! I've done all of this, taken this all on, precisely for tomorrow. I don't want these last moments spent bringing up memories, painful—"

"I know, I know... but I want to make sure you can do this, that you're ready."

I finally look him dead in the eyes, my face like ice, "I have killed before Axon. I have always followed his orders," my voice trailing as I hiss the last words, "I'm the only one that can do this."

Axon nods his head in agreement. "That's our girl... knock 'em dead," he pulls me into his side, taking us back to the roof edge. His body is hard, the years of training and fighting apparent. My body probably feels the same now — I have put on muscle in my legs and arms, strong and firm from all I've achieved. Training was harder than anything I could have imagined, and muscles were not the only thing I gained. Scars litter my body from burns to cuts and gashes, some of which are poorly healed. I'm not the same girl I used to be. But I have come out the other side with venom running through my veins.

Our cloaks flutter in the wind. Its nearing dawn and we should get back before the people of Altaras start to wake. I take another long look at the city below. They don't realise now but, when they rise, their lives will start to change forever. The city will change forever.

"You can do this, Elyria."

"I know." I say, my tone burning with confidence.

We climb skillfully down the side of the building using pipework and crevasses, jumping down without a sound. It only takes a few minutes to run back to the Sparrows' base, our legs carrying us as though we're in flight. We keep to the shadows, hiding from the cameras dotted amongst Altaras. Training made me memorise all of them — all eight hundred of them — what street they are in and to which direction they face.

It took a long time for them to allow me outside but, after months proving my hate for the Consulate, I now can come and go as I please. But only at night - the darkness on my side. Everyone thought I was dead; Eris said they held a funeral for me, and everyone cried. I don't know much more than that. I've never asked, I don't want to know - I've never even stepped foot near my old house, too upset to see the damage of my old burned home. To find out where my family now lives. I can't be distracted; I only allow myself to think of them when I sleep.

We reach the entrance, Axon letting me lead. In a house on an old rook street near the edge of the city, an elderly couple waits; the occupants are Sparrows and loyal to our cause. Blocked from the cameras view, they hide us from the Consulate and its guards, should they ever conduct a raid. I let myself in, Axon close behind. We check behind us a final time. Once reaching the bookcase at the back of the house, I press the button to release the secret trap door hidden behind it, taking the steep stairs all the way down in complete darkness — I know it off by heart now. When we reach the bottom, we're led into a corridor, home to the *cells*. Our rooms. Sparrows like Axon only use the rooms when they're too fatigued from combat; others use this as a base station, the meeting ground for planning and training. I'm the only one that lives down here. All of this is built underground, unknown to the Consulate. Right under their noses. The space is huge and ancient, a rabbit warren of rooms and meeting halls. It has been here for hundreds of years, just like the rebels.

Through one of the doors is a large, soundproof training hall. This is where my torture started. The walls are insulated so well, you would never know from above ground. Our technological advances helping to create this amazing base: the perfect bunker for a hidden rebellion group. Sparrows that fight here are harsh and deliver the unexpected... you wouldn't think an older woman could hit you so hard, but that's what the rebellion does to you; it makes you strong, determined to be the last one standing, even in your sixties. The armoury is heavily reinforced, all our weapons rigorously maintained. Over the years, the rebellion has benefitted from many high risk drop offs — old Consulate weapons, decommissioned but still worth their weight in gold to us. Whatever we find, we take.

We pass my room, but I have no plans to sleep just yet. I must talk with *him*. To finalise the plan. We get to his door, and I knock, waiting for a response. He's always awake, I've never known him to sleep.

"Come in!" a voice barks from behind the door.

I raise my eyebrows at Axon, both of us knowing exactly what resides behind that door, "Someone's in a bad mood."

Chapter Eleven

He hasn't changed over the past fifteen months, still the same man I met in the woods: the one who's beaten me countless times and turned my heart to stone, the one who's burnt my skin if I shed a single tear. The one who forced me to make my first kill.

The past year has been blood and torture, facing unimaginable pain. All down to this man. He is not a noble leader; he leads with vengeance and entices fear. A lot like the Consulate does. But I follow his orders - even if I fight back at first — I do it for the future of this rebellion. For Altaras. He always wears his tunics rolled at the sleeves, preferring dark colours of maroon and purples; his big arms are bulky slabs of bulging muscle, able to snap me like a twig. He probably would if the need arose, but at least I'd put up a good fight now. He's older than my father, I came to realise; his face is scarred and holds many secrets beneath his dark eyes, long black hair tied messily to the back of his head. Illuminated by the glow of candles, he sits in his big chair behind the large desk piled high with papers, maps, and blueprints: documents I have never seen the contents of.

He speaks in a low gruff voice, "Elyria, Axon... what do you want?"

I fold my arms in front of my chest. If training in this hell has taught me one thing, it's that you must stand strong. You must not show weakness — prove you are tough. But *luckily,* I don't have to pretend any more. *I am just that.*

"Just checking in. I wanted to have a chit-chat," I say, as I bump my shoulder to Axon. He does not look impressed. Axon is the silent one — subservient, a soldier who always obeys orders, never wanting to disappoint.

"I don't have time for your games. Speak, Elyria." He looks up from his papers, his eyes are dark and menacing. Lack of sleep and planning for a rebellion does that to people. I laugh and walk over to the chair in front of his desk, plopping myself down. I pick up a map and pretend to read it, but Axon snatches it from my hands, placing it back on the desk. I glare at him over my shoulder.

"Eris, I just want to finalize the plan, that's all. Double check everything is in here." I tap my head with a finger, a smirk across my face.

"You're too comfortable here Elyria, do you ever hear Axon using my name?" Eris says, gaze flitting between us both.

"No, but that's because you like me best," I answer with a grin, both to Eris and then back at Axon. "So Xannu has already given me my lengthy agenda. My dress is ready and waiting in my room, I'm awaiting the big chop and dying of my hair in the morning—" I pretend to wipe a tear, but Eris looks at me sternly. "—then I will dance and charm my way into the heart of *Jude Lightfall*." I finish with a wink, my smile plastered to my face.

Eris sighs, "Correct, Elyria. Now was that hard to remember?"

I pout in response, "Not at all."

"You will be polite and charming, luring him in. Say whatever you can to get yourself inside that boy's head. Use your body. Do whatever it takes." he says. "Understood?"

I can feel Axon tense at his words behind me; his feet shift on the concrete.

It would have been easier to not masquerade as someone else, considering Jude Lightfall had clearly taken a liking to me before. Eris' plan for me had evolved over time. The Sparrows had watched our encounter at the balls, and decided I was the perfect honey trap. After watching him for weeks, the only time they saw him lower his guard, drop his withdrawn and standoffish nature, was when I entered the picture. Getting to Jude means getting to his father. He's the one the Sparrows want. To implement this plan to perfection, I had to disappear. In everyone else's eyes, Elyria Nightingale died. To me — she was eradicated that first night in the cell. Eris wants me to get close to him, to find out his deepest, darkest secrets and once I've got my nails in — dig deep.

Overseeing the military and weaponry of the Consulate, Marik Lightfall is their Achilles heel: he knows everything and is gold dust to the Sparrows. Wiping out his influence is the key to this rebellion; my mission is to tear up their command and power from the inside. To kill Marik Lightfall, make a spectacle of his death on a live briefing for the whole city to see.

My time with the Sparrows has hardened me, and has turned my skin to steel and my heart to stone. I'm not the same nervous girl, I am a warrior cloaked in ice. All hope of a better future is set on this mission. If I can't execute this plan effectively, then so many more will be killed. But this is exactly why I trained for so long, polishing my skills to perfection. I will do this. I can do this. I was made to do this.
Eris slides a piece of paper across the desk. I stare at it before looking back up at him.
"Get this job done before the sun rises, Elyria."
A *job*. Now?

"You could have given this to me sooner," I snap, snatching up the paper and glancing at the words. It's a name and location. The name of someone that Eris wants taking care of. *Tonight.*

"Be a good little bird and do as you're told."

I exhale and stash the note in my pocket; Eris has sent me on sixteen of these missions. Seventeen kills totaled in the past year. He has taught me to become better than them at their own game. I've made quite the name for myself. The Consulate whispers rumours of the *Night Slayer*. The killer in the dark. The name makes my lips curl in a wicked grin. My bloodshed has been hidden from the public briefings for they fear me. Fear what I can do. I have the one thing they hate: power over them, and they are right to be terrified of me.

"What did he do?" I ask.

Eris lights a cigarette and inhales, blowing out the thick smoke from his nose. "He is the head of the orphanage; he just declared a food ban for the children."

My nostrils flare. He would starve children? "Why would he do that? We have more food than anyone knows what to do with! I'm guessing the city does not know of this *ban*?"

"There is something deeper going on here," he trails off. "People like him need to be eliminated. The ideology behind his power is getting out of hand, too violent. So, I want him gone." As if Eris can sense my objection, he contributes some more information. He makes it certain that I will have to kill him.

"What do you mean his ideology?"

"He does unthinkable things to those children. He does not deserve to live."

My throat burns with bile. My face contorting to a grimace. *He does not deserve to live.*

"How has he gotten away with this?"

"He alone holds the power there, he believes that with his money and station, he can do whatever he pleases with them, and no one challenges him. The children have no one else to protect them, so they are at his disposal."

I'm going to be sick.

"I'll accompany her," Axon says from behind me, but Eris shakes his head. "It is better if this is done alone. Now leave, dawn is soon upon us." Eris dismisses us with a flick of his wrist, like shooing a fly.

"Happily," I say, accepting my orders with a sarcastic bow, then storming from his office with Axon hot on my heels. He follows me to my room, not that I need a babysitter.

"I hate him," I seethe.

"Sleep, Elyria, you'll need the rest. I will take care of that," he says, pointing to the note stashed in my pocket.

"I don't need rest; I need to gut that man before I can even begin to think clearly," I hiss. "And Eris will go even crazier if he finds out I didn't execute his order."

Axon takes a deep breath and I wait for his retort. He must always fight back at me. Always challenging.

"Stop with the attitude birdie..."

"No attitude here," my irritation snapping out at him, I lift up my hood to signal this conversation is over, "I gotta go, see you in an hour — unless you're gone," I salute him before making my way back out of the Sparrows' nest and into the night.

Chapter Twelve

I run as fast as I can through the city, trying to beat the sun breaking over the wall. Eris' note contains a name and location. He wants me to kill this man in his sleep. It doesn't take me long to reach his home; he lives in the elite estate. He must be of some other importance to the Consulate for Eris to want him dead so soon.

I scan the buildings and decide that the top floor window is the best entry point. I fire up my grappling hook, embedding itself into the roof of the adjacent home allowing me to scale the building. On top of the flat roof, I coil up the rope and leave it concealed, still hooked into the concrete. Luckily, the homes are only a short distance apart so, with a running leap, I jump off the edge, landing on the other roof with my hands braced on the floor. I walk to the front of the home by the open window, sit on the ledge and peer over — only a short distance down — it's like they designed these homes to be broken into.

Lowering myself off the ledge, my hands grip the gutter pipe, and I scale down until my foot finds the window ledge. Slowly, I part the window open. I creep into the room, but not into the one I need. A child's room.

The elite boy sleeps soundlessly in a bed far too big for him; this man would starve orphaned children whilst his own sleeps comfortably in a four-poster bed. I don't let myself dwell on the *other* things he does to those children — it only makes me want to kill him more. Walking along the dark corridor, I follow the sounds of guttural snoring to a room at the end of the house. The door creaks as it opens, but the figures in the bed do not rise. I stand and watch them for a moment, but I don't have time to feel sorry for the woman who will wake up in a pool of her husband's blood tomorrow. His dead body lying stiff and cold beside her. Eris has made me into a monster. But this man, I am happy to kill.

I take out my dagger and cut his throat as he sleeps, spraying my hands with warm liquid. He doesn't make a sound; he does not wake or fight back as the blood spills out of him. He's dead in an instant. I swallow the lump at the back of my throat and run.

~

Axon is waiting outside my door when I return to the nest.

"You look like shit, *Nightslayer,*" he says with a lazy half-smile.

I roll my eyes at his teasing, "Yeah, well, I've had a pretty shitty night, Axon." I lower my hood. "You didn't need to wait up for me. Go back home."

Axon looks to find my eyes, but I divert my gaze. *Stop looking at me like that!* I wish to hiss at him. *Stop pining*! His angular eyes are so blue they shine like sapphires, a contrast to his jet-black hair. Hair that he's *always* pushing from his face during our combat training. Axon has been here with me through it all. Watched as I was thrown around like a rag doll, beaten and screamed at. He's seen me pass out from pain, and even been the one to inflict many of the bruises. But Axon is my lifeline in this hell. *That's all it is* — all we are to each other — the one to cover your back when you're fighting what's in front of you. I will not allow myself to feel otherwise, as nothing and no one can compromise this mission.

"I just wanted to make sure you were back safe."

"You can stop treating me like I'm some scared little girl," I move past him to shove open the door, "I think I have proven already that I can take care of myself." I slam it behind me and leave him standing in the corridor alone.

I throw my cloak to the side of the room; my frustration sets off like the flick of a switch. Eris has made me this way. I never want to be seen as weak or fragile. I want to pick fights, relieving this desperate need to release my anger on someone. Axon is always an easy target.

My nails unclench from my fist and blood trickles down my palm; a few drops splatter to the concrete. I hastily wipe them on my suit, before spotting an object left on the mattress. I crouch to pick it up. It's a beautiful gold throwing knife, swirls of metal carved into the handle for a more feminine and daintier appearance. With it lays a note:

'For my favourite assassin.'

Eris.

I shake my head with a look of disgust. Gifting me presents when I've done his dirty work — *typical.* Eris likes to do this when he thinks I'm in a bad mood. A reminder that he can give me what I can't get for myself: a luxury. I run my finger down the blade; it is one of the most exquisite weapons I have ever seen. Placing it on my dresser, I notice that Xannu has already hung up my dress. Xannu is Axon's older sister by four years, almost thirty. She was one of the first people to give me a powerful reminder of why I was here; her voice is commanding, and what she says goes. This lesson I learned many times — do not start an argument with her unless you want to fight for hours. Her words cut deep, just like my own spiteful tongue — or dagger.

After a few hard punches, and several bloodied noses, we understood one another. The fight was not to be had with each other, but to be saved for *them:* the Consulate, the board of Commanders.

Xannu and Axon grew up in the Sparrows' base, training most evenings with their father's approval. He was a committed rebel, loyal to Eris and the cause. However, his passion for vengeance got him killed when they were both young children. A mission had gone wrong near the gates, the Consulate guards gunned him down before he could surrender to death by his own hand. From the beginning, all Sparrows know that they must sacrifice themselves before they are captured. It's our *absolute* law. Equipped with a tiny pill concealed in the shoulder of our suits, it's easily accessed by a turn of the head. All you need is to bite down hard, and your life ends there.

Once their father died, they continued to live in their home without parents, living as children with grown up responsibilities, trying to carry on as normal. In Altaras, family missing or being killed for treason is not a rare occurrence, so older orphans living alone isn't uncommon. After his death, they would come more often to the base, training to become more skillful and stealthier, to fight back and protect each other, learning from Eris, being guided by him at a much younger age than I. That's as much as Axon will tell me; his guard is always up in discussions of his past. Xannu is a loyal servant to Eris, just like Axon, both eager to please, both indebted to him. Eager to follow their father's life-long mission. They would die to protect their leader.

The dress is exquisite. Xannu brought it back from the boutique she owns on the edge of the elite estate, crafting the fabrics like a true artist, cutting silks and lace as skillful as she can cut through skin. Eris' plans ensured his rebels could fly under the radar in Altaras; Sparrows working in places that are of use to the rebellion, and today I will benefit from her talents. Sparrows with proven academic value work in the Unity building; Idris Amal's secretary, Tissa, is a handy little spy. Networking in the schools and cafés, every Sparrow brings their own special talent to the cause.

The dress shop fits perfectly into this mission, with beautiful gowns at my disposal, free of charge of course.

The gown is a periwinkle blue, with soft silk flowing from the bodice, the shoulders with the same fabric draping to the ground. It has a low neckline and a tapered waist with gold detailing. A dress fit for a queen. I haven't worn something so beautiful since the last ball I attended. Clover's full moon dress — now, *that* was beautiful.

But this is regal.

I have been wearing my combat suits since the first day I came here. It will feel odd to change out of my supple skintight leather, bound to me like a second skin. My suit is interlaced with small compartments for my daggers, a sheath hanging down the side of my hip, perfect for my pistol. The leather is worn, comfortable in any movement; I will miss my suit in exchange for this tight-corseted, frivolous thing.

In this dress, I'll come out of the shadows and be under the spotlight for everyone to see. But that's the plan. Hide in plain sight, then attack like a viper. Dressed to kill.

Chapter Thirteen

I didn't get much sleep. Waking suddenly, my body jolts upright, mid scream. A vivid memory infiltrated my dreams, from when I first became her, locked in a dark cell for days. The images rose from my subconscious, as if I had returned to the room once again: screaming until my mouth was raw, not caring who heard me. After two days of no food or light, I was too tired to make a sound, the darkness my only comfort. Eris unlocked the door on the fourth day — the lesson, he said, was to not make a sound when captured.

I don't know how long I was screaming for, but I know no one has heard me. Slick with sweat, I toss the blanket to the ground, unable to shake the adrenaline from my system. Before breakfast, I'm already up and sparring in the training room. Zirk is my punching bag for the day. I can always count on him being here at any hour; he's older than Axon and younger than Eris, but is a much deadlier fight than both.

A few rounds later, I finish with him and start running laps around the hall. I run for so long that eventually Zirk leaves me to my own devices, filling me with peace. My stamina has grown much more than it once was, now running for hours when left alone. Running keeps the memories from filtering through the walls in my brain, soothing the adrenaline desperate to burst out. I focus on my breathing, on the movement of my arms, each muscle contracting within my legs to power me on.

"All that running will tire you for tonight."

I turn my head and Xannu is leaning against the door, her arms folded, and legs crossed at the ankles. She is the tallest woman I've ever met, standing just shy of five eleven; her legs are so long, her body so powerful, she towers over my measly five six. I used to be intimidated by her stature and beauty, but now I can beat her in any combat, despite my height. As our friendship grew, she revealed to me that she prefers women, and that men aren't her type in the *slightest*. Her openness surprised me. Her confidence whilst confessing something so personal made my fear of her quickly dissipate. She was *never* shy about her sexuality which made me admire her more.

"Just letting my energy out, I'm bouncing off the walls," I say as I slow my pace and join her by the wall. I take a sip of water and wipe the sweat from my brow.

Her sleek black hair is pulled into a tight ponytail; it makes her sharp features striking, dark eyes and a soul to match. I'm fiercely jealous that she can accentuate her eyes to perfection with her trademark dark kohl or red shadow. Today, her dark siren eyes are adorned with red powder, a forceful look to mirror her personality.

"Plus, it's not as if I'll be doing strenuous work; I'll be dancing the night away."

I grin, slinging my arm over her waist as I can't reach her shoulder. She shakes me off with a lighthearted shove.

"We have work to do, I have everything set in your room," she takes my bottle and swigs some water. "Let's go."

"I hate this part," I whine, following her out the door and down the corridor to my room. A chair has been placed in the middle with a few bowls of paste on the floor.

"Now sit."

"Maybe we could find a wig?" I suggest, but her expression is fierce.

"No."

"Just not the chop then, please," I beg, placing my hands together in prayer as I flutter my eyelashes.

"Begging may work on my brother, but not me," she starts undoing my braid. My long dark hair is always the same, plaited in fine braids woven around my head which then wind down the length of my hair, connecting in one long braid down my back, keeping it out of the way during vigorous activity.

Eris said I need to change my appearance so not to be recognised. I don't know what Xannu is planning, but it better be good.

"What colour is it going to be?" I ask as she starts applying the paste, thick to my head.

"You will see when it's finished," her answer is short, her tone clear that it's not up for further discussion.

"Okay, as long as you're not sabotaging me or making me look hideous. Eris would not be impressed," I tease.

"Be quiet Elyria, I'm concentrating."

"That's another thing I'm better at than you," I say with a laugh, "Multitasking."

I don't need to see her to know the expression on her face; I know exactly how to push her buttons.

After what feels like hours, the burning and itching of my scalp has stopped. My hair is finally washed and rinsed in the ice-cold water — the nest's generator is focused on the provision of electricity for our equipment rather than the luxury of hot water. In the bathroom mirror, I can see a rare smile form at her lips.

Taking off the towel, I'm left with bright white hair cascading down my shoulders.

"Oh my god," my tone is loud as I admire myself, turning my head from side to side, and applauding my new reflection.

"A different person, but with the same vanity," she says behind me, triumph laced in her tone.

"I am not vain," I protest sarcastically, throwing my hair off my shoulders. Beauty is one of my weapons and I'm not afraid to relish in its power. I don't even recognise myself; I look completely different. The icy white blond hair is a striking contrast against my olive skin. The training has given my face an angular edge I never had before. The only giveaway to my former identity is the Nightingale eyes. And, as if Xannu reads my mind, she places a small container in front of me. Opening the box there are two little gold eyes staring back.

"Contacts," she says as she waits by the door. "No one will recognize you're a Nightingale now. Oh, and you can sleep with them in at night."

Xannu finishes, the door shutting behind her.

I take the delicate contacts out of their holders; it takes me a few attempts, but I successfully place them in my eyes. In the mirror, a stranger looks back.

On top of the basin, Xannu has left some cosmetics. I take the gold dust and brush it over my eyes, my shoulders, and sprinkle some in my hair. A red liquid in a small container sits beside it; it must be for my lips, so I put a tiny drop on the centre of my mouth and blot it in, creating a pretty sheen. Dabbing perfumed oils of gardenia and jasmine all over my body to finish, I relish in the smell.

I walk out of the bathroom and back to my room, swishing my new hair behind me. My appearance fills me with so much confidence; I know I'll be able to seduce my way into Lightfall's heart.

Peeling off my suit and standing before the hanging gown, I examine the body that will wear it. My back, legs, and stomach are covered with scars — healing wounds and stitches — the network weaving across my skin. My body is now a roadmap of everything I've endured these past months. Xannu has cleverly made a gown to conceal them all for now. However, my deepest scars will always stay hidden.

I carefully step into the dress; the material is cool and soft against my skin. I already know I look good without even looking in a mirror. Xannu has done well. A knock at the door snaps me out of my trance.

"Come in," I say, as I slide on my heels.

There's a sharp intake of breath as Axon clears his throat. I look up at him, dressed in his combat suit and cloak with the hood down; a gun is strapped to his hip, his other weapons hidden in his suit, and his stature fills the doorframe.

"How do I look?" I tease, doing a spin in the middle of the room. My dress flows and spins with me.

"Different," he says, leaning against the door frame. Exactly like his sister.

"Good different?"

"Different, different."

I huff, "That's no fun; ever heard of giving a compliment?" I counter, raising my eyebrows.

"You look good, birdie," he says, reaching for a strand of my hair, "Alien."

Pulling away from him, the strand of hair runs through his fingers; I playfully swat his hand, "Hot alien." I correct as I flip the white strands over my shoulder. I'm glad Xannu didn't do the horrific chop.

A voice calls from outside the hall, "Stop flirting you two, we have to leave soon." Xannu tuts aloud.
"We were *not* flirting," I pull a face and put on my cloak. Axon laughs and tugs on his hood, shaking his head.
"She's right, its nightfall now. We should leave."
Before I go, I don't forget to place the tiny pill in one of the folds of material by my stomach. Easily concealed, but easy to access if things go wrong. Axon stares at my hands, now empty, his eyes exposing a flash of anguish as he leaves the room.

I don't stop by Eris' office as his words will only infuriate me. I must deliver my best performance while at the mansion; I don't want his animosity to ruin my mood.

Axon, Xannu and I make our way out of the base and through the secret passage. When everything is clear, we leave the safe house and make our way up to the mansion. Our cloaks and the shadows hide us from sight the whole way there. Ducking and weaving, I'm a little slower in my new outfit.

Axon and Xannu won't join me in the mansion; they'll be stationed outside — hidden yet ensuring everything goes to plan.

After a few miles, we round the corner and the mansion is in full view, perched on the hill. I almost stumble in my heels. I haven't seen it this close, or even been over this side of the city in so long. The memories of home start to rise, fighting to cloud my thoughts and judgement. But I force them down, bury them beneath my pain. No, I tell myself. Focus. Snapping out of my momentary daze, I take in the grand building. Just as I remember; the same rows of carriages line the road, waiting to get in: girls, boys, men, and women all preened and gagging to enter through the huge doors. The thought of their posturing makes me feel sick.

We duck into a side ally, all of us silent, all of us focused. Axon gives me one last nod before darting out and heading to his position. Xannu hangs back, concealed in the darkness. I can still see the blackness of her eyes glinting in the night.

"It's a masquerade, keep this on." She shoves a delicate gold mask into my hands. I nod my head in thanks as she too slinks to her hiding place.

I'm on my own now, I think, fixing the mask to my face and taking off my cloak. I abandon the safety of the shadows but luckily, I'm not afraid anymore.

Chapter Fourteen

Strutting to the mansion, I don't take the back entrance like before. I walk straight through the doors. The key to power is confidence and I now have lots of it. There are guards standing by the entryway, dressed head to toe in red. But no one asks for my name as I walk past them into the grand lobby. The ceiling is so high, I must crane my neck to see. All around me are people dressed in the finest of clothes, everyone making an extra effort to dress up for tonight's masquerade. A few glances come my way, admiring the gown most likely, but I shrug them off and walk down the corridor. Men gather, drinking by the staircase; they laugh, slapping each other's shoulders in amusement at whatever is said.

Sparrows will be here: undercover and watching. There are so many. It's maddening that we haven't taken over already; all of us lurking and waiting for the right moment to pounce. On Eris's command.

Heading straight towards the hall, I know the place like the back of my hand. The past year has been filled with studying maps, layouts of rooms and blueprints of Altaras' most important buildings: inside the Citadel, the Unity building and Centralis. All permanently engrained in my brain. The doors to the grand hall burst open and I quickly step aside as drink spills to the floor; two women dressed in pink and purple bound from the doors, laughing, and stumbling as they go. Drunk.

Cracking my neck, I step inside. The hall is the same as before: grand crystal chandeliers, tall ceilings with drapes adorning the huge windows. The doors to the gardens are closed this evening, probably due to the cold. The whole place is decorated with jewels and flowers. People are standing by tables, chatting and laughing. The music of the band is quiet and mellow, pleasant to hear for once. I can't remember the last time I heard music. Waiters zip around with platters of glasses and tiny foods for their guests to indulge in. Scanning the room, I confirm he's not here. I make my way over to the table, keeping aside from the crowds. A waiter dressed in white gloves offers me a drink; I haven't had this stuff in over a year. I take a sip and the bubbles pop in my mouth, but I don't want this to affect my alertness, so I won't take another.

Looking around the room once more, I survey the people present. I beg not to see someone I recognise for fear of them clouding my judgement — *I must stay on task.* But still, my eyes flutter across the room, just in case I see a girl with auburn hair. One more scan and I decide to divert the plan somewhat, I just hope Eris won't berate me for this. I place my glass down on the table and walk over to a boy at random; he's sat down with a group, quietly talking amidst the loudness of the ball.

"Want to dance?" I ask sweetly as I put a hand on his shoulder. He has amber eyes with auburn hair to match; it reminds me of Clover, but I shake the thought from my mind. He nods his head eagerly, standing and almost knocking someone's drink in the process. I giggle softly and offer him my hand, which he accepts.

We cross over to the dance floor, and he turns to me, holding my hand and waist.

"I'm not very good at the steps," he says nervously, looking to the ground.

"Well, it's a good job I am," I reply and take the lead in our movements.

The boy is sweet and follows my lead. We dance for two songs; his hands are slick with sweat. In the corner of my eye, I clock him. Not the boy currently stepping on my toes, but *him*, now entering the hall with a girl on his arm. Jude. Spinning quickly, I instantly feel Jude Lightfall's eyes on me. They rake up the back of my body, burning me like fire. I don't even need to look to know this.

He seems older now, his jaw tighter, shoulders broader. *Taller,* if that's even possible.

"Sorry I keep messing up the steps," the boy with the auburn hair says.

"Don't worry," I mumble, "I'm used to it."

We finish the last dance and I take my hand away from his and nod my head in thanks.

"You're the most beautiful girl I've ever seen," he says, his eyes not leaving the floor.

"You're very kind. Thank you for the dance. I enjoyed myself."

And it's true. I did. I dip my head and curtsy, and we go our separate ways; his eyes follow me in longing. Floating across the hall, I head closer to the doors and look out at the garden remembering its beauty, but it makes me sick. Sick of these people with such little care for the outside world, for the people that live in crumbling houses in the rooks' estates.

I feel a presence behind me and I know it's him before he utters a word.

"I've not seen you at one of these before," Jude Lightfall says; his voice is deep, laced with darkness and allure. I slowly turn on my heel; my eyes rove his entire body before meeting the gleam of his chocolate eyes, shielded by his black mask. I hold his gaze for a minute longer. Jude will never remember the face of Elyria Nightingale; we had spent so little time together over one year ago. People disappear in Altaras all the time. Plucking another glass from a waiter's tray, I take a sip and forget my earlier mental note to have no more. I'm ready to play my part in the game that's about to begin.

"That's because I've not been here before," I try and keep my tone seductive, eyeing him as I place the glass back onto the table beside me. He is taller than before — even taller than Axon, if that was even possible — maybe standing at almost six foot seven.

"Where have you been hiding, and why have I not known about it?" His tone is cocky and full of mischief. I'm sure he uses this exact same contrived act on all the pretty girls, and I bet they lap it up.

I match his game, undeniably fearless as I say, "Where did the girl hanging off your arm go?" My brows furrow, pretending to look around the room.

He smirks, and the corner of his mouth lifts slightly. "I like that you had your eyes on me. She means nothing now that you're here."

Of course, Jude has not changed; he has the same hint of arrogance as before, dismissing girls to get what he wants with no regard for them. I want to wipe that smug look right off his face. But instead, I laugh, "I bet you say that to all the girls. Do they fall at your feet when you whisper sweet nothings in their ear?"

His eyes grow darker as I talk, his lust for me growing with every word. I step closer to him, extending on my tiptoes. I'm still so much smaller than him in heels. Reaching up, I place a hand on his strong shoulder as I whisper, assuming control, "Dance with me?"

"Gladly," he replies, taking my hand and leading me back to the dance floor, "And just so you know, I won't be stepping on your toes. And I *always* lead." Confidence radiates off him as he spins me to face him, staring me down with those big dark eyes as we begin turning to the music. Our footsteps sync as if we have danced together all our lives. My dress floats around us like a cocoon.

Jude bends his head close to my ear, his breath hot at my neck, "You are breathtaking."

We dance all night. He spins and dips me; he tells me how my hair shines like ice against the light and my eyes are like gold dust. I charm him back, being as seductive and as sultry as I can. This charade of complimenting each other back and forth goes on for five more songs. I'm surprised he hasn't tired yet, and I am now bored of this pretense.

Eyes are on us the whole time, hawks studying their prey. They whisper and gawk — some even point. *Good,* I think. The sound of crying distracts me from my dance, and my eyes scan to the corner to see the poor girl Jude walked in with. She's huddled in the centre of a group of girls, sobbing into her hands. They shoot me daggers as they attempt to console their friend. I want to punish Jude for his dismissal of her, for making her cry, but think better of it.

"Let's go somewhere a little more private," I say once the dance has slowed.

Jude nods his head, and I lead him out to the gardens. He towers over me; he's a giant compared to my smaller stature. Once outside, I let go of his hand and walk out amongst the gardens, a parallel of the first time we met. Voices of the people inside fade as I walk further into the lawns. Flowers cascade from well-tended beds, woven beside the paths in neat rows.

"Tell me about yourself," Jude asks, following my movements yet keeping an arm's length away.

"There's not much to say about me. I live with my father. He works all day and I stay at home to study. I don't go to class. My father wished for me to home school rather than mixing with the other children." I pause and look over my shoulder, "I don't have siblings, do you?"

"No," he replies, "No siblings."

I turn from him and walk further ahead, "What about you? Tell me."

Jude puts his hands into his pockets before answering, "My father is quite an important man, it's a lot to live up to."

The mention of his father creates a bubbling fire in my stomach, but I must suppress my rage at this moment. I face Jude. His hair is a darker blond at night, but still shines in the moonlight. I reach up and attentively brush it out of his eyes. "Does this trouble you?" I ask him, and his demeanour instantly softens at my touch. I thought I would have to work a lot harder than this to gain his trust. But I know how to work my way through his walls, saying the right things at the right times. Making him talk.

"Sometimes."

"That's a shame," I whisper, my hand trails down his body to reach for his hand. "It's a good job I like boys that can live up to their father's expectations," I say through gritted teeth. "What's your name?"

"Jude Lightfall," he says, "and yours?"

He searches my eyes for any hint of recognition of his name, waiting for my reaction. But I brush it off like it's not a care to me.

My alias has been set for months, my data already in Altaras' system, all planted to perfection by Sparrows working in the Consulate. After all, Jude found out my real name after searching Lila up — he would do the same again.

"Rhea," I reply, our eyes not breaking contact, "Rhea Fellows."

"Well Rhea, it's a pleasure to meet you," his voice is low and raspy, a hint of a smile forms on his perfectly chiseled face.

I reach on my tiptoes to whisper in his ear, my lips so close I graze them on his lobe, "I'm glad you ran into me." He sucks in a short breath, and his hand shoots up to hold the back of my neck. My head is so close to his, if either of us move an inch, we'll be close enough to kiss.

"You'll have to know me for longer than one night to get a kiss from me," my voice is barely above a whisper, "plus, I'm much too smart to be seduced by you."

"And that's exactly why I like you," he says with a devilish grin.

"How many nights will I have to know you before you give me what we… *both* desire?" he asks, his breath mixing with my own. Touching my nose to his, he closes his eyes.

"At least five." I reply with a smile, the amusement clear in my tone. Weakly, I try to pull away, but he holds me to him. I *can* break away if I want to, if I really want to. I can take him to the floor before he's even had time to blink. But I don't; that's not what I've come here to do. It's the complete opposite.

"Fine. I like a challenge," he says, releasing his hold of me. I stand back to my original height, retreating from him as he collects himself with a crack of his neck. "Tomorrow, we will go for breakfast. I'll pick you up at your home," he says. Not asking. Telling me.

I chuckle, "Lunch, and I'll meet you there."
He smirks and reaches out to touch some hair around my face, "How have you already made me — of all people — beholden to your every word?"

"You flatter me Jude," my voice is naturally sultry as I speak. It's not hard to play a seducer; it comes easy to me, to tease the boy, to tell him what he wants to hear, playing a game of cat and mouse. "Jade gardens at lunch time," I say, my eyes glimmering, a smirk on my lips. "Oh — I adore pastries, if you really wish to impress me," I finish, backing away from him. His hand is left lingering in mid-air where my head once was. "Don't be late!"

He puts his hand to his mouth and calls to me, his voice sends a shiver down my spine, "I will always be early for you."
I leave him standing there in the dark. A smile forms on my lips, but I quickly shake it away.

Walking by the drunken women and the group of girls consoling their crying friend, I strut past with the biggest smile, goading them in my triumph. As I exit, I see the back of an auburn head, her hair up in a low bun showing off her slender neck, talking to a blond girl as I leave. My heart warms the slightest as I go, happy she is safe. I walk away from the men who are too loud for their own good, my silk gown fluttering behind me as I leave the mansion — and Jude Lightfall — returning to the Sparrows' nest to share the news of the first mission.

Chapter Fifteen

First encounter was a success," I exclaim, sitting across from him. I raise my legs to rest atop his desk and Eris' eyes glimmer with triumph — *pride* even? He's already been informed by a Sparrow.

"Yet would you expect anything less from Altaras' most feared assassin?" My tone is sarcastic, but there's a cockiness I can't help but emit.

"Don't get arrogant with me — that self-anointed title does nothing for your vanity." he says, reaching for a map on his messy desk.

"Not self-anointed," I correct, "You designated that title, if I remember rightly. Plus, a little confidence is good for the soul, Eris."

"It makes you sound weak and foolish to sing your own praises. You'll never be the best when you still have much to learn," he sneers.

My mood suddenly turns sour. I flex my fist; I want to snap at him, but acting on anger will only fuel his ego, knowing his words cut me. His mood wavers and rolls like a dice, never knowing if it will land on scorning me or singing my praises.

In the early days of my training, the Sparrows captured an Altaras guard that had landed on the wrong side of Eris. I can't remember if I was ever told the reason but the man was gagged and blindfolded for days, kept in one of the vacant cells in the Sparrows' nest. Eris would not put him out of his misery, yet we all knew he would never leave alive for what he may have seen or heard. Eris had informed me I was the only one allowed to end his suffering. After a week of hearing his moans and cries for help, I crept into his cell and put a knife through his throat — one quick motion, a tear trickling down my cheek as I removed the knife — to end his torture. I had done what he had asked of me, but spent the next week in solitary, as it wasn't to his plan. Eris will always get his way.

"We are to meet tomorrow at noon. Jade gardens," I say, memories from earlier flitting back. Eris puts down his map in frustration.

"I know of the plans Elyria, now leave. I have work to do."

I take my legs off his desk, and nod. "Goodnight," I say, before shutting the door, hearing no response back as I leave.

~

The next morning, I am awake before anyone arrives at the bunker, lapping the training room in a long, sweat-fueled run.

"Daggers first, then combat," a voice enters the training hall. Zirk sets an array of blades of all shapes and sizes on the table, laid out for my choosing. Each deadly once in my hand; each make my eyes light up with excitement. I jog over.

"You know how to brighten my morning Zirk," I pick up a small dagger with a razor-sharp point. I examine the piece of metal closely for a moment, then toss it at the furthest target at the end of the hall. I don't need to go closer to know I've hit the mark.

"Aim for the head next time," he says with a chuckle.

"That's not what I was aiming for," I smirk. The dagger pierces the outline of the man's body right in his private area.

Zirk's deep laugh hums throughout the hall, his brown eyes matching the shade of his dark skin. His shaved greying hair shows his age much more than his face does. Zirk has a softer nature than Eris; he's one of the warmest people I have met. His expertise and training have made me into a skilled fighter, always teaching me to be graceful with my moves and countermoves, to be as stealthy and precise as I can. "It's like a dance," he used to say. "You need to move with your opponent, read his next move, where his feet are placed and where his weight shifts, where his arms will strike." And he would proceed to manoeuvre my body into a blocking or attacking stance. The moves were always beautiful, and I will forever be grateful for his knowledge and the time he took to perfect my skills. Zirk would wait for me to stand before knocking me down again, whereas Eris would kick my already deflated body further into the floor, would crush my hand under his boot for falling. The two would train me in different ways, their fighting styles like day and night. Eris, the brute, focusing all on power and strength. But Zirk is the cat, skillfully waiting for the opponent to show their weakness to strike at the best moment. His strength comes hand in hand with skill. Both have taught me different ways; both have made me the fighter I am today.

Zirk and I throw all morning, one after the other in speed play. Adrenaline pumped, we then follow with obstacle training. Zirk releases the swinging targets with the press of a button; each change of direction challenges my aim as they move. But blades are my weapon of choice, so hitting bullseye on every shot is not unprecedented. I prefer how slick knives are compared to guns; silent and needing a higher level of skill to use, their steel beautiful but deadly.

Combat training finishes the morning's workout. When we fight, neither of us goes easy on the other; we know each other's weak spots after months of fighting together. I kick, he throws a punch. I block one move but fail at the next blow — it staggers me back, right in the stomach. I regain my stance and aim for his head, which he skillfully blocks. However, he doesn't anticipate my leg swiftly catching him by surprise and taking him to the ground. He falls hard on his back. After a few seconds of catching our breath, I offer my arm to help him up.

"You went easy on me today," I say, walking towards my drink.

He nods his head in agreement, his breath harder to catch from the blow. "I could say the same for you," he says narrowing his eyes at me. "Eris told me to keep exposed areas free of harm, no bruises to that face of yours."

I suppress a laugh, "Eris going easy on me? Now that's a surprise."

We share a knowing look.

"He does care for you," Zirk assures me, his eyes softening at my look of disgust.

"He's just dedicated to the cause; he cares for nothing but that," I say cracking my neck and rolling out my shoulders. "I don't think he knows of that emotion or any emotion other than anger."

"Eris is a complex man. This place has made him so."

"There are other ways to lead than inflicting fear and violence."

"Says the assassin training to kill Marik Lightfall," he retorts with a knowing look that I want to swipe off his face.

"Good job I'm not a leader then," I force with gritted teeth, before heading out of the hall, and swishing my braid behind me.

I wash my sweat ridden body and clean the dirt off my skin; the water here has always been ice cold. You would think with the Sparrows' use of tech, we could get a hot water line down here. But no. The freezing liquid travels down my skin, washing away the frustrations of this morning. Whilst drying off, I look at the mirror. My crimson eyes shine against my fresh white hair; I look deadly. Like a demon sent from hell, I look unstoppable. I'm not used to this reflection yet, and probably won't be for a while. The past year has taken its toll on the girl who now looks back at me; she has changed so much, completely different to who she was before. The sadness has left her eyes, replaced with passion and anger — this new look suits the ferocity there. It reflects the fire in her heart.

Today I decide to braid my hair down my back and place the contacts back in my eyes. Xannu has brought me back more cosmetics from the city. After a year of not caring about my appearance, it feels odd to make an effort again. Adornment has been a foreign concept to me, but I now allow myself to relish in the time: a great distraction from my looming thoughts. I brush some silver dust over my eyes and shoulders, finishing with a coral tint to the lips.

Back in my room, Xannu has left a dress. She must have dropped it off whilst I was training with Zirk. The dress is a plain black skirt with a corset top and puffed sleeves to hide my scars. The bodice is lace and it's back tied with satin ribbons. Another beautiful piece she has crafted.

Once changed, I put on some flat shoes — no heels for a walk in the park — and fasten my cloak. Axon is already waiting outside of my room.

"Took you long enough," he says, still leaning against the wall.

"You're exaggerating — it doesn't take that long for me to look this good," the confidence radiates off me. He chuckles behind me — the sound makes my insides warm... just a fraction.

We leave the bunker the same way as always, but this time more cautious since its daylight. I haven't been out in the sun yet — only when its dark. It takes my eyes a few moments to adjust to the natural light: Axon has come to the base so many times, not just at night, and he's used to it. I lift my hood and leave the house before him; we shouldn't be seen together, just in case, so he follows my steps a few feet behind.

It takes us an hour to walk to the gardens, located on the north end of Altaras. We are in good time, so our pace is normal and slow to blend in. The walk is peaceful as I take in the buildings in broad day light, the children running up and down the cobbled paths. The Guards patrolling the housing estates make my hand unconsciously hover over the dagger placed on my thigh. Guards patrolling in groups to instill a constant fear in the people of Altaras. But I don't have that same feeling towards them as the civilians do — I walk straight past with my head held high, fearless.

Chapter Sixteen

The entrance to the gardens is warded by tall iron gates with white jasmines weaving between them, crawling to the top to emit a delightful smell as you enter. I don't have to turn to know Axon is leaving, maintaining a safe distance, hidden somewhere outside of the perimeter. The gardens are beautiful, its flowers are unlike those at Centralis; these are stunning and wild, not defined and cut to perfection, but growing in a unified jungle. The green of the lawns stretches into the horizon, filled with majestic trees: oaks, maples, and willow grow tall in the distance, whilst a huge banyan casts its sporadic branches, its canopy of glossy large leaves, growing strong in the middle — the focal point of Jade gardens. Flower beds strew the pathways, a beautiful array of wildflowers mixing colours in a fiery frenzy. Before the Sparrows, I came here several times with my family.

Entering the iron gates, I look around for Jude but to also scope out my surroundings. To my left, amongst the line of oaks, Jude waits. Delicate moss hangs from the branches, dense canopies almost concealing the boy smartly dressed in trousers and a dark tunic as he lies upon a white blanket, picnic basket beside him. His legs are stretched, his hand blocking the late autumn sun from his face. In this light, Jude's hair shines bright; the light blond reflects amongst his darker strands, creating a shimmer of gold. I study him for a few moments; here, his nature is calm and peaceful when no one is watching. As I walk over, I mentally clock the two men standing near, close enough if the need arose, far enough away to not interfere, keeping their eyes on Jude. *Bodyguards.*

Jude lowers his hands from shading his eyes and pulls his body up to rest back on his arms.
"Don't let me wake you from your sleep," I say, standing over him, now blocking the sun from view and shading his body with my own.

"Not sleeping, just resting from this awful hangover," he says.

"So, you had fun after I left then?" I say, crossing my arms over my chest. He pats the space next to him for me to sit. I obey and take a seat.

"I was only drowning my sorrows after you departed," he replies. I chuckle and push his shoulder playfully.

"I hope there's food in the basket; I'm starving," Jude sits up, pulls the huge basket towards us, and opens the lid. The show of arrogance, the cocky performance from last night has dropped and he smiles — a genuine smile.

"Close your eyes," he says, and I laugh whilst holding a hand up to cover them. Moments later, he curls his fingers in mine and pulls my hand away, unveiling a grand array of fruits and pastries, as well as two glasses and a bottle. I smile. This is just what I needed.

"This is a lot of food; we won't be able to eat it all!" I gasp, locking his eyes with mine. He places my hand down to rest beside me, pulling his own back. Jude is calmer, and more relaxed today; his front has been relaxed — and what is left, I much prefer.
"Well, we'll just have to spend hours here then and not leave until it's all gone." Jude picks up a white ceramic plate and starts piling it with berries and a couple of pastries on top, passing it to me before filling his own. I bring an almond croissant dusted with powdered sugar to my lips, inhaling the

sweet smell of butter as I take a bite, almost gasping at the flavour. I haven't had food like this for so long. Surviving on the basic food provided by the Sparrows in the bunker: chunks of bread, beans, and lentils — anything that lasts underground for a long time.

"Good, right?" he laughs, taking a bite of his own pastry, "I hope I've satisfied your need for baked goods?"

I look to him with delight in my eyes, "You have outdone yourself Lightfall, I could eat ten of these."

Jude laughs deeply as he takes another bite, "I can get you as many as you wish. Our cooks make the best food in Altaras."

This sours my mood. Jude is the son of a brute — a rich man who causes so much suffering and, here I am, indulging in pastries and laughing in the sun. I place the plate down and reach for a glass of the liquid; it smells like elderflower and mint. Without him noticing, I dip my finger in the drink, but my nail comes back clear. A paint designed by the Sparrows coats my nails, a change in the colour detects signs of poisons or narcotics. A fascinating and useful invention. And I now, force of habit, never leave without it.

"You really have the most unique eyes," Jude says as he reaches over and moves a strand of hair that has fallen from my braid, "They glow in the sun."

"My mother's eyes," I counter. Xannu, without a doubt, picked the right colour to attract him and capture his interest in me.

"You say you live with your father. What happened to her?" he asks, his hand still playing with the strand of hair by my ear. I look to meet his eyes, which grow soft at this question. His demeanour from last night has changed, but that could just be from the hangover.

"She died when I was small, I don't really remember her," I say. A sort of truth — she may as well be dead to me; Eris will never allow me to see her again until this is all over.

"I bet you miss her."

I look to the ground. The flashes of memories across my mind make my stomach turn. I think of them, but I'm too frightened to see what has become of them, what it will do to my spirit. I allow the truth to spill out of me — save the lies for *necessity*, "Terribly."

"I'm sorry for your loss," he says, brows furrowed. "I don't know what I would do without my mother. I was a child who often got sick, she would stay with me throughout the nights and the long boring days, not once leaving my side. My father was barely around because of work, but her, she's this family's saviour; she's our glue."

I look up into his dark eyes just then, shining with flecks of gold. They soften as he speaks of his mother, of his childhood. But Jude quickly changes the subject, knowing he has divulged too much too soon.

"When you walked into the hall, I was annoyed that another boy danced with you first," he confesses with a cheeky grin. "I told Izabella to leave, that I did not want to be with her. Then, I went straight for you. We were dating for a month, but it was nothing serious." he laughs, running his hand through his hair, and my eyes go wide. "You were floating around the middle of that room, with a smile so bright your face lit up, dancing to the music like no one else in the world mattered... Your dress was so enchanting as you spun. I knew you had to be mine." he finishes.

We had already known Jude had ties with Izabella, but Eris was certain he would leave her for me. That I would be the one to get under his skin. His dismissive talk of her makes me want to chastise him, but instead I reach up and brush some hair out of his eyes, my tone laced with mischief as I say, "Well, unfortunately for her, I'm glad she's gone."

His lips pull into a half smile, "Her mother will be so disappointed, she has wanted to match us for years."

"Does your mother look for matches?" I ask, genuinely curious of his answer.

"Not really. She didn't let me go to the balls until I turned twenty-one. She's protective, always worried I'll get swept away by it all."

"And did you?" I counter, "Did you get swept away by it?"

"No, I can't stand it, to be honest. I hate the balls; it all feels so… disingenuous. But it's a place to have a few drinks and it's a reason to leave the house."

I contemplate his answer, trying to unpick it — this boy is a labyrinth. In our first two encounters, he seemed so cocky and self-righteous. I thought him to be pretentious — the arrogant son of an important and powerful man. He feels it's all *disingenuous*?

"Do you not enjoy the riches of this place then? Isn't that what elites are born to love?"

"I certainly enjoy the grand and finer things. But I could easily live without it all. It means very little to me."

"Even live without the bodyguards?" I say with raised brows, nodding towards the two men standing by the entrance to the gardens. Their backs are to us, but I can tell by the placement of their arms, poised by their pockets — their weapons are within reach. They are alert, waiting for any sign of danger.

Jude rolls his eyes, then cracks his neck. The movement captivates me, "I can't stand them. Father enforces it for our protection."

I nod my head in understanding, "I see." I wonder if I should push the conversation more towards his father to see if he will divulge. I decide to push.

"And what would you do if you weren't an elite? If your father was not so well known?"

Jude looks out towards the vast space of open grass, like he is imagining his alternate future. "I'll get back to you on that one, Rhea."

My eyes study his, my eyes furrow briefly at how he says my new name so charmingly, remembering for a moment at how he said my true name all that time ago — so much more enchantingly. I nod my head in understanding. The change in his tone indicates he no longer wishes to speak about his father.

"And you? What do you wish to do with your life?" His brows are raised, genuinely wishing to know the answer. The expression differs to his normal smirk and more brazen approach. I think for a few moments before responding, skeptical about how to approach this. I could answer with the elite girl dream — I would like to raise a family and be a devoted housewife. Or I could tell a slither of the truth, just to see how he reacts. If training taught me one thing, it was to choose when to lie and when to tell the truth. I chose the latter.

"I think I'd like to work in the Unity Building, be an advisor or something," I reply, diverting my eyes from his stare and laughing to myself. "I know it's a silly dream, only an elite could do something like that... but I like a challenge." I finish and wait for Jude to laugh or comment that it would be an impossible idea — typical of a response from Eris.

But instead, he says, "That's good, because then I could watch you at the briefings every morning for hours."

I laugh and push his side, a little harder than last time and he almost falls back. Jude laughs as he steadies himself. "I mean it, I think you'd be good. I listen to every word you say, I would probably do anything you tell me. I'm sure everyone in Altaras would do the same."

Nodding my head, those deep brown eyes of his drift to mine once more and we gaze at one another for a while longer.

"Meet my mother?" he asks lazily, falling back to lie on the blanket. I watch him for a moment. Can it really be this easy? To slip into his life? My hesitance to reply makes him say something else. "She'd like you; I just know it."

He pulls me down, so I lie next to him, our shoulders touching, both looking up at the oak leaves and the tiny fronds of moss wisping around our heads. Sunlight trickles through the branches, the sky peeking from behind them. My eyes move from the sky to face him. I study his strong jaw as he looks up, every feature hard and chiseled.

"Okay," I say, entwining our hands together.

Chapter Seventeen

Still lying on the blanket under the tree, our hands remain clasped together. It's not long before I decide it's time to go. I have another engagement to further the mission, so I am done here. I shift to sit up, but Jude holds my arm down. I must remember to act feeble in this situation, so I stay still.

"Tonight," the words murmur lazily out of his mouth. Telling, not asking again. I chuckle, turning my head to face his; he does the same, our faces so close together now.

"Some would say you're rather keen, Mr. Lightfall."

"Always for you," his voice is deep, enchanting, as he rolls back to look at the sky. "Why wait?" His eyes squint at the light pouring through the leaves.

"Tomorrow, tonight is too early for me to get an outfit ready!" I answer, my voice light and full of amusement as I gesture to my dress, "Where should I meet you?"

Jude sits up and I follow. He stands with ease and offers me a hand to help me off the ground, which I accept. Standing before one another, our height — without my heels — is even more laughable; he's nearly a foot taller than me, and I'm not even that short!

"I will let mother know of our plans; she will want to have a dinner prepared to perfection by the cooks. You will join us at the house, and I can send a carriage."

"No that's okay, I prefer to walk."

He nods his head as I say this.

"Really? Alright then, give me your arm."

Puzzled, he pulls out a pen from his pocket and begins to write down his address. The ink stains my forearm.

"8 o'clock," he concludes as he finishes writing, clicking the pen shut. I glance at the address; it was unnecessary as I already knew it from our intel, the route already in my head from the constant study of Altaras' maps. I nod and glance to his face once more, backing away from him. Leaving the sanctuary of the Jade gardens, it doesn't take long before I can feel Axon behind me. It's still light out, so it's safer if he keeps his distance and doesn't make contact until we are back at base.

The long walk back gives me time to think. The events have puzzled my mind; Eris has told me over and over how bad these people are; I have witnessed the horrors that happen in Altaras — to its people. But Jude? He seems different; he doesn't act like his father, or even seem proud to talk about him.

I push these thoughts down. I can't think like this. I can't compromise this mission with overthinking and deviating from the plan. Too many people are relying on me to kill Marik Lightfall. Even if he isn't like his father, Jude will soon despise the ground I walk on. He may want to kill me himself.

Back at the safe house and concealed inside, I wait a few moments for Axon to enter before unlocking the hidden door. Immediately, I sense the shift in his body language. He seems tense.

"What's wrong? Weren't you watching? It went better than expected; I got in!" I grab his arm with excitement, a smile plastered on my face. But he shakes me off and pushes past me, pulling down his hood to reveal his mop of black hair.

"What's with the attitude?" I ask, annoyance bubbling inside me.

He stands by the bookcase, his hair falling in front of his eyes, "I was on a roof nearby, I followed orders and watched the whole thing." His tone is not the same as normal. Something's off.

"Then what's your deal?"

"My *deal* is that I had to watch you roll around eating pastries with Lightfall for two hours," he snaps.

I shove past him and open the trap door, crossing my arms in front of my chest, "That's exactly what Eris told me to do!"

Axon rolls his eyes and lets out a frustrated sigh. "But that doesn't mean I have to enjoy watching it. I hate Lightfall, that's all."

"*Enjoy*? What are you talking about? You know what I have been tasked with, and all it entails... your actions are confusing me."

How can he be mad? He knows the lengths I must go to gain Jude's trust. He has no right to be annoyed with me; he has no say in what I do.

"Likewise, Birdie."

Without a final glance, he sulks down the pitch-black staircase as I roll my eyes and close the trap door behind me, following him into the darkness.

Axon opens the door of the bunker, an influx of light pouring in. But I don't let this go, the irritation from his actions and words compel me to continue, "Axon why are you mad at this?" I grab his shoulder, forcing him to face me. His cloak is scratchy under my touch, the fabric worn and old. He lets out a breath, his muscles contracting as he searches for the right words.

"Eris' plan..." he says, his jaw tightening with each word, "I just don't want Lightfall to..." Axon starts but is interrupted by the slam of a door.

Zirk appears at the end of the hall; his manner is rigid which only means Eris is in a bad mood.
"Meeting. Now!" he orders sternly, his face showing the urgency of his command. It's not like Zirk to raise his voice.
I look to Axon again and his face has relaxed, obviously not wanting to continue our conversation or finish what he planned to say. Axon hates to be on the wrong side of Eris, so never keeps him waiting. Arguing with Eris is even worse than arguing with me.
This meeting room was the first place Eris hit me.
I remember the shock of it. No one had ever done that to me before. The act was showcased in front of the other Sparrows, done to degrade me and demonstrate his influence and dominance. I had once been terrified of this room. Now I walk in, head high.

"Nice of you to join us," Eris spits, without even a turn in our direction.

"I just finished with Lightfall," I answer back, sulking over to the available chair to his right. I deliberately scrape it back against the concrete, making a teeth-clenching sound. It makes me want to smile – but I think better of it.

"Well done, little bird." Eris says low under his breath. An obvious compliment he hopes will go unnoticed by the other Sparrows to maintain his fierce demeanour. I allow myself to smile, proud that he is finally pleased with me, if only for a split second. But I know in my soul that I should not feel proud of his validation, not after all he has and continues to do to me. I should spit his approval right back at him and not want it, yet I'm ashamed to say I do.
The meeting hall smells of mildew, earth, and thick cigarette smoke. A smell I have grown accustomed to over the past year

but still grimace at. When I leave, I use twice as many perfumed oils to get the stench out of my hair.

On my first day here, I never would have thought I would sit amongst these people. But here I am, at his right hand. Eris, in his twisted ways, now values me more than the other Sparrows for my mission is paramount. Of upmost importance in getting this revolution started.

Axon takes his place, standing to the side of Eris, concealed by shadows but watching on. He never takes his seat, always hovering behind Eris. Zirk and Xannu sit opposite us on the round table. Other Sparrows have joined today including Dumah and Israfil — both much older than I, in their thirties, having been Sparrows for over a decade. Tissa is here too, dressed in a cloak: beneath it is a bright orange dress and gold dupatta; she sticks out like a sore thumb compared to our black and gloomy attire. She's like a canary in a coal mine. Her dark tanned skin is beautiful against the colour of her dress, sitting alongside Dumah, whose complexion is dark and striking. The two are always close; his massive physique completely protects and shelters Tissa, always.

Tissa, with her tiny mouse-like frame and quiet words is one of the most important people in this room. She works in the Unity building: the secretary for Idris Amal; her job and what she hears are critical to the rebels. I don't see her much — only on matters of serious concern which means tonight must come with important intel.

Vera sits on Eris' left, her hair grey and thin with age, cheeks hollow, deep-set wrinkles covering her face and rimming her amber eyes. She's been a Sparrow longer than everyone here, often proudly reminding everyone that she has watched every step of Eris' rise through the ranks to become our leader.

Eris' face is tense, his fists clench with elbows flexed on the table. He holds up a finger, and with a repetitive flick, signals Axon; he swiftly responds and appears with dark brown liquid, filling Eris' glass without a word. Eris downs it in a gulp, to which it is refilled, and again he drains the glass. All of us are seated around the table, pretending not to notice. We avoid his eyes as Axon returns to the shadows after filling his glass again.

Eris must know something — something bad if he plans to drain his cup so quick. His wild hair is pulled back into a band, accentuating the long scar across his face. We wait for him to start as my gaze flashes to Xannu who avoids my eye contact, her dark kohl eyes set on Eris.

"Tissa has come with some... disheartening news," he spits out.

Tissa looks down at her hands covered in red henna and silver rings resting in her lap; her short, wavy cropped hair falls forward onto her face, "I..." she starts but then stumbles. Eris speaks over her.

"The Consulate has captured Jakk." He slams his fist on the table, the glasses trembling in answer. My toes curl at the revelation, but my face doesn't show any sign of emotion. I look around the room at each of the Sparrows, but their expressions are blank, the same as mine. None of us make a sound, waiting for him to finish. "He was caught in the Unity building."

Dumah shakes his head and folds his arms, a look of confusion on his face. A simple expression that mirrors the thoughts of all of us. *What was Jakk doing in the Unity building?*

Jakk is our youngest Sparrow; I learned, not long after being here, that he was the one to give me my message that night at the ball. He's only eleven. And he's been *captured* by the Consulate.

"Our training has taught him well; I hope for our sake — and his — he knows what he needs to do and takes the pill. If not, he will be executed in front of the crowds." Eris finishes.

We sit in silence before a voice breaks the tension, "Don't they want to interrogate him?" Israfil says to Tissa, "This all seems so quick?" His wiry body leans towards the table as he braces his slender forearms in front of him. Tissa looks to Eris for permission to speak and he nods, no words spoken as he instead takes a long drag of his now lit cigarette, blowing thick smoke into the room.

Tissa clears her throat and tucks a short lock of dark hair behind her ear; her hazel doe eyes are sorrowful, "Everyone at the building was shocked to see a boy so out of place. We all saw it happen. Jakk was standing in the middle of the foyer, his arm was raised and he was chanting," she rushes, glancing around the room at our faces. Tissa is soft; she is not a fighter like us. Only a messenger. "He was saying 'Rebel with us, rebel with us. Join our rebellion!' over and over like a song. It was so shocking; I couldn't believe he was doing it—"

"Get to the point, Tissa." Eris orders, anger sparking off him. She cowers at Dumah's side, but nods.

"Sorry, yes. The guards quickly escorted him out, but the whole scene started a panic. Idris had no communication with any of the others in front of me, but he was in meetings in his office the whole day. I do know that a mandatory Consulate briefing is airing live tonight. I think we all know what that means."

"Why would he do that? That's not like Jakk?" I question, looking to Eris for confirmation. Jakk, the boy who would often visit the nest when Eris needed a message delivered, who would always have a shy smile on his face when Axon ruffled his hair, or when I gave him my last chunk of bread. Eris' gaze is set straight in front of him, looking at no one. It makes no sense; why would Jakk do this?

"I don't know," she answers with a shake of her head.

"We don't know," Eris starts, "But, in an hour, we may see that boy shot in the head for crimes against the Consulate. Or by now, he may have already confessed."

"If we run, we could make it to the..." Dumah starts but Eris cuts him off.

"We do not show sympathy to traitors."

His words shut us all up. Any hope of saving Jakk is diminished with his order.

"They don't know anything; they can only guess—" Vera starts to speak but is silenced by the fury in Eris's eyes.

"The Sparrows have been here for hundreds of years, longer than any of us have been alive, hidden in their midst, and NOW we have been exposed to the Consulate," he seethes, venom spitting from his tongue after every word. Vera only nods her head in defeat. I cross my arms over my chest, fighting the urge to rip his head off for taking his anger out on us.

"They are going to be on the highest alert now. Our plans have gone to shit!" he spits, rising from his chair and throwing it across the room with a bang. The veins in his neck and forearms bulge as though ready to burst at any second.

Vera turns to Eris, "Let's wait until the announcement," she tries to calm him down as he paces the room, but his body is tense with anger, making us all uneasy.

Chapter Eighteen

We sit in silence for the next hour, not wanting to anger Eris more or heighten the tension within the room. A shiver trickles down my spine as a red flash announces that the viewing is ready to proceed. The Sparrows before us had well equipped the room, the screen lighting up whenever a briefing is aired, keeping those underground in the loop. The holographic images illuminate the table from all angles, designed so we all can see the scene unfolding before us, from wherever we are seated.

Tissa sucks in a sharp breath as the image of a bound Jakk kneeling before the Unity building is shown. The crowd of Altaras are not visible on the screen, but we all know they are silently watching, horrified at what they are about to witness. Israfil runs a hand through his long blond hair as we exchange a silent look. The board of commanders are sat in their raised chairs before him, his little head cloaked in a fabric bag to conceal his identity from the rest of Altaras. He looks so small.

Idris clears his throat, standing on his platform, ready to give his speech. "Today, there has been an act of treason." he starts, looking directly into the camera. "The person before you has acted against the Consulate. Against you — the people of Altaras."

I look along the line of commanders, ten of them sat high in their chairs. My eyes dart to Marik Lightfall; his face is fixed, not on the boy in front of him, but to the side as though he can't bear to look at him. Would Jude be proud of his father in this moment? Does he stand by him through everything?

Idris continues, "These acts of defiance will never be tolerated here and any deviance from our rules will suffer the same consequence," he says, eyes burning with fury.
Eris punches the wall as he finishes, the sound echoing throughout the hall. A message to us.

Marik Lightfall stands, tightly grasping his bony hands. "It is my honour to extinguish this piece of vermin from our sacred land," he says, his tone laced with a hint of contempt as he steps down from his platform and strides towards Jakk's kneeling body. He revels in this, taking pleasure in ending a life. Jakk's life.

In the room, Tissa holds a hand over her mouth, her eyes brimming with tears as Dumah's hand rests on her shoulder. Marik positions himself to the side of Jakk, bending down and whispering something in his ear. Then, he straightens and pulls out a gun from the inside of his jacket. He aims the barrel at Jakk's head — at least this will be quick.

He waits a second before turning to the camera, directly staring down its lens. His gun remains pointed at Jakk's head; I look at him, loathing his very existence. But he does something unexpected — he lowers his gun. Tissa sucks in a breath; Xannu's brows are furrowed, her expression mirroring my own confusion.

Marik Lightfall steps back, and the stage swarms with Altaras guards, deep red uniforms marching into view. I count twelve guards, from all directions with guns at their sides. They make a crescent around the back of Jakk's small body, positioning themselves so that they too can face the camera. He looks so small up there, and the trembling of his body is visible to all. A puddle pools around his knees.

I swallow the bile that starts to rise. Tissa is crying softly now as Dumah whispers in her ear, trying to calm her sobs amongst the silence now filling the room.

Marik Lightfall stands to the side of the stage, his arms crossed in front of him. A slight smile pulls up at the corner of his mouth, this face is not Jude's. Jude's smile is charming and roguish, Marik has a smile of pure evil, "This is what we do to traitors."

And the guards open fire.

So many bullets used, all of them decimating that poor boy's innocent body. No one deserves this. The act is hideous, inhumane — a barbaric tactic used by sadistic men to inflict the greatest fear.

After the guards' rounds are emptied, the noise of the attack ceases. The room is deadly quiet. Blood starts pooling and drowns Jakk's lifeless body in a sea of red. Only then does the camera switch off and the screen turns black.

"Fuck!" Eris shouts.

I look around to my fellow Sparrows, their expressions are quiet and morose.

"He didn't deserve that," says Vera, "we will be more careful."

"That boy was a traitor; he betrayed our cause." Eris spits, walking past the table and into the centre of the room. "We will have less movement at the base; no more coming and going; we can't attract any attention. Tissa, you can't be seen travelling any more. I will send Sparrows to you. Elyria, you are going to speed this mission up, I want that man dead by the end of this week," Eris says, his words slick with venom. "Gut him and make him scream."

I nod my head in understanding. I don't even argue. I agree with every part of my being.

"Done," I reply, leaning back in my chair. Eris nods his head and storms out of the room, slamming the door on his way out. We sit in stunned silence.

"If I get the chance I could act tomorrow..." I start, but Vera cuts me off.

"No. It needs to be broadcasted," she looks to all of us, her expression full of emotion. "It needs to be shown to the city."

I nod my head, Dumah and Israfil murmuring agreement.

"Keep to the plan, Elyria. You do it at a briefing," Zirk says as he looks to me. The first time he has spoken since the execution of Jaak. "Marik Lightfall is at every one. He needs to be made a spectacle of."

"Eris is angry, as we all are. What we — what Altaras just witnessed — was barbaric and merciless. The whole city will be on alert."

Vera looks to Tissa, who now wipes her teary eyes with the back of her hands. "Act the same; we don't divert from the plan. We just have to be more vigilant."

"And Jude?" I say, glancing between the Sparrows before me.

"Vera's right," Israfil says, his eyes a sorrowful blue as he looks to me. "Keep to the plan; act like you believed what just happened was the right thing. Say whatever you need to earn his trust."

I nod my head in understanding, "I have a dinner with his mother tomorrow evening."

"I'll get an assortment of dresses; I don't think I will chance returning here every day," Xannu adds, finally breaking her silence.

"Jakk was a good boy, I cannot understand what happened today, but we will find out. For his sake," Vera says, her tone resolute and calm.

Xannu's next question makes my stomach turn.

"Does he have any family?" she asks Vera. Her worry for his family, driven by her own experience; Axon and her, small and confused as to why their father was not returning home flashes in my mind. Xannu suddenly forced to become the pillar of strength for them both. I wince.

"He has no one. He lived in the orphanage," she replies, and I can sense it breaks even her cold heart to say it. To imagine Jakk living amongst other children with no family to go home to breaks my heart. Like so many other children living in the orphanages dotted around the city — their parents killed for treason or imprisoned due to the Consulate's orders.

The room returns to silence as we all try to process what just happened. Dumah gets up from his chair and leaves the room, only to return a few moments later with a bottle. He begins to fill our glasses with the dark brown liquid, setting the now empty bottle down onto the table. He raises a glass.

"To Jakk. The Sparrows will remember you," he says, before drinking the whole glass in one. For whatever reason, Jakk decided to go out on his own and act in a way that could have harmed our mission, our rebellion, and so much more. My only conclusion as to why the Consulate did not address his words in the briefing was to buy themselves more time. To keep the rebels without a voice and platform. By not mentioning us, less questions are raised. But surely people must wonder what he had done so wrong.

Jakk was still a Sparrow, and his life was taken because of it. I look to my left and even Axon joins in with the toast; yet still, he leans against the wall, apart from us.

"To Jakk," we all say, consuming the liquid whole.

Chapter Nineteen

I look like I belong here. My hair is curled, small braids laced around my head; the forest green dress is snug to my body, the fabric falls straight down, past my thighs as gold piping edges the high neck with its peephole detail. The skin of my cleavage is exposed, also highlighting my dainty crescent moon necklace: gold to match my eyes.

It was left on my mattress without a note. But I know what it means. It's his way of an apology. Eris gifted me the jewellery: my praise for the mission, an apology for also being a brute. Validation washes over me, but again so does the looming guilt for wanting it in the first place.

The dress has long sleeves which are tight to my arms but float at the wrists, draping to the floor to meet the long silk folds of the skirt. The fine material is so delicate it could rip with the slightest tug. The only detail which sets me apart from these people is the cold hard metal of the dagger sheathed to my thigh, pressing against my skin. Its access is easy through a hidden incision in the fabric cleverly crafted by Xannu. My heels are tall, but I walk with grace up the steps of the huge manor. Two granite lion statues guard the home, their bodies bigger than a carriage. This mansion, situated inside the Citadel, is not unlike the one hosting the balls each month, but it is home to the Lightfalls. Giant white pillars covered in marble tiles adorn either side of the doors, their height just over twenty feet. The house has ornate metal railings surrounding the perimeter – the elite never seems to tire of hiding behind walls. Guards stand by the entrance, asking for my name before I'm permitted to enter. The front door opens as I reach the last step up, a woman standing in my path.

"Hello Miss Fellows, he's waiting for you in the library," the woman says. She doesn't appear a threat; her manner is kind and welcoming — paid to be just that.

"Thank you," I reply as I cross the threshold, studying my surroundings as I do. The foyer is bigger than the training hall and whilst there's a huge staircase in the middle, the room is mostly empty. The walls are void of décor, little other than clinical white paint. "And where is the library?" I ask, passing the woman, my skirts trailing behind me.

"Up the stairs and take two lefts," she says cheerily, closing the door behind me. I would have thought her to be less positive, considering the man she works for is so cruel. He really must pay well. I nod my head in thanks, giving her a genuine smile before making my way up. Temptation itches at me to explore whilst I'm alone, to take a right, open every door, rifle through every drawer and rustle through every paper I find. I push the need down and follow the woman's instructions: two lefts and I am faced with the open door to the biggest library I have ever seen.

The shock almost knocks me back. So many books. I enter the room, my eyes wide in bewilderment. The floor to ceiling shelves are lined with books of all sizes; dark red covers are embellished with gold and navy blue, some with worn cracked spines. I run my fingers across the line closest to me, picking one up and smelling the cover. In the middle of the room, I turn — the carpet floor is so soft under foot. A figure stands on the raised platform, his back to me, peering out through the huge windows.

"I've not even read them all."

I place the book back into its original spot and walk towards him. "How could you not?" My tone is genuine, "I would be here all day if I could." *Books!* Incredible. Something that's been so heavily censored by the Consulate.

I walk directly to stand behind the boy before me. My proximity makes him tense, as though he can already feel the fast beat of my heart. His hair is a halo of blond, glistening, the light reflecting off it.

"I can make that a reality," Jude says as he turns to face me. The sun creates a shimmer on his high cheekbones; his eyes look hazel in this light, illuminating the soft flecks of gold and green found there.

"Only if you stay here with me all day while I read. At my beck and call, bringing coffees and *lots* of bake goods," I tease. I try keep my tone flirtatious and his forearms tense at my words. "What are they about?" I nod to the stacks of leatherbound pages.

He steps closer to me, "Mostly apothecary books. That's my mother's doing, she loves medicinal plants: healing and wellbeing, that sort of thing." A hint of a smile creeps across his lips, then falters as he carries on. "My father has his strategy books, tactical planning, mechanics, and the like. The history of Altaras and so forth," he meets my gaze, "Boring factual stuff mostly."

His mother's interest for herbal remedies and recipes for healing surprises me. How could she be with a man that kills and tortures, if she has a passion for medicine?

"No, it's amazing. What do the history books say about Altaras?"

"There's one..." he starts, moving towards the shelf searching for a book with furrowed brows as his fingertips trace each binding. The action is so normal, yet so entrancing. I can't take my eyes from him.

"This," he says as he pulls down a navy leather bound book, "is a log from one of the first Commanders — the Rostam line. He was a direct descendant of one of the original elders. Rostam writes about how the elders formed the Consulate after years of disagreements. The city needed structure, so the Consulate was developed to oversee and govern its people."

"That's fascinating," I reply, spilling my genuine excitement over the book as I study its cover: *The Early History of Altaras*. "Do you have more books on the elders?" I stare at the leather book in my grasp.

Jude chuckles at my enthusiasm, the sound is pleasing to my ears, and I feel a flush trace my cheeks.

"Yeah, a few, but they aren't that interesting. I wouldn't get your hopes up for a good read."

"I think it's important to know our history. Altaras needed leadership. Control." My tone flattens at my own words — some truth at first, but the latter rises bitterly in my throat, choking my true feelings about our leadership, of his father's actions. Jude's hand reaches for mine, but he hastily withdraws it, as though he thinks better than to touch me.

"What's wrong?" I search his eyes for answers. "Jude?"

He turns back to the window, looking out to what I now see is a garden. A garden composed of lush green lawns and adorned with trees and flowers. Placing the book on the nearest table, I reach up and put a hand to his shoulder, stepping round to face him once more.

"My father is a wicked man," he starts, snorting in disgust and cracking his neck, "I assume you saw the spectacle he put on last night."

My heart tightens — innocent Jakk, his lifeless body, cut down like a rabid animal. This side of Jude I did not expect. I never assumed he would be upset, or even angry about his father's conduct. I try to think of the best way to navigate this situation. I could try to reason with his father's actions to seem in agreement with his ideology and avoid any suspicion, but being his confidante seems like a better approach.

I inhale and reach up to gently stroke Jude Lightfall's face — an action my body has no control over. Attentively brushing my fingertips over his cheek, I hold his face in the palm of my hand.

"His actions are not a reflection on you." I say as I caress his jaw, his eyes fluttering closed at my touch.

He reaches up and places his hand over my own, "They are."

I should hate this boy. I am programmed to. I should want to kill him — I *should* kill him, for his father should suffer, like he has made so many others. But I fear my head has no control over my body at this very moment. Or at any moment when it comes to Jude Lightfall.

"Then be better than him," I whisper, meeting his eyes. "Prove yourself." His eyes lower to the floor.

To lighten the mood, I step back, a genuine smile on my face as I turn in front of him, spinning to showcase the dress and my body.

"I got this today; do you think your mother will be impressed?" I laugh and stop to face him. The dress pools at my feet.

"She will indeed," he grins, and I can see the light gradually returning to his eyes. I offer out my hand and walk in the direction of the doors to leave the library. "Let's go eat, I'm starving."

"As you wish, Rhea."

We walk down the stairs, our hands still entwined as Jude Lightfall leads me to the dining room. Pushing open the doors, we enter a regal room with a long oak table topped with many bursting plates of vegetables, fruits, meats, and breads. The food alone can fill twenty mouths, not just three. I look to him, but he has already read my mind. "Four of us. Father will also be joining."

At his words, my blood turns cold, and my pulse quickens. I'm going to be in the same room as Marik Lightfall. "I didn't realise he would be joining," I say, to cover up the drumming of my heart in my ears.

"He wanted to meet you."

I want to scream, to tighten my grip around Jude's hand and squeeze so hard he groans.

"You'll impress him," he says, walking me to a seat at the table. He pulls out my chair and beckons for me to sit. "It will be fine."

I grind my teeth and hold in my fury. It may be fine, or I may throw my dagger at his chest before we even have dessert. Just as the thought comes, the doors to the far right of the room swing as the maid pushes them open. Two people emerge. I hold in a breath as Jude gestures for me to rise.

Chapter Twenty

A honey blond, elegant woman walks in through the left, her light airy emerald dress highlighting the green of her eyes. She's much smaller than Jude, smaller than me even, but her frame is strong, and she walks with purpose. Ethereal, almost. They look alike, but Jude's hair is more ice toned like his father. They both have high cheekbones, full rosy lips, tanned skin from the sun. She's gorgeous, but she's also married to the most hated man in Altaras. The devil walks beside her, his dark navy suit tailored to perfection. Even more so in person, wickedness pours from his face — angry at the world. His tilted chin indicates his inflated sense of pride, a constant grimace on his lips. He looks nothing like Jude, apart from how tall he is. Other than this, the resemblance dies there. He has a slender face with pointed, sharp features. His short white hair gelled in place, so solid even the wind couldn't move it.

Jude clears his throat when they are seated; Marik at the head of the table, and his mother opposite us. "Father, Mother, this is Rhea Fellows," he gestures to me, and I nod my head to each of them.

"It's a pleasure to meet you," I say sweetly, urging down the bile that rises in my throat.

"Fellows… I don't recall that name," Marik says as he takes his seat, waving his arm impatiently for the maid to serve his food. I want to jump across the table and strangle him, but I clear my throat and brush my hands across my dress, wiping the sweat from my palms.

"My father and I live in the agriculture sector," I start, recalling the intricate backstory I was forced to memorise. "He retired a few years ago. We live a quiet life."

I look to his father. He does not meet my stare, instead focusing on the food in front of him.

Without looking up, he says, "That explains the scars on your hands. I would hate a quiet life."

My eyes flash to my fingers, covered in both rings and marks much lighter than my olive tone; I raise my eyebrows at the slightly offensive comment. The one thing I wouldn't be able to hide without gloves. Jude coughs, and his mother tries to cover up the insult.

"A lot quieter than our lives," she chuckles. "You'll have to teach us some of that life."

I smile, looking to her. She seems so different from Marik, her nature soft and elegant. How has she put up with him for so many years?

Marik scoffs at his wife's words, making us all look over to him, "I'm afraid quiet lives have little purpose, Odessa; would you really want to give up all of this for a life that contributes little?"

I bite my tongue, not saying a word, only looking into the eyes of a delusional man. One who has no idea what the rooks or medis suffer with every single day. Who can sit here in his manor and laugh at their — our — expense?

But what surprises me is the sharp intake of breath from beside me as Jude says, "I might just come and live in the fields with you." Sarcasm drips from his words. This comment is not intended for me, but for the man sat at the head of the table. "How about that, father? Should we leave this big house and live in a small hut on a farm, which actually contributes to the lives of Altaras?"

Jude's comment stings as I don't live in a field, a hut or anything of the sort. His intent is clearly to evoke a response, but it's not directed at me. My eyes dart to his father to gauge a reaction; he tightens his grip on the fork slathered in meat, cooked so rare that blood drips from it. It pools on the white plate; his mouth slightly ajar, his nostrils flaring as he eyes his meal with a cold stare.

"No kids there for you to murder." Jude spits across the table.

His mother gasps, clearly shocked by his outburst. I move my hand to grip his under the table and squeeze.

"That's enough Jude," his mother says, her tone harsh, "Not with our guest present."

She glares at him, but Jude's eyes are trained on his father, both faces tight with anger. Marik Lightfall puts a mouthful of meat in his gob and chews. The vein at his neck bulges.

"But I suppose you can still slaughter the pigs. Anything to get your fix, father."

Marik slams his palm on the table. The maids across the room shudder, and I look to his mother whose eyes are now closed. Like she knows exactly what will happen next.

"Do not speak to me that way, boy."

"What will you do about it?" Jude taunts. I squeeze his hand again; he grips my fingers in a tight cocoon, a protection from the poison that is his father.

"I have lost my appetite," Marik says. He scrapes his chair back and wipes his mouth with the back of his hand; as he walks past, I hold my breath, but the faint stench of bloodied meat and musk fills the air as he goes. I resist the urge to spin out of my chair and launch my dagger at him.

Once he leaves, it's like the room exhales the breath we're all holding.

"Mother, I apologise for the outburst..." Jude starts, but she interrupts him.

"That was uncalled for Jude. You embarrassed him. You embarrassed me. And you embarrassed Miss Fellows," she says, before following her husband through the doors.

Jude cracks his neck and takes a mouthful of the wine in front of him, gulping half the glass in one go.

"Jude," I start, looking up to him. His face portrays nothing but anger.

"I'm sorry Rhea, I could not just sit there and pretend I was happy in his company for the next hour."

"You don't need to apologise," I say. Gently, I squeeze his tense hand, and he returns the gesture, brushing his thumb over mine. "Family is a tricky thing."

"No one's family is as tricky as mine."

My appetite totally eroded, I stand and pull Jude up with me. "Show me around?" I ask, attempting to change the subject.

He wipes his mouth on a napkin, leading the way out of the dining hall. "Let's go."

Jude takes me to the gardens, a place we often seem to end up in. It makes me wonder if he would've brought Elyria here too. Would our lives have been consumed by dinners and garden visits if I was not taken by the Sparrows? But gardens are a place that we both seem to gravitate towards — soothed by nature. Perfectly trimmed hedges border the gardens, some cut in intricate spirals, others in pristine lines. Delicate flowers overflow the cobbled paths, each lining its way to meet the other in an intricate maze; a climbing vine winds its way around a stone rotunda, the bright purple flowers scenting the evening air. In the middle of the garden, an ornate fountain entwined with jasmine decorates the space, it's water a constant trickle: soothing to the ear. As we get closer, flashes of colour bob beneath the surface.

"Fish," Jude mutters, dipping his hand in.

"Won't they get sucked through the fountain?" I ask, peering at the flashes of gold, swimming beneath the lily pads. "No, they're quite safe. Don't worry," he chuckles. I contain my own amusement. Above us the clouds have started to shift, swirling and bleak — sign of a stormy night ahead.

I ponder what I should say next, how I should navigate this conversation, and if I should delve deeper into this mission.

"Do you like your father?" I ask, the bold statement hot on my lips.

Jude is silent for a moment, then rolls his shoulders. "I haven't spoken the words to answer that out loud before," he says finally, looking to the water. That tells me all I need to know.

"You don't have to," I assure him, trying to offer any semblance of comfort that I can. "Blood shouldn't bond you forever."

My hand runs through the soft stream of water, my gold rings glisten as the fish swim up against my fingers, my hand jerking back in surprise at one touching my fingertip. Jude laughs and flicks some water up at me, covering my dress in droplets.

"This dress is expensive you know..." I tease as I flick water back at him, droplets falling on his face. He grins, and to my dismay, it's a beautiful sight.

"I will buy you any dress you desire," he replies, a wicked smirk creeping on his lips.

I stare up at him, but the moment is broken as heavy rain starts pouring, covering us in a shower of water. We both look up and then to each other. My smile is big and bright. His blond hair is wet and slicked against his head, droplets cascading down the strands and into his eyes. I get the sudden urge to reach out and move the wet strands from his eyes, to touch his full wet lips with my own. The unsettling feeling of kissing him in this moment builds low in my stomach, it makes my fingers tingle and my head swim with dizziness. Not a kiss for the mission — for what I *want*. My own selfish need to be touched. But I can't let myself think like this. I *can't*. I sense Jude moving towards me, eyes raking over my body. He wants this too. The need is evident in his eyes.

So, thinking with my head and stepping back, I grab his hand to disturb him from his thoughts and pull us towards shelter. Jude picks up speed, and so does the rain, its droplets cooling my now-burning skin. Once inside, water pools at our feet, creating puddles where we step. Jude's eyes are on me once more, and the burning sensation quickly returns.

"Jude, ask the maid for some spare clothes. She can clean up in the guest room." his mother's voice startles us from above; she stands attentively on the staircase.

Jude straightens and wipes a hand through his damp hair. "Of course, mother," he says, looking between us, "can we propose that you stay the night? I think it's safer here than going out in that storm."

I take a moment to respond; Eris will be furious if I don't return tonight, and I don't even want to think about Axon's reaction. I look up to his mother, her hands are clasped delicately, resting poised on her stomach. This could be good for getting some intel; I can appease Eris with whatever information I find tonight.

"If that is okay with you?" I ask her, moving the wet hair stuck to my face. In this moment, I feel ridiculous, like she caught two children kissing in the rain. I search for Jude's hand and interlock our fingers, a slow smile forming on my lips. "I'm sure my father will understand that the storm is too dangerous," I say as the lightning cracks. The sound booms through the manor.

"You're welcome to stay, of course. Jude, may I speak to you while our guest gets changed?"

Jude nods his head once then turns his attention back to me. "This way," he says.

He offers me his arm and I follow.

Chapter Twenty-One

Jude takes me up the stairs and to the right of the staircase. Instead of the first left towards the library, we walk along the corridor lined with doors. We take the fourth left, and he ushers me in. The bedroom is regal; a four-poster bed is situated at the back of the room; huge red curtains drape the big window overlooking the gardens. The covers are pulled back; there are plush white pillows looking comfier than anything I've ever set my eyes on. In the middle of the room sits a large Kashan rug: dark red mixed with gold, it almost hits wall to wall. If this is the guest bedroom, I wonder how the master bedroom looks. A door to the right of the room is ajar; I can make out the outline of a bathtub atop a marble-tiled floor.

Jude clears his throat, "You can clean up in here, I will have the maid bring you some dry clothes."

"Thank you for being so kind." I turn to face Jude leaning up against the door frame, his arms crossed in front of him. "You can't be here when I change, you know. Go to bed." I move to playfully push him out of the room. He grabs my wrist and leans down to meet my ear, "But I wish I could." The amusement rings clear in his voice.

I bite my cheek from smiling too much. Damn him and his heart raising words.

"Get out, you're making puddles on the floor." I retort, finally pushing him from the room. I go to close the door, but he lodges his hand by the frame.

"As you wish, but one day I won't be so gracious," he says as I shake my head and close the door in his face. I quickly press my ear to the wood, detecting the faint sound of him chuckling as he carries on down the hallway.

Bending down, I unstrap the heels from my feet and sigh as my toes meet the soft carpet. I pad on tiptoes to the bathroom, bunching up my soaked dress so as not to make any more mess. The bathroom is stark white compared to the darkness of the bedroom; a white tub sits in the middle of the room, white countertops, and a huge mirror. The bathroom is already stocked with soaps and oils, and I open each one. It's like inhaling a little piece of heaven: lavender, almond, rosemary, and vanilla fill my senses. I close my eyes in delight. Placing the bottles back on the counter, I turn the faucet and begin to run a bath. A *bath!* I can't remember the last time I had anything other than an ice-cold shower. Picking an amber-coloured bottle, I dip my nail into the liquid, and it comes back clear. Safe to use. I then empty the contents into the running water. Reaching my hands up to the clasps of my dress, the material falls to the floor in a heap. I unbuckle the dagger strapped to my thigh, laying the leather and metal on the counter, and submerging myself gradually into the steaming hot water.

I release a long sigh, the water heating my sore muscles and bones, instantly soothing as though it can heal every ache and pain. I dip my head back and let the water consume my body, only returning to the surface once I'm out of air. Checking the other bottles — a force of habit now — I rub them over my body, and feel the bumps and dents over my skin. I rub some over my hair and the fragrance makes me close my eyes. I savour the smell.

After the water in the tub turns cold, it's time to dry off. I find towels in the cabinet and wrap them around my body, not forgetting to fasten the dagger back to my thigh, whilst exiting the room. Right on time, there's a soft knock at the door and the same woman who greeted me at the stairs enters, carrying a stack of materials of deep jeweled tones.

"These are Mrs. Lightfall's old summer clothes, please — take your pick." She places them on the bed and quickly exits.

The first garment I pick up is a black silk sleep robe. I decide this will do and put the cool material on my body, fastening it at the waist. My wet hair drips down my back as I wander around the room. I look under the bed, in every wardrobe, every cabinet, behind every curtain, and even pull back edges of the huge rug. But I find nothing of importance. I will have to wait till the middle of the night to explore; I can easily conjure an excuse as to why I'm out. Looking for water, or something along those lines. Deciding this is going to be a long few hours, I go to bed and turn off the ceiling light, settling above the covers. I rest my back against the mahogany headboard; if I'm going to stay here, I may as well make myself comfortable. I switch the side lamp on, creating a soft glow to the room but my thoughts are interrupted by another knock. Yet this time, there's no pause as the door swings open. Jude stands in the doorway holding a metal tray.

"Thought you may be hungry as we missed dinner." He walks to the bed and places the tray in front of my feet. This is the most casual I have ever seen him: cream tunic, dark trousers, and sleeves rolled at the elbows. Jude takes off the silver cloth to reveal bread, olives, and cheese. My stomach growls in thanks.

"Have you eaten?" I ask, finally taking my eyes off the plate that's making my mouth water.

"No, not yet—" he answers, so I quickly interrupt him.

"Join me?" I ask, patting the bed.

"Very well." He closes the door behind him, then positions himself before me. He lies on his stomach, plopping an olive into his mouth as I reach to pull a chunk of bread from the platter, smelling it. To Jude, this must seem a normal habit, but for me, I'm smelling for poisons or narcotics mixed in with the food. Detecting nothing suspicious, I take a huge bite. I hear Jude chuckling as I do; he tears off some bread and eats it.

"Was your mother upset?" I ask, continuing to tear off chunks.

Jude is quiet for a moment. "Nothing she isn't used to. He's a hard man to endure; I apologise that he mentioned your scars."

I can imagine, I want to say but think better of it. "I see them every day; it's nothing I'm not used to." I flex my fingers, admiring them. "Your mother is different... nicer."

My comment makes his mouth turn up at the edges.

"Well, I think your scars make you look strong like you've fought a battle and won," he replies. "Yes, she's very different; they're polar opposites."

I nod my head in agreement. "How did they meet?"

"At a ball, their parents made a match. Both of their families are elites." he answers, rolling to face the ceiling, his head close to my legs. "And yours?"

"Their parents didn't create a match. My mother met him in class. They grew up together," I tell the story of my actual parents, not the ones I made up. For once, I decide to be truthful but I'm not sure why. "They were friends first, my father always told me how he would follow mother around just hoping she would one day return the same feelings. And that day did come... but not for a while." A smile grows on my lips.

"That's a great love story," Jude says. "They loved each other very much?"

"They did."

"My parent's story is incomparable to that," he says, "She puts up with him, that's all."

My heart pulls; he has been brought up in a home with a cruel father and a mother who does not love her husband. "But she loves you," I say, reaching down and moving some of the hair out of his eyes.

"I had a sister."

My hand freezes, hovering above his head.

"She died three years before I was born."

His mother didn't look that old; she must have been so young when she had her. I don't question him; I just let him continue with his story.

"I think that's what made him sour. Losing her made him so angry because he couldn't save her." I stroke his head whilst he talks, his eyes fluttering closed at my touch, as though soothing him just with a stroke of my fingertip.

"Losing Khala made him hate me."

"I'm sure he doesn't hate you," I interrupt, my fingers tangling in his hair.

"I hate him for the father he never was. He hates me for the son I will never be."

I nod my head in silent understanding. Maybe Eris is wrong. Perhaps Jude Lightfall is just misunderstood, he portrays nothing of his father's wickedness. My fingers entwined in his hair, my mind searches every shared moment for a hint of deceit or malice on his behalf. And I find nothing. His anger for his father is evident; is this why he was kept away from

Altaras for so long? Hidden from the spotlight. He hates his own father and is not afraid to tell him so. Every fiber of my being pulls me to the conclusion that I should protect Jude Lightfall. Somehow, I want to protect him. Even if it costs me Eris and the Sparrows' trust.

Chapter Twenty-Two

I sense it's past midnight. Jude has drifted into an unplanned sleep; I listen to the sound of his light snore and feel the gradual heaviness of his body. I remove my hand from his hair and move the bracelet which adorns my wrist. The gold metal is heavy against my skin. I find the green emerald and pluck at it with my nail, the jewel falling into my palm and revealing a tiny vial in its place. With nimble fingers, I remove its lid and roll the contents onto my lips, the liquid cool against my skin. Keeping my mouth closed, I place the vial and emeralds back to their original form and click it closed. With swift movements, I raise up on my knees and hover over Jude's sleeping form, my hands placed either side of his head. Soft snores escape his sleeping lips, his warm breath stroking my face. I study his upside-down head, his full lips, and his long dark eyelashes. I close the distance between us with a light kiss of our lips. The feathery sensation is warm but quick as the liquid from the vial coats his lips, and filters through his system. The narcotic is sure to keep him in a deep sleep for hours.

Quickly, I remove myself from the bed, careful not to disturb him. He remains still, and I rush to the bathroom to wash the potion from my lips. Through the walls, I can hear Jude's snores from the bed, so I pad softly across the bathroom tiles, open the bedroom door, and step out into the darkness of the Lightfall manor.

A faint glow is cast from a side lamp from the end of the hall, persuading me to take a right, following the lighted path. My bare feet are silent as I creep along the corridor and past the landing. The light from the windows highlights the stairs and foyer below. I check for any signs of movement and run swiftly to the other side. This is where the Lightfalls rest. I can feel it in my bones. All I will have to do is open the right door and slit his throat whilst he sleeps. But Eris would kill me for that. It would ruin his plan to make a spectacle of his death. Checking each door, I almost give up, sensing no sounds or disturbance throughout the entire floor. At the end of the hall, a small glow appears under the door frame, its light increasingly apparent as I draw closer. I don't want the person — or people — to be alerted of my presence so I don't dare move past it. I hug the wall instead, my ear pressed close to the frame. I try to breathe as little as possible to interpret the murmurs travelling through the walls, focusing only on the voices. My fingers grip the paneling so hard, I'm sure they're now white.

"You don't know that." A woman's voice — Mrs. Lightfall. There is the persistent thrum of footsteps pacing along the floorboards.

"He has been sharp tongued since he was a boy." A booming, gruff voice. Marik Lightfall. Their conversation goes back and forth, it's mainly incoherent until I catch the last part of Marik Lightfall's words, his voice rising.

"The people of Altaras are told what they are told to keep them at bay. We will figure out ways to grow the crops and find a new water source. It will be a time of hardship but —"

"And what will you tell them when the food runs out? That the ground is becoming desolate and infertile, but you have no explanation as to why you cannot trade outside the walls? Or why you cannot fix the problems we have caused!"

"We will start with population control—"
"Don't you dare! No more killing to solve your mistakes, Marik." Her voice is on the brink of hysterics, "This will cause unrest. People will question this."

"The decision has been made." His response is flat. Final.

I want to scream, to break down the door and confront this devil, this inhuman *thing* that resides just inches away from me. But that's not what I'm here to do, I'm here to be a spy, to listen and wait in the shadows and attack when it is asked of me.
"When do you leave?" she says.

"In the morning, it will happen through the night, all rooks and medis have been chosen."

I hold my breath. Mrs. Lightfall's voice is so quiet as another few sentences are exchanged.

"It is cruel." I hear her say.

"It's the only way."
What's happening through the night? Another torture? Murder? Is someone being held for questioning?

"Odessa, you may be my wife, but your opinion doesn't matter. The commanders decide what's best for Altaras… I need to work. You should leave."
Bile rises to my throat, but I swallow it down to keep myself from retching, steadying myself on the wall for fear of falling. The revelation… it *can't* be true. This is barbaric, a vile act from someone who does not deserve to have the power to enact this kind of hideous crime. Not bothering to hear the rest of the conversation, I sprint back down the hall to the guest room, light on the pads of my feet to prevent any noise. My heart hammers in my ears, the blood rushing to my head. This isn't *real.*

I reach my room and close the door behind me, resting my back against it as I slide to the ground. I curl up, hugging my knees to my chest, taking shallow breaths to calm myself. I match my breathing to the sound of Jude snoring only ten feet away, still passed out flat on his back.

This changes *everything.* The lies, the deception. It's so ingrained in this city, in its people.

Population control. A food shortage. How can this be happening? Altaras is the wealthiest city in Ceraea; how could this be such a problem that the only option is mass killing? It can't be. My breathing steadies as my mind filters through what I've just heard. We must act before the Commanders enact their barbaric plan.

By the time I uncurl myself from the ball on the floor, the tears that have fallen are salted on my cheeks, my eyes now puffy and sore. The light from dawn has started to peek through the windows and the narcotic in Jude's system will wear off soon. I climb back into bed and tug the covers high over my face, putting myself as far away from his sleeping body as possible without falling out.

Thoughts pound in my head and to soothe them, I concentrate on Jude's breathing, the rhythmic pattern of sound that calms my heartrate. It's not long until exhaustion hits me, and my mind ceases to think, a dreamless sleep taking over.

~

I awake to rustling. Instinctively, my hand moves to the dagger still strapped to my thigh, but I halt when I see Jude sitting at the end of the bed staring at me.

"Good morning." His lips pull into a seductive smirk. His hair is tousled, clothes wrinkled from sleep.

"Morning," I reply, suddenly uncomfortable that I stayed the night as I lean against the headboard. I fell *asleep* in the enemy's house. I could have woken up screaming from my nightmares... but for some reason, last night I didn't. I can sleep with my contacts in... that would be hard to explain if he discovered my eyes were no longer gold.

"Normally, I don't let girls sleep over so early on..." he says, his tone cocky and amused.

I roll my eyes and pull the covers tight around me.

"You wish," I yawn. I must have only slept an hour or so.

"I do wish," he chirps, his swagger still present — even this early in the morning. Where does he find the energy?

"Breakfast will be in the dining room when you're ready."

I groan, sinking into the silky bed linen as he exits the room; I don't want to let myself enjoy the riches, the fancy beds or the luscious food. So many people have died because of Marik and his orders, but here I am, sleeping under the enemy's roof. So many live in lack, fearing the implications of having no money. Yet here, the Lightfall's bathe in it. Shame rattles through me. But it's so hard to resist the lavishness of it all when it's served to you on a literal silver platter.

I change into one of his mother's dresses, choosing a lavender colour to complement my olive complexion. Plus, it has sleeves. I run a brush through my white hair and splash some water on my tired eyes. No cosmetics today so my bare face will have to do but, luckily, I don't need them. Always using my beauty as a weapon...

Down the mahogany staircase, I'm greeted by the delicate play of piano music. The tune is sad, sorrowful, and slow —

the melody is captivating. The dining room doors are wide open so I can see the culprit of this beautiful masterpiece. Jude sits at the grand piano, his back to me as he plays. His fingers move gently yet purposefully over the keys. I close my eyes and listen intently to the melody. I even feel my body sway but snap out of it as I walk over to him. His eyes are closed as he plays, his head slowly moving to the sound with furrowed eyebrows. As the song begins to slow, he opens his eyes. They widen when he sees me.

"I didn't know you played," giving him a small smile. Jude smirks and straightens his back, flexing his fingers, "I've had a lot of time to learn."

"It's beautiful," I reply, "Do you have any other gifts? Gifts you've kept quiet from me?" I move away from Jude and sit at the table: fruits, pastries and juices adorn the table. Jude gets up from the stool, bending down so his lips hover at my ear. "You'll have to wait and see."

I cross my legs as the shiver passes over my body, smiling as he places some fruits onto my plate, then picks up a sfogliatella. I bite into its many layers, moaning at the warmth and flavour of the pastry.

"This is so good," I praise, my mouth full of crispy perfection. Jude chuckles as he takes a seat beside me; he fills his cup with coffee from the decanter, then fills mine. I take a sip as the hot liquid coats my throat.

"Do you have any hidden talents, Rhea?" he asks between sips, his eyes focused on me, face set in a roguish grin. I ponder his question. Does throwing knives and being able to kill a person with my bare hands count?

"No talents, but I do enjoy sketching."

"Drawing is a talent." He bites into an apple, his white teeth piercing the ruby red skin, "Do you paint as well?"

"A hobby," I retort, "I can't say I'm that good an artist to call it a talent, but I like to sketch nature, especially the flowers my father would bring home." I smile at the real memory. "I use water colours sometimes, but not always. Just to accentuate the petal's colours."

"Do you sketch often?"

Since being a Sparrow, I've not been allowed the luxury of such a thing.

"Not recently no," I deflate a fraction. There's not much time to sketch and paint when you're being trained to kill in an underground bunker. "I haven't had the time," I finish. Another truth. Another lie.

Jude nods his head at my answer, turning his chair to face me, "What's your favourite colour?"

I laugh at his simple question, "You're really asking me what my favourite colour is?"

"Yes," he answers firmly, bringing the cup of coffee to his lips. Like he's just asked me the most important question in the world.

"Green," I say. "Like deep green: trees, vines and sprouting leaves right as they come alive." I close my eyes and picture a forest of evergreen. When they open, Jude's eyes are curious as he watches me.

I'm suddenly embarrassed and look away, before directing the conversation back to him. "What about your favourite colour?"

He waits a few moments before answering like this is a question he's thought about many times, "Yellow. But not bright yellow like the sun. Yellow like a sunrise, when it's pastel and warm."

I bite my cheek to stop from smiling. I would not have guessed Jude Lightfall's favourite colour to be sunrise yellow.

"So now the important information is out of the way," I say, grinning. "I must return home. My father will worry." Despite the talks of music and paintings and colours, I have not forgotten the information gathered from last night. I must tell Eris.

Jude nods his head, "And let me guess, you wish to walk home?" Amusement is laced in his tone as he surveys me.

"Always," I smile and stand from my chair. Jude does the same, our bodies so close that I can smell the coffee on his breath. Warmth radiates from him, as he towers over me. We look to each other, and we can both feel this *thing* between us, a flicker of a spark, a growing heat in the pit of our stomachs, the warmth of this feeling radiates off the both of us.

"Let me walk you out."

I obey, walking to the foyer. The maid that greeted me yesterday is standing by the door, holding my cloak and wet dress.

"I didn't have time to clean it miss," she says, holding it out for me. Her eyes are downcast to the ground as she speaks. Putting on my cloak, I take the wet pile from her hands.

"Don't be silly. I can have it cleaned at home. Thank you." I smile and the older woman smiles fondly back, her eyes crinkling at the corners.

Jude clears his throat, standing with his hands behind his back. "Come tomorrow at noon."

I hold in a grin at his instructions, "You can't get enough of me Lightfall."

His chocolate eyes fall to my own. "No, it seems I can't escape this spell you have me under." He places his hand gently around the nape of my neck, lowering his face to my cheek. He flutters his lips, millimetres away, his warm breath sending shivers down my spine. His lips are soft as they kiss my cheek; he returns to his normal stature, releasing his grip.

"Goodbye Jude," I say, the sound just merely above a whisper.

I turn quickly and leave through the open door. The old maid's cheeks redden after witnessing our encounter, but I don't care.

"Thank you," I nod to her kindly as I leave Lightfall manor. Heading back to the dark bunkers of the Sparrows.

Chapter Twenty-Three

Where the fuck have you been?" Eris' voice bellows, his face outraged and full of fury.

"I was doing my job," I yawn, rubbing my eyes, not in the mood for Eris' bluntness. "It was raining, so Jude asked me to stay, I thought it would be best to further our plan."

"No word was sent. I was going to send Axon and Xannu to look for you. You could have been killed."

"How could I send word if I was at the manor?" I frustratedly snap back.

Eris looks to me, anger flashes in his eyes, "Don't play smart with me girl."

But defiance flows in my veins, "Then don't act like I don't know what I'm doing. Don't act like you care about my welfare either," I snap, anger bubbling over. My frustration is interrupted by Eris's unleashed fury as he slams his fist to the desk, the movement making his cup topple over. I resist the urge to flinch.

"Marik Lightfall was there," I announce. The mention of his name alters Eris' eyes from fury to curiosity. "He didn't reveal much at first; he had an argument with Jude, and then he left. I saw nothing of him for the rest of the evening." Eris leans away from the desk and rolls his eyes. "But," I say with a knowing smirk, "I slipped Jude a sleeping narcotic and did a little exploring." Eris is silent then, waiting for me to continue. "I heard some very interesting things..." I tease, dragging the sentence for dramatic effect.

"Spit it out girl," his anger never subsides for long.

I chuckle at that before my mood clouds. "He said something about our food supply running out. He was talking about population control. And I'm guessing that means a lot of killing to try counteracting the food issue." I wait for his reaction as the information rolls off my tongue. He ponders what I have to say. The revelation of mandatory executions is huge. It could be the turning point for the rebellion.

"We need more information," he replies flatly. I hold in my temper.

"Odessa Lightfall said that our water source is drying up. That the ground is becoming infertile. Did you know this?" I ask. "I thought our soil was the best in the whole of Ceraea. That people were once killing each other just to live upon this land and the riches it gave."

"Altaras' water source is collected by pipework that flows from the hill under the Mansion across the city. The wells and tunnels are deep underground and can't be seen by the naked eye. So yes, it is possible that they may be drying up and limiting the soil for crops to grow on the southern end." Eris shakes his head. I can see the cogs turning in his brain, trying to decide our next move, "Population control is one way of delaying the issue — less mouths to feed. Tissa will be informed; we will have to wait till they make an announcement before we can act. We can't go in blind."

Eris opens his desk drawer and pulls out a cigarette, lighting the end and taking a drag; the thick smoke surrounds us; I try not to gag.

"He said it will happen through the night. He left this morning, but I don't know what for," I relay the conversation I overheard.

Eris nods and I take this as my cue to leave. Stalking to the door, he says, "Well done, little bird. That necklace does look divine on you." he finishes, not looking up from the papers now gripped in his hands.

My fists clench, the points of my nails digging into the palms of my hands. I want to rip out his throat, smash my fist into his face, and claw his eyes out with my nails. He probably wishes to do the same but, unluckily for him, I'm valuable here. I close the door swiftly behind me yet, despite my inner protests, his twisted praise brings a hint of a smile to my lips.

Axon and Xannu stand outside Eris' office. Their expressions hard. Evidently, they're pissed off. With me.

"We thought you were captured, Elyria," Axon snaps as I brush past them with a roll of my eyes. Axon follows me down the corridor, his bulky frame close to mine as I stand outside my door; Xannu waits at a distance behind.

"Well, I wasn't. It was just raining. Relax, Axon," I go to put a hand on his forearm, but pull back quickly, and fold my arms instead. "They would have a hard time trying to kill me anyway."

Xannu storms past us both, "Combat in ten."

I give Axon a short half smile as I open the door, "You don't need to worry about me, I can handle myself."

He sighs; I think I see the glimpse of a slight smile on his lips. He can't stay mad at me for long.

"I always worry about you, Birdie," Axon says. I shake the comment off. I don't need anyone worrying about me, I want to shout back. But his words mean nothing, he's just saying what I would say to any other Sparrow in this place. We look out for each other.

I change into my Sparrow suit, the leather feeling like home, and meet Axon and Xannu in the training hall. Xannu stands by the mats as she waits for me, wrapping her fists in tape. Her hair is pulled back in her signature pony, ready for a fight. Axon's fists are already wrapped as he ducks to my height, whispering in my ear, "She ended things with Briar, so go easy on her."

I nod my head in acknowledgement to which Axon walks ahead. Xannu and Briar were dating for a while. She says it was never serious, but I think she was afraid to let herself be vulnerable. How can you be vulnerable with a life like ours? A rebel living a dangerous, secretive life, unable to fully open up — unless your partner is also a Sparrow, like Tissa and Dumah.

I join Xannu at the sparring mat. "Sorry about Briar." She shrugs her shoulders, "It's safer for her. It's not like I could ever be with her, not really. Why prolong it?"

"Maybe just the physical then?" I tease.

Xannu laughs with a shake of her head, "She's too emotional for that."

I smile back, the mood officially lifted. In the corner of the room, I try to avert my eyes from a now shirtless Axon punching a bag. Sweat glimmers off his toned body, his muscles rippling with each strike.

"You shouldn't mess with him either," Xannu says. I detect a slight firmness to her voice and furrow my brows.

"What are you talking about?" My defenses are up as I start to tape my own hands. Xannu nods pointedly towards Axon. My gaze flutters between them both, landing back to her striking eyes.

"I'm not messing with him," I protest, my tone matching hers. "He knows nothing can happen between us."

She shakes her head, holding up her fists, "He would do anything for you. Don't take that for granted."

Her comment makes me frustrated. Why would she say this? He knows we can only be friends. I would do anything to protect him.

"I would die for him," I say, holding up my own fists as we start to circle one another, "As I would also die for you — much to your dismay, Xannu."

She rolls her eyes, suppressing a smile. Her tough act doesn't work on me.

"Unfortunately, I would not do the same," she jibes as she throws a punch. I swiftly dodge it and regain my stance. She throws another jab, this time towards my stomach, but I know her fight. I block it, and then another, as she rapidly swings for my face.

"You would *so* die for me. I bet you both were itching to storm over to Lightfall manor to rescue me," I muse to tire her out. Her fights are quick and hard, but she exhausts easily. Her ego distracts her from mastering self-control.

"Only to put a bullet in Altaras' guards, or Marik. Not for your sake."

We attack and defend for another round. My forearms start to burn at the constant impact of blocking her punches, her kicks. She jabs again, but I block, then move for the attack, hitting her in the stomach. She staggers back, then launches — her leg swiftly kicks my leg out from under me. Falling on my back, a smile lands on my lips. She used my own move against me! The falter is short-lived as I use the low momentum to take out her legs with my own. Xannu falls and I quickly roll so her arm is caught between my own in a tight grip. She thrashes, her stomach pressed to the ground. I kneel up so her legs are trapped beneath mine, my weight pinning her as I rest back. The kill position.

"And you're dead," I say, untangling my legs and lifting the weight from her body.
She groans in response and rises from the floor, brushing her suit with her palms.

"If I had a gun in my hands, we all know who would be dead first," she warns, walking over to get a drink.
I chuckle at her response, "Yes Xannu but if I had my knives, I wouldn't bet on it."
And with that, she rolls her eyes and heads to the shooting range.

The afternoon carries on as normal; we train all day. Zirk joins much later, along with Israfil, and we go over tactics and strategy. Israfil is our powder man. A nickname given to him for his interest — and specialty — when creating explosives and ammunition. He can fight, but he's the brains rather than muscle. Looking at blueprints of the layout of the Citadel, we strategise over how to act in an attack, who covers what ground, and what are our entry and exit points. Coordination is imperative.
The Citadel is enclosed and fortified by a wall — much smaller than the one surrounding Altaras — giving good opportunity to be at a higher level when infiltrating, especially if we have numbers on our side — which we will do, especially when the truth regarding the population control comes to light. Centralis sits in the centre, the Unity building and the Consulate Building on either side, along with the other Commanders' homes, Lightfall manor being one of them. The area is huge. It will take an army to conquer.

After strategy, I leave the training hall and prepare some dinner in the makeshift kitchen, taking just enough from the stock we have. It's small and holds little fresh food, most of it laden with preservatives, but nevertheless, its fuel. I grab a tin of soup and a chunk of bread and head back to my room, devouring the meal as soon as I sit down. I groan. This is nothing like the food served at Lightfall manor.

Eris would have already passed the information to Tissa through one of his other Sparrows. I will be called if he needs me, I can rest. I undo my suit, stripping it off and changing into an oversized linen shirt to sleep in. The action depletes my last reserves; I finally realise how tired I really am. Lying flat on my back, I stare at the ceiling. A mould patch has started to grow in one of the corners; whilst I lie here, waiting for sleep, I think of how many more times I'll look at this ceiling. How many more times will I sleep in this box room? Will I ever leave and find my family? Will I die before I get the chance?

Sleep must have consumed me as suddenly, the nightmares of my past torment arise. I wake back up screaming, my throat raw, my skin slick with sweat. Eris had the flame to my fingers, burning me each time, my lip trembled, ingraining the pain in me if my eyes started leaking. 'Crying is for the weak, little bird. Crying is for cowards,' he said as the flame scorches my palms.

Chapter Twenty-Four

Up at the crack of dawn, my morning starts hard and fast: running laps, punching bag and rope work, and finishes with the chance to throw some daggers before my free time is up. Duty calls. Once I've washed, I start brushing my hair, braiding the front pieces to form a crown around the back of my head; the rest of it falls in curls down my back. I lace rings and gems within the braids, whilst knowing these gold jewels would suit my natural hair much better.

I put the gold contacts in, masking my red eyes, and wiping a dust of cosmetics over my cheeks and lips. I rub some jasmine and gardenia oils across my skin to hide the musk of the underground and the damp that probably lingers deep in my bones.

There, waiting for me in my room, is a sage dress with cream silk ribbons to tie the corset at the back. The green lace combines perfectly with the silk and the small cream floral embellishments which adorn the front. Long sage sleeves drip down into a sheer fabric — opaque enough to see the olive tone of my skin, but still covering the sight of my faded scars. Xannu never fails to make a masterpiece.

At noon, I arrive at the Lightfall manor. The same maid that greeted me holds open the doors as I thank her.

"Just wait here, Mr Lightfall will be with you shortly."

I nod my head, and she scuttles away, returning to her cooking or cleaning or whatever her task is for the day.

"Hello trouble," I crane my neck to see Jude with his arms braced on the white porcelain bannister. He looks down at me with amusement in his eyes, and a roguish grin settled on his face. He wears his signature dark tunic rolled at the sleeves, with a pair of black trousers to match.

"Hello Jude," I clasp my hands in front of me innocently, but he continues to eye me up and down. "Are you going to keep me waiting down here whilst you just gawk?"

"I'm just admiring you, is that a crime Miss Fellows?" his voice is dripping with confidence, a slight smirk on his lips.

"Not a crime. Look all you want then," I reply, stretching out my arms as I spin in a graceful circle.

After a few moments of a silent wistful stare, he straightens and walks down the staircase, offering me his arm. Leading us across the foyer, in a different direction to the dining hall, we walk down a short corridor and into a large room filled with light. The sight is magical. Huge ceramic pots are dotted everywhere, showcasing the leafy foliage of a wonderful array of plants — all different sizes — huge monstera plants with big glossy leaves, exotic palms, and ferns unfurling their delicate fronds from within. As we tread across the coloured tiles deeper into the room, tiny terracotta flowerpots perch on wrought iron stands. Plants I don't even know the names of litter the room in all directions. Overhead, a huge skylight exposes the sky above; the sun beams through, its rays creating a warm atmosphere, even in the winter. The walls are embellished with gold ornamental artworks that shine against the light. The tiles are a mix of burnt umber and terracotta, creating a warm earthy tone to the room.

"Mother's favorite place," Jude says with admiration laced in his tone, waking me from my trance of admiration. "She spends most of her time here planting or journaling her flowers. But she's let us use it for this afternoon."

I look to him, his blond halo glowing in the light, and his dark eyes now looking bright and hazel; flecks of gold swim in them as he studies my reaction.

"It's remarkable. It looks nothing like the rest of the house."

The ambiance of the room is warm and homely, not like the regal form and fancy nature of the other rooms. I think back to the guest room.

"Mother's touch," Jude breaks eye contact and moves further into the room. I follow him, through the overhanging vines and past the huge leaves. To the side of the room, an easel has been set up. Did Jude do this for me? A blush forms on my cheeks as he gestures for me to sit. He pulls a white apron around my waist and gently fastens it at the back.

"I thought you would enjoy a day of art."

Meeting his gaze, my eyes soften. This is not gathering intel for the rebels — Eris would not be pleased that I spent my day painting. But I have gone so long without real enjoyment. Throwing knives and being kicked to the floor does not bring the same happiness that painting does.

"Jude, this is very lovely of you."

He nods his head, "I just thought of how you said you haven't drawn in a while. So, now you can."

Jude places some watercolors, kohls and pencils on the stool beside me.

"Who knew Jude Lightfall could be so considerate?" I tease. I pick up a thin pencil and eye it, before placing it back down in its set.

"Only to those I like the company of."

I look into his eyes, those eyes that are kind and thoughtful, the eyes that would see me as a monster if he found out my true intentions for being here. Jude picks a tiny plant from a shelf; it has tiny silver orbs growing out of each stem, like full moons, "This is called a Moondancer."

"I've never seen that before," I say, studying the strange plant.

"And this is a Blood blossom." He holds a crimson flower in a glass vial, its head full of petals tapered at the ends. "This plant can cure blood poisonings when fermented in a tea."

I gape at the delicate flower, "That's amazing. How did she find it? I have never seen flowers like these grow in any of the gardens."

He sets down the Blood blossom and steps away from me, "If I told you, I might have to kill you."

A half-smile grows on his lips.

I purse my lips. Oh, he could try.

Chapter Twenty-Five

We spend the day sketching and painting different flowers in Odessa Lightfall's greenhouse. I don't find out any secrets. I don't look for anything or sneak around trying to search for information. I just sketch. And paint. I eat the little treats Jude passes to me whilst I work. I even pretend not to notice him staring at me as he too pretends to read his book. I enjoy myself.

The sun is starting to set, a warm orange glow cast through the skylight. I put down my paintbrush in the jar of murky water and look at my finished painting: a blush-coloured bunch of peonies. A small smile escapes my lips.

"You should be an artist," Jude says, coming up behind me and observing my work. I push his shoulder playfully.

"Don't joke."

"I'm being serious," he picks up the other sketch of the Blood blossom I had completed first — the water colour not doing justice to the deep red of the petals, but nevertheless a fair replica. On the bottom of the page reads, 'Jude' in my neatest handwriting. The detail makes his eyes crinkle as his smile reaches them. Happy? Proud, maybe?

"My mother could hire you to draw for her when she does her botanical journaling. She could write and you could sketch. An encyclopedia of sorts, maybe."

I smile at the thought, the idea of a rich future filled with power and art. Life with Jude could be so easy. He makes everything so simple. But it's not the reality. Not when a coldblooded killer lives under the same roof as him. A man happy to take the lives of innocent people. Children. Outside of Jude's world, injustice and lies still live within the city, no matter if his presence makes me forget all that. I'm getting swept up by him; I need to remember why I'm here.

Rising from the stool, I stretch my back and start to untie the apron from my dress.

"I've had a wonderful time, Jude. Thank you." I admit. And I mean it.

Jude's gaze meets mine, deep pools of brown burning into me. His words are a lethal caress as he says, "I feel like life didn't truly start until you." His voice is low and deep as the words come out. My heart tightens in response; my chest aches. I squeeze my eyes shut to block it out. Not to let my guard down. I have tricked this boy with false feelings. All for what? To get to his father? Is this worth it? Perhaps playing with his emotions is just as cruel as putting a blade through his heart. My head is only filled with turmoil, my emotions beginning to cloud my judgement.

"Jude—" I start, but I'm cut off as he cups my cheek with his large hand. A lump forms in the back of my throat. The warmth from his fingers is like a narcotic, eradicating all sense from my brain.

"You don't need to say anything, I just wanted you to know," his tone is lustful as I suck in a breath.

I open my eyes but avert his gaze, "I should go. Can we meet tomorrow?"

Jude furrows his brows for a split second at my pause but with his charming smile, he only answers, "Dinner will be served at seven."

~

"Elyria sit," Eris booms as I enter the meeting room. I had already changed out of my dress, replacing it with dark linen tunic and trousers. I am not in the mood to train this evening.

Looking around the table, a few Sparrows are seated: Vera, Zirk, Tissa and Xannu sit, whilst Axon stands in the shadows. Israfil and Dumah are absent. Tissa looks charming in her lemon-yellow dress, compelling her dark skin to glow with beauty. Dainty gold Jakarta's hang off her ears. There's another Sparrow — one who has never shown their face in the bunker. They have mousy brown hair styled with a fringe and deep-set eyes, their name is unknown to me as they sit between Xannu and Tissa. There are lots of Sparrows I have never met, dotted all over the city, but having one in the Sparrows nest is uncommon.

I stalk over to my chair at Eris' right, leaning back and folding my legs in front of me. Eris' body is rigid, radiating power and anger. Tonight should be interesting.

"Information has been brought to our attention," he says.

Tissa shrinks in her chair, but this time Dumah is not here to comfort her.

"Elyria heard the Lightfalls discussing how the city will be plagued with famine: no water or food," he pauses, assessing the room, studying each of our faces. Xannu holds her face strong, no waiver of emotion detected. Vera looks concerned as she watches Eris.

"Tissa discovered that the Consulate will select fifty random individuals from the city at the end of each month to execute. To delay the food crisis."

No one speaks, but I can feel the tension as it rises. My jaw clenches; my toes curl at the revelation.

Fifty. Fifty people killed each month. Its barbaric. Inhumane. No one will willingly let this happen. And if the Consulate thinks we believe the choice is random — that the elites aren't exempt from the culling — they will be wrong.

"A briefing will be held in the morning — the people… they've already been chosen," Tissa says as she turns the silver ring on her finger, an anxiety trait I'm very accustomed too. Twirling it round and round, attempting to settle her nerves. I turn to face her, as do the other Sparrows at the table. Even Xannu looks surprised.

"What are the Commanders going to tell us? That fifty people are somehow missing each month?" my tone is hostile — infuriated.

Tissa nods her head, hair falling to her face, "Yes, exactly that."

"But people will start asking questions. No one will stand for this! How can the Consulate make this decision? How will they get away with this?"

"They have already taken the fifty," the unknown Sparrow adds in with a monotone voice. No emotion resides behind the words. "They took my father and brother last night. They're being held in the Citadel in a compound underground."

Xannu's eyes flick in the person's direction in silent assessment before quickly averting her gaze. I'm confused by this stranger who knows so much.

"How do you know about an underground compound?"

"Because I work there," the Sparrow says, finally looking to me with hollow eyes, light brown, matching their straight hair cut into a shaggy uneven bob, a flicker of freckles covering their nose.

"You're an Altaras guard?"

"Yes. My name is Seven. Nice to meet you all, finally. It's been a long time without knowing others like me, wanting this rebellion." Seven's voice is calm but full of determination.
"Well, you've joined at the right time, Seven. It's nice to meet you too." I smile and nod in understanding.
Eris finally speaks up, "Elyria and Xannu, you will join Seven on a little covert mission."
I glance to him, waiting for him to relay his orders.

"You will enter the Citadel. I want those people freed."
Eris has gone mad. But, before I start to question the logistics of this plan, he continues, "I had a Sparrow make me one of these," he reaches into his pocket and pulls out a little cube, chucking it into the middle of the table where it rolls to a standstill.

"What is that?" Vera says as she picks up the device, inspecting it with her bony fingers.

"That," Eris sneers, leaning back in his chair, "is a camera."
I've never seen one so small. Eris doesn't need to explain. I know his mind and what he wants out of us. He wants us to show the city. To capture the truth of the Consulate's evil plan.

"You three will get inside that compound and kill as many Altaras scum as you wish. We have done a lot of sitting around with no action. That ends tonight," his voice is strong and commanding. We all listen intently as he continues, "Israfil is already making and placing bombs around the Citadel walls as we speak."
Eris' eyes flick to Xannu whose expression conveys my own feelings about this mission. "Is there a problem Xannu?"
She straightens before answering, "No sir."

"Then wipe that look off your face."

"Yes sir."

Axon emerges from the shadows and clears his throat, "I can assist."

The comment is directed to Eris, his words spoken with strength and conviction. Like a true soldier. But Eris shakes his head, "No, you will stay here, I have another job for you." *What job?* Axon only nods in response, remaining silent.

"Leave in ten. Zirk, go over the maps with them before they leave." He goes to leave the room, but pauses at the door, uttering his final words, "this city will burn for what they have done."

"I suggest we jump the east wall — it provides us with closer range to reach the compound," Seven suggests.

Zirk unrolls the map, splaying the blueprint of the Citadel out across the table. It shows the buildings, entrances, exits, corridors...

"Here is the East wall," Zirk says, pointing to the right of the map.

Seven stands and points to a smaller building, "The compound is under this building here. It has one entrance and one exit. But hopefully, if your *powder man* gets his aim right, he can blow a hole through this wall here," Seven draws an imaginary line to the building, "And we can leave through the East wall with the second blast."

"Where are we going to hide fifty people?" I say to no one in particular.

Zirk looks up. This is the part of the plan that Eris has not perfected, obviously.

"We have a few safe houses around the city. Axon, you will direct some of the groups to each once we're back." Axon only nods in response, "Then the others will come here."

This plan is crazy. It's rash. We can barely squeeze in here, let alone with fifty others.

"I have a feeling this mission will speed up the rebellion," Vera says. Her tone is concerned — hesitant. "I don't think we'll be in here long."

"This is going to start the war. Isn't it?" I say flatly, bracing my forearms across the table. Stating what we all know to be true. This act will start the fire, igniting the rebellion in full force. Vera only looks to me with sorrowful eyes. She does not need to answer, I know it in her gaze.

"How many guards will be stationed?" Xannu says, breaking her silence.

Seven clears their throat, "One at the compound door; three or four will be inside the prison. More will enter when it starts, but I'm not sure how many."

I look to Seven with a forceful smirk, "It won't matter, we'll take them all down."

Seven returns the smile, a gleam of fury lit in their eyes.

Once we finalise our strategy, I exit the meeting room and change into my suit. My white hair is braided back — four braids intertwining into a singular one. I put in my gold contacts and swipe black powder across my eyelids. Brandishing myself in war paint. I adorn my cloak and head to the armoury. Xannu and Seven are already here, strapping their bodies with deadly blades and guns. I pick my daggers up, placing them in the suit compartments, and sheath several knives to my thighs. Xannu passes me a pistol which I place at my hip.

"You all look menacing," Axon half smiles, leaning against the armoury door. He wears his normal tunic and cloak, but I know his body too is concealed with weapons. I look between Xannu and Seven. "We do look badass." I clip my gun into place.

"Be safe, little brother," Xannu pushes him out of the way, and pulls up her mouth covering.

Axon chuckles but his eyes still trail the ground as he says to us, "Aim straight," then flicks my chin with his thumb as I walk past.

"Always," I reply over my shoulder with a matching half smile. Pulling my covering up, I stalk down the hallway: ready to light the spark.

Chapter Twenty-Six

The three of us look deadly as we stand in front of the Citadel wall. Dressed in black and covered in an arsenal of weapons; Seven gives us the signal and we aim our grappling hooks up, shooting in synchronisation as the metal embeds within the wall. No guards are stationed, but there will be cameras. Our detection will, however, be too late. Israfil will have already detonated the first bomb by the time anyone raises an alert of our presence. Climbing up the wall is effortless; the wind rushes at my face as I propel myself upwards. Then, as I swing my leg over the wall, my body descends quickly to the ground.

Following Seven's lead, we dart across the open grass, the darkness of the night concealing our movements as we run to one of the closest buildings for cover. The Citadel is such an open space, the fact the compound is so close to the Eastern wall is a shocking design fault from them. But a great win for us.

We run to the next building which houses the compound. It's a small concrete structure with a guard stationed outside. His blood red uniform glistens in the moonlight. Quickly, Xannu steps out from the shadows, holding a pipe to her lips. She blows the dart with precision and force, the poison embedding itself into the guard's neck. His eyes look panicked and wide, his mouth stretching to shout for help as he desperately reaches to pull the dart out. But the paralysing effect of the narcotic is already in his blood stream. He drops to the ground in an instant. We sprint out from the shadows, Xannu pulling the dart from the guard's neck and returning it to her suit. I drag the dead man's body from the entrance by his legs, all the way to the shadows of another building. Discarding his remains to be found by another.

Seven punches in a code at the door to the concrete building, which then opens with a click. We swiftly run inside and close it behind us. They lead us down the corridor. I keep two daggers raised. Xannu follows, pistols gripped tightly in her hands. The corridor is dimly lit, the walls and floors both made of cement. At the end of the corridor is a door, opened by Seven after giving the all clear.

We're greeted by a dark metal staircase which cascades into a spiral, so far down that my eyes squint to see through the darkness. Is this a prison? Our boots make a clang against the metal as we walk down the staircase; at each level, there are doors. A figure in blood-red is suddenly upon us. Before anyone can think or breathe, my dagger soars, landing in his skull. He drops with a thud. Xannu nudges me with her gun, a silent praise. We pass the body, stepping over his crumpled form as I reach down and extract my dagger from his head, wiping the blood on my suit as we progress forward.

Down on the lower levels, I see the prisoners. A man crouches in the corner of one of the rooms, holding his head with bound hands. Another younger looking boy sits with his back against the wall, his face and hands covered in blood.

"Prisoners of Altaras," Seven says, "For attempted treason."

I clench my jaw reaching for the handle to open the door, but Seven pushes my arm away.

"What are you doing?" I hiss, "If we're saving fifty, what's the harm in saving this lot too?"

"We can't save them all." they reply curtly, walking on, gun raised.

I take a breath, trying to still my mind and repel my stubbornness, trying to repress the guilt for leaving these people behind. Following Seven's lead, I shove the little camera through the window, capturing the sight of the prisoners. We pass more doors and more people, leaving them to rot in their dungeons as we walk ahead. Finally, at the entrance to the lowest ground level, Seven halts us before we descend the stairs. Through the grilles, there are four guards standing at each side of the corridor; they talk among themselves, guns hanging low at their sides.

The three of us look between each other, conferring the silent plan. Xannu's eyes burn with fury; coated in kohl, she looks sinister, mirroring my own look of pure wrath. We get into position, silently, whilst they are distracted by their own chatter. Then, we let our lead fly. Each of us hit a guard square in the head as one by one, they fall to the ground. The sound of Xannu and Seven's bullets ring out in the air.

We race down the stairs towards the locked doors, quietly — soundlessly — like the hearts of the guards that beat no more. There are no windows, but we already know what awaits us on the other side of the door. I nod to each of them and open the first. I pause. Faces stare back at me. Many faces: men, women, and children. Expressions of fear haunt their red-rimmed eyes, shaking as they weep. With a lump in my throat, I quickly point the camera in their direction and scan the room, then retract it back into my suit pocket.

"It's okay." I press a finger to my mouth, "Stay quiet, we've come to help." I hope their crying stops soon, at least until we make it back to safety.

Xannu and Seven open the remaining doors while I keep watch of the stairwell. No guards descend; no footsteps are heard. The crowd of people huddle together, their bodies shaking with panic and distress. All of them are now squashed towards me — as far as they can get from the wall where Seven stands. Seven checks their watch and holds up a hand, showing three fingers and using their other to move the fringe from their eyes.

"Everyone get down. Cover your heads," I order; my tone is hushed, but firm as I address them.

Everyone ducks. Men and women cover the heads of children. I see Xannu holding the hand of a little boy, talking to him whilst his small frame shakes with panic. These poor people: innocent, harmless civilians. Seven moves quickly from the far wall, holding out their arm with a pointed finger raised. They open their mouth to shout, but the blast goes off before the words leave their lips, and Seven's body is launched into the crowd.

And people begin screaming.

Chapter Twenty-Seven

Rubble litters the hallway and dust flies in the air. It chokes us, we're blinded; fine particles engulf my senses as I try to quickly blink away the smoke. The crowd is in alarm until the dust settles, panic subsiding once they begin to realise they're unharmed.

"Follow me. Quickly!" Xannu shouts, leading the crowd from the *giant* hole in the wall. Israfil clearly could have used a smaller detonation, but he chose to be dramatic. Knowing time is not on our side, we hurry people out; Seven stands — unharmed by the blast — and rushes forward, climbing over chunks of concrete. Holding back, I guard the rear of the crowd, ensuring everyone makes their way out. The bomb that blew up the wall reveals the entrance to a tunnel — Seven's knowledge of this a lifesaver. Another rabbit warren of underground tunnels, there must be a whole network under Altaras?

Up ahead, I see people run. Running so fast and frantic, knowing their lives depend on it. And I am grateful for their frantic speed. The tunnel stretches and, as I draw closer, I spot another stairwell. People clamber up, racing and pushing to escape.

Shouting and heavy boots echo behind me. Quickly, I whirl yet see nothing. The guards will have us cornered if we don't get up that staircase *fast*. Crouching down, I aim my gun; they will have to shoot blind.

The sounds draw nearer, and I can just about see the red of their suits when I fire. Shooting at each one. Hoping that there

are not too many charging down to greet me. Praying I make it out of here alive.
The closest guard fires a shot right towards my head but, last minute, I dodge. Bodies crumple at their end, falling on top of each other as I hit them — thighs, heads, anywhere to render them useless. Thankfully lady luck is smiling on us, helped by the hefty residue of smoke and dust in the air at their end of the tunnel; none of their shots strike. They really are shooting blind, yet I have perfect sight.
Another two guards fall and the shouting ceases. The only sound being that of my gun as it rings in my ears. I assess the space before me, confirming there are no others before I wait a few moments and stand. I sprint so fast down the tunnel towards the exit my braid slaps against my back. The stairwell is clear of people as I race up it, two steps at a time until I reach the top.
The light through an open door illuminates my escape. As I edge out, I see the trail of the crowd in the distance, running towards the Eastern wall. To my right, another explosion rings out. A Consulate building sets alight as debris and shrapnel flies in every direction — near enough to feel the impact and see the guards run towards the racing flames and people flee the burning building, screaming for help. Reds and oranges illuminate the night sky as thick black smoke rises — a beacon for all.

Wiping the sweat from my forehead, I sprint towards the Eastern wall, praying that Israfil's final explosion comes soon. It doesn't take long to reach the crowd and I spot Xannu's jet black hair as she stands at the head of the crowd. It's silent for a moment as we wait in the shadows. Concealed by darkness. Protected by night. The Citadel has been infiltrated and the Altaras guards are now distracted by the blazing Consulate building. Finally, the last detonator explodes — a blast to the East wall. The final blast for now. Bricks and dust consume us as the wall crumbles, revealing another hole. Our escape.

Seven and Xannu lead the pack, sprinting for the exit. Men carry children as they all run as fast as they can through and over the mound of rubble.

"Ten of you that way — follow her!" Xannu shouts as the crowd splits, changing directions as they run. Seven takes a left through the trees, leading a group to safety, while Xannu leads the others. I run at a slower pace now, so to not overtake the people in front of me; instead, I protect their backs as we run through the trees. Xannu starts to slow as she turns, another two figures emerging from behind us: Axon and Dumah. Warmth fills my body knowing that everything is going according to plan.

Xannu signals me forward, so I sprint to the front of the gathered crowd.

"We each take ten now. Elyria, back to the base. We will meet you back soon," Dumah says, his hood has fallen exposing his short shaven head.

"Careful of the cameras," I salute to my Sparrows and turn, calling forward a handful of people to follow me. We dart on between the trees.

It doesn't take us long before we're out of the tree line. Homes of the elites are situated here, and we need to get away from here as quickly as we can. I need to get us back to the Sparrow base.

I turn to face my group, looking to each of their faces. But my heart stops - my body turning to stone as one face peers back at me. Her unmistakable Nightingale eyes. Looking back at me like my reflection always does.

Lila.

A lump starts to form at the back of my throat as I instantly recognise her glossy blond hair, reflecting the moonlight. *She's grown so much.* My heart shatters and my chest tightens; rage and anger boil in my veins. My *sister* was going to be executed. It takes every fiber of my being to not collapse right there, to sob and clutch her tightly. How did she end up amongst the group to be culled? I take my eyes off her for a moment to regain control. I silently thank Xannu for my gold contacts, praying Lila does not recognise me.

"We're going to keep to the shadows, quiet as we can," I explain, pushing past the pain to focus on the task at hand. I point up to one of the buildings where a red light casts a steady glow, "Remember, that right there, is a camera. There's a lot of them around the city and we need to get out of here undetected, or the Consulate will track us down. If they find out where we hide, this will all be for nothing. Understood?" My eyes drift to Lila. She looks petrified but nods her head along with the rest.

"Okay, single file." I say, my tone firm with the instruction.

For safe measure, I raise my gun to the camera pointed directly at us and shoot it down.

Then, we run. They follow my every move — clumsily, not as stealthily as I would like — but we make it out of the elite housing circle, turning south in the direction of the Sparrow base and managing to keep out of sight. It takes longer than expected to reach the base and as I peer round the corner, a figure clad in blood red runs down the path directly towards us in the dark. I curse whilst motioning for everyone to get down and hide along the side of the house. They follow my command, one woman covering her mouth with her hands which tremble violently as she muffles her cries.

The guard must be on patrol here. If I kill him, it will mark this area as the path we took; the Consulate could question or raid nearby homes, potentially discovering our base.

So, I decide we stay low, and wait.

Our breathing slows in unison — I place a finger to my mouth as the guard runs past, refusing to look in the direction of the shadows; I know where he is headed — the Citadel. I exhale as he leaves our proximity, watching his figure retreat up the hill and far away from us.

Quickly, I stand and usher the group forward.

There's the house — across the cobblestone road — where an old couple now wait patiently at their table with expectant eyes. Their relief is evident upon our arrival, and as he opens the secret passage for us, I smile to the elderly man in silent thanks.

Beckoning the group over, I lead them down the stairs, and through the corridor. Down into the meeting room, I swing open the door where Eris sits in his chair. Cigarette in hand.

"Hello everyone. I see my little bird made sure you arrived here safely," he takes a slow drag before blowing out smoke. "I know you're all frightened, but the rebellion has saved you. *We* have saved you."

Eris stands from his chair, putting on a performance. I turn to face the people we brought here; some of them are panting, hands on their chests as they try to restore their breathing.

"We are the future of this city. The rebellion has saved your lives," he says as he walks closer to them. "You will have to stay here, hidden for a while until it's safe for your return."

I look to Lila; her face is stunned and wide eyed. A part of me craves to go to her, to explain everything. But my body is rigid, my feet planted firmly, staying here in the dark so it is safer for her, clueless to what I have become.

"The others will join us soon but make yourselves at home."

Eris starts to leave the meeting room, but I flank him, joining him in the doorway.

"My sister's here."

His muscular body towers over me as he turns on his heel. "A family reunion then," he says with a hint of amusement.

I furrow my brows, "I don't want her to know I'm here," I say flatly. Lila being here — knowing I was never dead — it could ruin everything. It could distract me and break me. I can't go through that. I will not hurt her more than she's probably already hurting.

"Can she go home?" The pleading is evident in my question. I have never asked anything of him, never wanted anything so much that I would now beg Eris for it.

Eris stares at me, his dark eyes burning holes. "Don't ask such a stupid question, Elyria. She cannot go home. She will never go home now," he spits, turning and walking back towards his office. I follow, marching right behind him with my fists clenched at my sides.

"My family will keep her hidden. Don't keep her from them. Please, this is all I will ever ask of you," I plead, begging for my wish to be answered. "I don't ask much from you. But I will ask for this one thing," my voice lowers as I end my speech. "Please Eris."

Eris's arm pauses at the handle for a few moments, likely deliberating the one favour I have ever asked of him. He opens the door, steps around and faces me once more. His frame fills up the entrance to his office, his body radiating absolute control as he stands there, looking down on me, like I have just insulted him, "No Elyria, she will not go home. She stays here. That is an order. You seem to forget all that I have done for you, you insult me with the favours you ask."

Then, he slams the door in my face, finishing the fight before I even begin. I close my eyes for a second and take in what he's just said.

Lila isn't going home.

Favours! I have never asked him for *anything!* I have obeyed *every command* – even if it came with some back chat or a groan.

I exhale through my nose, trying to steady my breathing, but to no avail. Breath escapes from my lungs at dizzying speed, my head swimming.

I will not cry; I am not allowed to cry.

I slam my fist against his door; there may not even be a home she can go back to soon. What we have done tonight will have changed everything. I place my forehead against the door, exhaling and fighting the urge to storm in there and rip Eris' head off.

We, the Sparrows, made our appearance. Our first public act of rebellion towards the Consulate. The assassinations Eris had tasked me with were nothing compared to this trail of destruction across the Citadel. Finally, we have made a difference, saved all these people awaiting death. This is a good thing. Lila is *safe* down here.

I take another long breath, inhaling and exhaling deep through my nose; I flex my fists, anger washing over me.

These people are safe because of us. We have done the right thing.

Chapter Twenty-Eight

Initially, I don't return to the people in the meeting room, nor do I bother returning to Eris — he clearly doesn't want to be bothered. I sit and wait in the corridor of the bunker, legs stuck out in front of me as I spin my dagger between my fingers waiting for the others to return.

Two hours pass before the metal bunker door swings open and a bloodied Xannu slumps through the door. Jumping to my feet, her group stagger behind her — they seem fine, uninjured.

"Are you okay? What happened?" I ask, my eyes shooting to the gash on her forehead, blood trickling down her face. It makes her striking features look even more menacing, but still not a single hair out of place. Xannu pulls off her face covering, baring her perfectly straight white teeth in a devilish smile as she slings an arm over my shoulder, walking us back up the corridor. I throw my head back in a grin, a grin just as mad as hers. *We did it.*

"Two guards ran into us just up on the Southside. They were in close range, but I handled them," she says, opening the door to the meeting hall.

I laugh at her amusing approach to near death, "They got close though," I say referring to the gash on her head.

"Not close enough,"

We walk into the meeting hall; the group of people remain seated on the floor where I left them. Some that were lying down have now woken from their sleep. I try not to look but my eyes dart to the blond girl sat with her back against the wall. The once confident, loud sister I knew is not in this room with me. A petrified girl sits in her place. I quickly turn to Xannu, reaching up to whisper out of earshot from the rest of those filing in behind us. "My sister is here."

Then I return to my normal stature, walking to our chairs at the table. Xannu knows instantly what this means. She nods once with understanding, following me to her seat.

"Did you guys hide somewhere for a while?" I ask her once we sit down. We face the gathered crowd who have already started to talk amongst themselves, reliving the past few hours of their escape as we speak.

Xannu nods her head, "Yes, we went to a safe house at the South End. Eris had already given me the location. We waited there for an hour or so then made our way back up here."

"No patrols of guards?" I ask, folding my arms in front of me and leaning back in my chair.

"Other than the two who we ran into, none. It was like a ghost town."

I contemplate her answer. Why are there no guards looking for us? However, my thoughts are interrupted by the hall door opening as Dumah and Seven walk in, seemingly unharmed as they lead their groups to join the others. Seven looks dishevelled — their full fringe now sticks out in odd angles, slick with sweat, whilst Dumah is out of breath as he staggers over, his dark skin glistening with sweat.

"Nice of you to join us," I say, gesturing to the empty seats at the table.

"You had the easy route Elyria; we've been running around the city trying to divert those fuckers," Dumah says as he plonks himself down in a chair with a sigh.

"All I'm hearing is excuses," the teasing ring is evident in my tone.

Seven brushes their fingers through their messy hair - *thank God* - and sits with their shoulders slumped with exhaustion. Xannu's eyes shift to Seven; she looks over them, searching and scanning Seven's body, their face — for a moment too long to go unnoticed by my observant eyes. She quickly averts her attention before anyone notices, but I clocked her movements.

"Eris already gave his speech to my group, they are probably filling the others in now," I say, nodding towards the civilians. Most of them probably don't know each other, but collective trauma can really forge close bonds.

Dumah rests his head in his hands as he tries to catch his breath whilst Xannu chuckles beside me. "You should join us in training more often, Dumah. It's taking a while for you to catch your breath there."

I stifle a laugh along with her. Dumah looks up and gives us a half smile, his skin crinkling at the eyes just as he flips us the finger.

"You girls were good in there," Seven says as they clear their throat; Seven looks younger now, maybe a similar age to Axon? "Good aim, blondie."

"Didn't suffer through all this training to miss," I counter, a hint of sarcasm in my tone. We give a silent nod to each other: a silent thanks.

Axon is taking longer to return — longer than expected. After a few hours waiting, Dumah is passed out in his chair, whilst Xannu's head bobs as she tries to keep herself from nodding off completely.

Seven and I, however, stay silently awake. Their family is with Axon, so I'm sure the anxiety regarding their safe return prevents sleep from taking hold. I look to the crowd of sleeping people, their bodies curled under shreds of blankets on the concrete. Children use the bodies of others as pillows. Mostly, I watch Lila; she sleeps soundlessly on the cold concrete, now amongst the group.

Lila is here. In the Sparrows' base. My parents wouldn't have willingly let her get taken, so how did she get here? My mind mulls over these endless questions as I compulsively turn my gold rings round and round, trying to settle the thoughts festering in my mind.

After a few more hours, perhaps dawn or early morning, commotion erupts in the other room. Axon opens the door soon after and I release the anxious breath I didn't know I was holding. Stepping over the bodies that fill the floor in front of me my pace quickens as he greets me with open arms, his hug tight and strong. I melt into him.

"Glad to see you're alright Birdie," he says into my neck; his hot breath warms my cold skin.

"You too," I murmur, "Lila is here."

As I look to him, his surprised sapphire eyes look back, but I say nothing else on the matter. "Glad you made it back in one piece as well," I say, pulling out of his grip and pushing his side.

"Took you long enough," Xannu says as she waltzes over to give her brother a hug.

Axon laughs releasing her, "I was right on time. Get that stitched up." He pokes a finger to her forehead, and she swats his hand away, rolling her eyes.

Axon's group walk in from behind him and, as they do, Seven jumps to their feet, racing over to a man and teenage boy, hugging them both tightly. The scene makes them look childlike as the tension they harbour evaporates. There's a collective breath: a sigh of relief of being together once more.

Sevens' face is slick with tears as they come up for air. My jaw clenches — the Consulate is barbaric for trying to tear families apart, killing innocent people and thinking everyone will sit back and let it happen. Eris entering the meeting hall distracts my anger as the Sparrows sit back at the table. He stands before us, speaking to the crowd of scared people.

"You have all had quite an ordeal. But you are safe now, and we plan to keep it that way."

A man older than Eris pushes through the crowd of people, "What is the plan? To keep us in this place forever? This is no better than that dungeon we just escaped from!" he shouts, gaining some murmurs of agreement from the group.

Another shouts, "Are we going to live in Penury? Are you going to get us out?

This sparks louder chatter and some sobs, "I don't want to be a Penurian!" one boy cries.

Eris' jaw tenses and the muscles in his arms contract; he does not like to be questioned. "And yet you escaped only due to my Sparrows," he replies, gesturing to us behind him. "The camera, little bird." Eris says, directing his speech to me. I toss the device to his outstretched hand as he catches and raises it in front of him.

"My little bird here captured the whole mission on this camera." He shows the crowd the device; another performance for him, yet it seems to work as the people's eyes widen in surprise and wonder. "We will broadcast your imprisonment to the city, exposing the Consulate for what they truly are. Killers who lie to you. After this, we will all be free of their torment and control."

Taking my attention off Eris, some individuals start to cheer, clapping and holding each other in celebration. The man that questioned Eris now shrinks back into the crowd, but I fear that the people here do not understand the full extent of Eris' plan which cannot be as simple as he makes it out to be. There will surely be more death and turmoil to follow — the broadcast won't simply free us; we will have to fight for it. And these people may be underground longer than they anticipate.

Chapter Twenty-Nine

The day that follows the rescue mission is tiresome. Xannu finally got her head stitched by Axon; word also arrived that Israfil made it to a safe house and is okay but laying low until he's needed again. The rescued civilians were on high alert for the first few hours, scared of being found. We gave them cans of stew and beans - our bunkers now stocked with food to last us all for at least a few weeks. The people took rest; whilst most slept the entire day, others divulged in quiet chatter amongst themselves.
Without a word to us, Eris took the camera and locked himself back in his office; I assume he has another Sparrow in the city that can hack into the broadcast and play our own footage - the skill set for that beyond my expertise. There is no word of a morning briefing, or any announcement of what happened last night. The Consulate and board of Commanders stay silent for the time being which causes a deep feeling of uncertainty of when and how they will react. I run laps in the training hall to take my mind off the fact that Lila is in the Sparrows' bunker with me, resisting the urge to go to her and confess everything. After what feels like hours of running, the time to meet Jude arrives. Dressed in a blood red gown, I exit the bunker — more guards than normal patrol the streets on my way to the Lightfall manor, but not one guard looks at me with suspicion as I walk the cobbled paths. I hide in plain sight.

On arrival to the manor, the maid greets me at the door. However, her eyes do not shine with the same warm welcoming as they did previously. Her manner is off, and anxiety radiates from her; she looks to the ground and avoids my eyes, yet still says hello as she beckons me in.

"Hello Rhea," Jude's voice rings as I enter. He stands wearing a dark suit which, as I get closer, is a deep shade of blue. Delicately embroidered gold swirl the lapels. A smile grows on my face as I meet his gaze.

"Hello Jude."

He holds out his arm for me then leads me towards the dining hall.

"My father is not in the best of moods," he says in a low voice.

My insides twist. He's here. I don't mention that I know anything of the explosions, or anything that could evoke more questioning.

I only nod my head and say sweetly, "That's okay, I'm here with you and that's all that matters."

A half smile appears on his lips at my comment, as he ducks his head and whispers, "I have a surprise for you later. And that dress looks magnificent on you."

My heart jumps a fraction as I meet those eyes that bore into my soul as he watches me, but our connection is swiftly disrupted by the opening of the hall doors. Marik and Odessa Lightfall are already seated at the table — their plates empty as they wait. Marik is the epitome of evil as he sits, staring out in front of him. Now I can see why the maid was off. Marik is drunk, his eyes glassy — probably in utter disbelief and rage with the stunt we executed last night.

"Sorry, am I late?" I ask, glancing between them and Jude.

"Not at all," Odessa says softly, "we are just early."

I smile and nod my head, following Jude who pulls back my chair and gestures me to sit. I divert my eyes from Marik Lightfall as the maids quickly rush to start plating our food. One of them starts to reach for a cut of meat to place on my plate before I stop her, "I don't eat meat," I say. She utters her apologies and reaches instead for the heaped pile of potatoes and roasted vegetables.

"You don't eat meat?" Marik Lightfall asks across the table, his mouth full of food as he talks. Roast beef, to be exact. I purse my lips and look to him, "No I never have." I smile. His sinister eyes do not glance over as I reply, he's uninterested and continues to eat.

Odessa chimes in, "But you say your father works in the agriculture sector?"

"That doesn't mean she's obliged to eat meat," Jude says through a slight laugh. His mother smiles, chuckling alongside him.

"I guess you're right, my apologies Rhea."

I place a few carrots and parsnips in my mouth, savouring the flavour as a sweet and salty explosion burst in my mouth. The cold soup cans back at the bunker never compared to the spread of luxuries here. For a city on the brink of starvation, there always seems to be more food on this table for three than a family of eight could even eat. I could ask Jude to take some rolls back with me — for my father, of course — not that a few rolls would feed fifty people, but it could make a difference.

We eat in silence for a while. My plate is cleared as the maid offers me seconds, which I decline. Given the circumstances, indulging on more food than I require seems wrong.

Marik breaks our silence with a question. "What do you wish to do with your life, Rhea?" He swigs from his glass and eyes me from across the table. I cock my head, knowing exactly what to say to get under his skin.

"I want to work for the Consulate. I want to make a difference with my life — to help people." I look to Jude with a triumphant smile, "The role of Commander seems like it would get the job done."

From the corner of my eye, Odessa shifts in her seat as Marik laughs deep and low, as if I had just told the most humorous of jokes. Leaning back in his chair, he sneers, "The role of a secretary might be more suited to you."

I grimace at his degrading comment, "Is that job role unattainable to me then?" I ask.

He places his elbow on the table, his blue eyes cutting deep into my soul as his stare meets mine.

"A girl will never be a Commander. That is just how we have, and will continue to do things, in Altaras."

"Father," Jude says, his voice raised in warning. But, unfortunately for the Lightfalls, I'm enjoying this conversation with Marik. Finally talking to the devil himself.

"Maybe a female Commander is just what Altaras needs," I goad, flashing my pearly whites.

Marik Lightfall flares his nostrils as my words obviously strike a nerve. His voice is raised as he replies, his laughter gone. Spite drips from his words. "Men have built this city. Men have fought for this city. Men protect the city from the Penury. And men will continue to govern this city!"

It is Jude who speaks next, his tone cold, deadly, as the command rips from his tongue. "Be careful how you speak to her, Father." Body stiffened with anger, directed at the man

that raised him, he says, "There are no rules about a female working as a commander; it just hasn't been done yet."
Jude rubs his thumb across the back of my hand as he says this; he thinks his father's words have wounded me, but really, they've spurred me on. A grin settles on my face. I know I should not say this; as a spy, I could potentially compromise the mission. But, as a girl too used to being degraded by men, my words are fire as I respond.

"I think that could be the problem with Altaras. Too many men making all the decisions."
Marik and I lock eyes in a deathly stare, but I continue to smile politely; anger oozes from him, the drunkenness seems to amplify it, but Jude interrupts our standoff once more. "We're done with this conversation now," he commands, giving his father a cold glare.

Odessa breaks her silence by speaking to me, trying to shift the tension. "Jude showed me your watercolours. They are remarkable."
I blink away the anger directed at Marik and smile at Odessa, the comment almost makes my cheeks redden. The praise is music to my ears. I love to be the best at what I do in every respect, but my art is something I hold close to my chest. I always protect that part of myself in fear of others judging it too harshly.

"Thank you very much," I say, pushing my white hair off my shoulder as I speak, "I loved your greenhouse, its beautiful. You have quite a collection."
Jude plays with my ring, his thumb turning the gold band. He looks directly at me as he says, "She's effortlessly talented."
My cheeks redden more with his praise, "Jude tells me of your interest in apothecary." I say, diverting the attention back to his mother, whose hands are delicately placed in her lap. She

smiles, but it doesn't reach the eyes. "I found comfort in nature after a loss. Finding nature helped me to heal, and then uncovering its healing powers has been a joy."

I nod my head, not needing to say anything to show my understanding. My heart tightens for her, for the loss of her child. It sours as Marik Lightfall huffs at the end of the table. He has taken so many children from their parents, ended so many lives whilst knowing the loss of a child firsthand.

Marik stays silent for the rest of the evening, refilling his drink every few minutes. A lot like my own father, but Marik's drinking is laced with anger rather than sadness. The dinner becomes tense as Jude and his mother chat to replace the silence. I chime in when needed, but my thoughts stay on Marik Lightfall: how he sits there, bored, and uninterested in his family, as his mind works overtime. Is he plotting his next move? Would he even flinch if I were to throw my dagger at him, penetrating his skull as his head slams down, blood pouring into his plate? No, he probably wouldn't.

"Would you like to join me?" Jude asks.

"Yes of course," I reply, not knowing what he even refers to. Jude rises from his chair and helps me out of my own.

"Thank you for dinner, Mr. and Mrs. Lightfall. I thoroughly enjoyed myself," I praise as we leave the room. Odessa smiles at me, her honey blond hair shining in the light as she speaks.

"You're welcome any time, Rhea. And please, do bring me more of your paintings, I'd love to see them."

"I will, thank you."

However, Marik Lightfall intercepts our leaving with his next words, "Rhea, did you hear the bombs last night down in the fields?"

My blood runs cold. Why is he taunting me? Does he know?

"Father!" Jude shouts sternly as he steps forward, shooting him a warning look. "You're drunk. Think about what you're saying."

Marik Lightfall stands from his chair, the legs scraping back with the urgency of his movements. "Jude here will make a fine Citadel Sergeant with that attitude. Don't you think girls? He just got the appointment today," he says smugly. Jude's hands clench tightly at his side.

"Father, stop this." he seethes, but Marik Lightfall carries on.

"It was a simple question for Miss Fellows," he says, looking to us. His eyes are glassy from all the alcohol consumed. My head is telling me not to say something stupid, to not provoke him. But how long will playing this naïve card work for?

"No sir. I don't know what you're talking about." I say, manipulating my voice to be as timid and shy as possible. *Act dumb.*

Jude drains his glass and slams it so hard on the table I'm surprised it doesn't smash to pieces. "That's enough."

"Don't be foolish, girl. Everyone heard the explosions and saw the rising smoke last night. Are you harbouring fugitives down in your fields?" his voice slurs as he speaks, his drunkenness tainting his normal illusion of calmness and, evidently, his cognitive ability. Now he seems hysterical — hysterical enough to let things slip.

"What are you talking about?" I question him, my guard remains up but still I goad for more information. My voice is high as my eyes dart between the Lightfalls. "What explosions? What fugitives?" Odessa has a look of pure shock on her face, whilst Jude looks angry. She stands and walks towards Marik Lightfall, but he bats her away with his arm like a fly. Then, Marik Lightfall makes a mistake.

He says something he will regret as soon as he sobers. "You must know about the food shortages girl. You live in the fields, for God's sake! Has your father harboured the people we were supposed to kill? Those rebels may have taken one group, but there are plenty of more people to choose from."

Everyone's mouths fall open in shock, including my own. Marik Lightfall admitting the Consulate secrets at the dinner table? I bite my cheeks so hard to stop myself from laughing.

"Marik. Out." Odessa orders, pulling at his arm once more, "Now."

"Come Rhea," Jude says as he ushers me out.

Chapter Thirty

We rush out of the dinner hall, Jude dragging me by the hand down a long corridor until we are alone.

"What the hell is he talking about Jude?" I ask, my eyes searching his. Jude takes a deep breath and runs a hand through his hair, pacing in front of me before speaking. "I don't know what to say. That was a shit show."

"Explain," my voice is curt as I cross my arms in front of me.

Jude inhales a long breath through his nose, his mind ticking over what to say. What to divulge.

"Fuck," the word shoots out of his mouth as he paces a few more steps. "There was an incident last night. A rebel group broke into the Citadel and broke some people out."

This is something I had not anticipated, but it could work in my favour; I need to get Jude on my side, I need him to trust Rhea with every breath. Even if it kills me a little to do so.

"What people?" I pry, stepping towards him and holding onto his hand. He goes rigid at my touch, then softens.

"There is a food shortage in the city, it's been happening for years. The commanders decided that fifty people will be executed each month to limit the food consumption. The rebels broke the people out," he explains, his jaw tightening as he speaks.

My eyes go wide, as though the information is new to me. Like I wasn't the one to free those people. I cover my mouth with my hand in shock. “This can’t be true!” my voice is shrill. “Killing fifty people! Every month! What rebels?”

“I know. I know. It’s a fucking nightmare. I didn’t want you to find out this way. It’s so much to take in, I know.” His hand tightens over my own and I shake my head, looking away from him.

“This is barbaric,” I let out, then I remember Marik Lightfall’s other detail. “He said you’re a sergeant now. Is that true? Are you going to have a say in killing these people Jude?”

Jude turns my chin, so I face him. “He’s making me do this. I start in a few days. But don’t worry, you and your father will be safe. I will make sure of it.” His deep voice echoes in my mind.

“Are the elites safe from being picked then? Do they only plan to kill the poorest of Altaras?” my voice cracks at the end — a genuine crack as the hurt caused from this plan begins to filter through the lies, filter through the façade of Rhea Fellows.

“The elites will be safe, yes,” he says, closing his eyes as though the words cause him pain. He tries to pull me closer, but I jerk away.

“Jude, I cannot,” I snap, a tear threatening to fall. “I cannot live happily amongst your family when what they are planning is so barbaric! How could I? Knowing that the only reason I am safe from this cull is because you have a liking for me.”

My tears are hot and stream down my face, the truth and lies mixing and merging. “I cannot feel for someone who’s path is destined for murder. Someone who will wake up each day to attend a meeting — to decide the group of innocents they plan to kill each month.”

He reaches a hand to wipe the tears away; his touch is so soft, I crave it. I want to lean into it. But the anger won't stop the bubbling inside of me, or the hate and frustration that courses through my veins. I ball my fists at my sides, unable to look at him, or to see the look on his face. I turn away and pull from his grasp, walking down the corridor.

Jude follows swiftly behind; he grabs my arm and spins me to face him. "Shout at me!" he yells, "scream till your lungs hurt! I will happily and gladly take it, but don't shut me out." He grips my face, his hands so big they cover my whole jaw. "Please. Please just talk with me."

"I have nothing else to say to you! I can't change who you are! You're a Lightfall — *another* Lightfall on a path of murder!" I shout, a sob threatening to break. "I need someone who does good for this world. Not the opposite," my voice lowers as I speak, I say the next words as I know it will cut him deeply. "It's in your blood to hate."

The words rip out of my mouth. My fury shouldn't be aimed at Jude. I know this. But taking it out on him is the closest thing I have to taking it out on his father. My words are finally full of truth; everything I have wanted to say to him about this awful place, the horrors of the Consulate and hatred for his father pools out of me. Marik Lightfall would have *killed* my sister if I hadn't broken her out. If I hadn't saved her.

"You want me to change?" he shouts. He takes a step closer to me, but my feet are rooted to the spot. I'm unable to move from beneath his powerful gaze. "I would change every single atom in my body for you, if it meant I could be the person you need."

Our eyes don't break contact, his deep brown eyes staring into my soul, trying to break my every being with just a look.

"I can't lose you," he whispers. "I would leave it all behind. I would do anything, say anything, if it leaves me with you. I need you to trust me. I'm nothing like him." he lets out, just before he pulls my face to meet his lips. And I finally, *fully* surrender to him.

The kiss annihilates me.

Like two racing flames fighting for dominance, neither one of us wants to gasp for air for fear of breaking the seal. Desire and lust clash together at once; hands and arms flail, grabbing desperately at each other, as though we simply cannot get enough. Lips crash and move as one. All my anger suddenly blows out like a match, only to be replaced with the desperate ache to be closer to him. All sense is lost when it comes to Jude Lightfall, especially when his lips are on mine.

He grabs the back of my neck to tilt my head more towards him. My hands graze his shoulders as I reach up to meet his lips once more. He dips his head to be closer to me, his body towers over mine, even on my tip toes.

Jude breaks the kiss, only for a moment, to rasp, "I will never get enough of you," then joins us again in this fiery dance.

With every fiber of my being, I build the strength to pull away. Still tangled in him, I tilt my chin, so our eyes meet again. He caresses the back of my hair, moving his hands to stroke the side of my face, to brush his fingers over my lips.

"Rhea, you have my heart," he gently kisses my lips, "it will always be yours."

I pull at his chest, kissing him once more; the words tumble out of me, my judgement clouding what I should do or say in this moment. The thoughts of Marik Lightfall and our argument over the culling has vanished like a match into water. In this moment, all I think of is hope when it comes to Jude Lightfall.

Our foreheads touch as I close my eyes. Uttering the words, I know I should not. My guard and all sense of self begins to crack. *Is this real?*

"Promise me," I whisper.

"I'm yours," he replies.

Chapter Thirty-One

Jude Lightfall leads us back to his mother's greenhouse, our fingers interlocked as we walk. His hand is warm and firm, as he caresses his thumb over my hand.

"Is this where my surprise is?" I tease, changing the subject of what had happened only hours earlier: the screaming match, the revelation of his father's plans. He opens the door, and the room seems to be more majestic at nightfall. Moonlight casts a silver glow on the centre of the room, like a spotlight shining down. We walk in further, my long red skirts floating behind me.

"It might be," he says, his voice hinted with amusement.

We stand directly under the skylight, and I look up. The moon is so bright, nestled among the thousands of stars littering the sky: sparkling and shining like a painting.

My gaze is diverted by the feel of Jude's eyes on me, staring at me in wonder.

"What?" I say, laughing, a smile plastered to my face.

Jude Lightfall's eyes bore into my own, looking at me so intently as he speaks, "Out of all of the stars and the moons, you are the one that shines the brightest."

His eyes glow darker as he draws closer to me, the warmth radiating from him. He reaches into his jacket pocket and pulls out a gold chain, holding each end between his fingertips. Dangling in the centre is a delicate gold sun pendant, encrusted with swirling rays. The fine metal curves at the end of each point, a bright green emerald placed in the centre. Delicate yet intricate. Jude places the amulet around my neck, fastening the clasp at my nape. The cool of the gold hits below my collar bone. The perfect length.

"I saw your crescent moon, so I thought you should have the sun to match," he says, slowly removing his hands from the back of my neck. His fingers gently graze across my exposed skin. My fingers go up to touch the crescent moon Eris had gifted me, sitting just above the sun pendant; they were meant to be worn together. My fingers touch the amulet, rubbing my thumb over the green gem.

"This is too much Jude," I say, my eyes and heart softening.

His face shines — that half smile that makes my knees want to buckle, "Nothing is too much for you. It was my mothers and she wanted me to give it to someone that I cared about." His fingers dance across my cheek, and my heart squeezes, the guilt already starting to consume me — even when I wish it wouldn't.

"And there has been no one else you've ever thought to give this too?" I ask, for my own curiosity. Does he remember Elyria? Would he have given this to her?

Jude's eyes flicker a moment, as if he was lost in a memory, but instead of answering he holds my face with both of his hands — the *size* of those hands, big enough to cover my entire head.

Lightly kissing my lips, he whispers, "I care a lot about you. Stay with me tonight?" He kisses my lips once more; his hands still cup my face as he does so; the warmth radiates my whole body as I shudder from his touch.

I shouldn't. I can't let myself feel this way. My body and mind seem at constant conflict when it comes to Jude. The only thing that settles my conscience is the thought of getting more information from Marik Lightfall tonight. So, for the sole purpose of the mission — and not my body's desire to stay — I agree.

"But only sleeping Mr. Lightfall," I say, a wicked gleam flashes in my eyes. "No funny business."

His full lips flutter against my earlobe, "Does kissing count?" I feel the hint of a smile against my ear as he softly chuckles. I want to melt, but I swat him away.

"If you keep your hands to yourself, there *may* be some kissing." I laugh. He looks to me, with his molten brown eyes; they rake up my body and land on my own.

"You can change your mind," he says, leading me out of the greenhouse.

We stand in Jude's room, it's not plain, but it's not regal like the rest of the house. It has a few books stacked messily on a shelf — some half opened, face down, some with bookmarks sticking out. As though he's reading them all at the same time. Pages and pages of handwritten notes are piled high; the writing messier as the pages continue, like his brain is working faster than his hand. Etchings and scribbles are strewn on the floor in messy heaps. *Jude writes?*

My mouth can't help itself, the words tumble out, "What is all of this?" I gesture to the stacks with well-worn curled edges. Jude flashes his signature half smile but avoids my eyes as they trail the ground instead, like I've just caught him doing something he shouldn't be. Embarrassed that I've seen this part of him.

"It's just something I've been working on," Jude runs a hand through his hair. "Just some ideas, its nothing substantial yet."

I smile and look at the stacks of pages. *A few*, I smile to myself, *this is more than a few*. The desire I have to devour each page, to see into the mind of Jude Lightfall, is overwhelming. But I understand what it's like to want to protect your art, to keep it safe until you're ready to share it. So, instead, I say, "I'd love to read them when you're ready to show me."

Jude looks up and the faintest sign of a blush resides on his cheeks. It's a gut wrenchingly beautiful sight to see.

Taking in the rest of the room, dark oak wood furniture matches the polished wood floors; there's a huge four poster bed with curtains drawn around it, the voiles fine enough to see through. A glossy piano sits in the far corner, the stool upholstered with a midnight blue velvet fabric, and sheet music scatters the floor.

I wonder how many nights he spends playing his piano, how many mornings he wakes to read a book, or write at his desk or in bed under the sheets. His life is so different to mine, yet it would be so easy to slip into it. I shake my head, brushing away the thoughts. Amidst the luxuries, there are lies. Beyond this room, the devil himself sleeps only a few feet away. It's easy to forget all the bad when it's cloaked in dreams and fantasy.

"You wore this last time, is that okay for now?" he says as he hands me the black silk robe his mother had given me. Our hands brush together at the exchange.

I nod my head, "Of course, I'll go change."

I take the material and head towards his bathroom, when I hear, "I do adore you in red, though."

Over my shoulder, I look back at his wicked grin — his tempting smile — yet close the door behind me.

The tiles are dark in this bathroom, unlike the white marble of the guest room. The granite shines a deep jet black against the large gold mirror hanging above the sink. I quickly change but decide to take off my thigh dagger, just in case his

hands *do* get the better of him. I neatly fold it away within the fabric of my dress; looking at my reflection, the two pendants shine against my olive skin as I bring my fingers to each one. I need to keep my head clear, and my heart out of this.
Suddenly, when I re-enter his room, there are lit candles everywhere, placed haphazardly on top of books and on the floor. They encase the room in a soft glow of warm orange light. Jude lays on his bed, the jacket and tunic chucked to the floor, exposing his bare, muscular chest. It's as though his body is carved from marble, each line and definition so perfect as though he was sent from the heavens. I bite the inside of my cheek to stop myself from gawking. Many black ink drawings swirl around his body; his tattoos were hidden until now. My nails dig into my palms to calm the racing of my stupid heart.

He props his arm above his head to watch me as I close the door, his hair sits messily across his forehead, nearly shielding his eyes.

"Impressive," I joke as my eyes rake down his body in an obvious stare. I join him on the bed, then my mind briefly drifts to Axon and how Jude surprisingly looks more muscular than him. I shake my head, eliminating the thought.

"I have to occupy myself somehow in this place when you're not here." Jude smiles.

"I like to run," I admit. Another truth falling from my lips. "It makes me think less."

Jude nods his head, "I know the feeling. Do you run a lot?" he asks, as our faces draw closer together, his body shifting closer towards me.

"Yes, most days. I run around the fields; I love the feel of the wind in my hair. Feeling free is the best part."

He smiles at that, his eyes closing as he lazily pulls me to him, so my body rests on his own. Jude's chest is a solid force as I lay on his bare skin, the muscles hard under my touch. I swirl my finger over the black ink.

"What are these?" I say softly, tracing the drawings, each one is beautifully detailed. Over his bicep, the image of a human heart, an image of a dragon with its wings splayed in flight over his shoulder.

"Some don't mean anything — some do," he says, the sound of his voice vibrates through my body with a hum. I move from him and push his body up so that he's seated in front of me. I want to get a better look at each one. I trace my fingers over what looks like an inscription, it covers his whole back in beautiful swirls and designs.

"This one is incredible," I whisper, mainly to myself.

"My sister," he says, his voice changing as he speaks. "The story of her. And her death."

My brows furrow in confusion, "It doesn't make sense though, I can't read it?" I ask, examining the strange words.

He lies back down once my fingers leave his skin, "The Consulate keeps some of the ancient books hidden so, unfortunately, not everyone will get to know the tales of our ancestors unless they were passed down through the generations of those lucky enough to have read them." His muscles contract under me with each word. Frustration maybe? Does he feel angry at the Consulate's deliberate hording of information? He carries on, "The ink is in an ancient language from before Altaras was built, a group that joined the town; they merged with the elders so many years before they made their journey here. There's a book in their language."

My eyes light up at the information. Ancient Languages. Knowledge of life before this place. I should have known artefacts and books were kept from us. The less we know, the less we ask…

"Why did you use their language to tell her story if it's not your own?' I ask, settling back down to his chest.
He runs a hand down my silk cladded arm as he speaks, "I liked that I could have a part of Khala etched into my skin, to hold her memory with me forever. The way our ancestors respected their dead was to detail their death on the body as a reminder, to keep them close, in a language unknown to most. And I want to keep their memory alive, whilst having her with me forever. They had their secrets. Khala is mine. I brought the two together."
I think about what he says: how the death of his sister, whom he never even met, has shaped his life. How he wants to preserve her memory onto his body as a permanent reminder.

"That's beautiful Jude. I think Khala would be proud of you," I am unable to stop the words, surprising myself with what I say as the truth of what I think of Jude comes out in this moment. "The ideology of the ancient people is wonderful — you should keep her memory with you. I just hope that the knowledge of their customs lies hidden within some families. Maybe some even remember the language," I close my eyes and try to believe what I'm saying is true. To let ancient customs and languages die is a terrible crime. We have been blinded, and we need to fight for freedom. To choose to grow, to be a city with many different opinions, customs, and languages. That will make us powerful. Knowledge is power, as my father would say.

"We need to do something Jude. We can't live like this," I whisper into his chest. He smells of freshly cut grass, of rain, of mint... all rolled into one. Jude smells of a fresh day, of nature.

"It's going to be okay, Rhea; you don't have to worry. I'll take care of you."

He kisses the top of my head and I nod into his chest, breathing in his scent, savoring it. *Grass and rain.* Wishing he could be right but knowing how wrong he is.

Chapter Thirty-Two

I spend hours of listening to the rise and fall of Jude's chest, feeling the warmth radiate off his body before I know he's sound asleep. *So, this is what peace feels like,* I say to myself. I wait a long time before I peel the dead weight of his arms from me and sit up from the bed. Once again, I kiss the sleeping narcotic onto his lips, quickly washing it off my own before I leave the room.

Creeping down the hallway on my tip toes, it's again so quiet in the manor. The only noise is that of my own breathing but, just like last time, I go to Marik Lightfall's office. Yet, instead of the light under the door, the whole corridor is without any sign of the Lightfalls.

Biting my lip, I think of what to do. They must be in bed. I could search the house — or I could go outside and find any signs of light. I choose the latter and pad down the stairs. I scurry to the doors that lead to the gardens — no guards stand watch; no maids or chefs are awake to stop me in my tracks. The night air sends prickles across my skin, the wind whips the hair around my face. My bare feet walk across the freezing paving stones, then gravel, as I tread around the manor in search for Marik and Odessa's bedroom.

On the far side of the house, there's a small glow on the top floor. That could be it. It's as though the Lightfalls sought to invite prying eyes as a vine of wisteria grows just below the window. Gripping the solid trunk, it sways under my weight, but the climb is easy, my bare feet deft on the branches. My silk robe floating in the wind, I threaten to expose my position at any moment.

Once, at a safe distance away, I steady myself on a strong branch, looping my arm around another. Just like Eris and I — the Lightfalls never sleep. Thankful that their window isn't soundproof, every word they say is within earshot.

"He thinks we should tell them that the patrol was attacked, that the people of Penury have grown even more savage and have acted in violence against us. Some of the guards will not be returning home." Marik Lightfall's voice says. The alcohol must have somehow found a way out of his system as no words are slurred.

"How will they not return?" Odessa questions, her tone hushed.

Marik Lightfall waits a few moments, thinking of the right thing to say to his wife, "Don't be naive Odessa, we will take them out."

My grip tightens on the branch, the bark digging into my palm as I listen, as I take in his words. Marik Lightfall is going to kill his own guards? All for the sake of a ruse, to keep up the animosity for Penury? I dig my nails in hard to distract myself from the anger brewing, to continue listening to their conversation.

"I'm not being naïve, Marik." More steps fill the room as though she's pacing back and forth. "I am perfectly aware of the age-old deception you all cloaked around Altaras, don't think me a fool."

"Then don't act like one," he spits, his voice rising. A long pause fills the room. I would do anything to just see the looks on each of their faces.

"You're the only actor here, Marik."

"We do this for the people. The lies are for the people... If they knew, the city would burn — even more than it has already started to, there would be anarchy in the streets. The deceit is the only way to keep the peace!" he spits.

"There is no peace!" Odessa's voice teeters on hysterical. "The rebel group just bombed Citadel buildings! They are making you look a fool. You don't even know where they are, let alone when they'll strike again!"

A loud bang makes my fingers curl as Marik Lightfall hits something solid. A wall? A desk maybe?

"People are already starting to uncover more than you think. They are so close to taking everything we have," she says.

We have broken him. His power is starting to crack and soon it will shatter for he has no plan, no next step on how to solve his little problem of us. Of the rebellion.

"And what of their families?" Odessa starts the argument back up, her voice no longer soft but sparked with frustration as she delivers her final blow. "What of the mothers and children who wait weeks to see their fathers and husbands return? Only for them to be hidden underground, waiting for your order to go back? What are we to do when the water runs dry and there are too many mouths to feed *without* anything to feed them with? Or when your plan of population control does not actually solve our problem, and the rebels just break them out again? Will you finally get the courage to open those gates, Marik?"

An ember of anger was rapidly catching fire, igniting me, reducing the person I used to be to ash. The gates don't open. We never leave through the gates. I feel like my head will burst, but those words... I heard it so clearly. *Will you finally get the courage to open those gates?* Bile rises to the back of my mouth.

The gates have never opened.

Hidden underground? My own father is a *god damn liar.* Tears threaten to fall down my cheeks, but my fury keeps them at bay. My need for answers spurs me on as my fists grip the branches so tightly, I fear it will snap. I steady myself and clench my jaw. I need answers. *Now.*

Before Jude awakes, I change back into my blood red gown. I walk to him, his mouth slightly open in peaceful sleep. I study the rise and fall of his chest, the way he breathes and the intricate markings that cover his body. The light blond hair that falls against his eyes in waves and the perfect eyebrows that shape his face.

Jude would have told me. He would have told me this lie, same as he told me of the culling. Right? But I'm uncertain. The little trust I had in him now has me questioning everything Jude has ever said. And that makes me the worst rebel spy there has ever been.

Before I go, I find a pen amongst his scattered things and write a message on Jude's arm, like he did to mine back in the Jade gardens. I need to talk to Eris. I need to tell him everything I have just learned. This information will change *everything*.

'Didn't want to wake you, Jade tomorrow – R'

And I leave the Lightfall manor in the dead of night.

Running home, my mind is occupied by anger and confusion, but I stop dead in my tracks as boots stomp against the cobbles. Since the rescue mission, there have been more patrols, and I have just stumbled on one of them. Two red suits walk towards me. Quickly, I spin on my heel and quietly

walk back the way I came, still hidden in the shadows of the buildings. Picking up my pace, I hurriedly walk into a side alley. They will spot me if I don't get ahead of them soon. And, just like my night couldn't get any worse, another set of guards turn a corner directly in front of me: three more red suits blocking my exit now as they unknowingly close in.
I groan under my breath, and silently curse at myself for walking into this trap, unable to hide myself in this alley now. The guards get closer and sense my presence. I unsheathe the dagger at my thigh holding it close to my side, tightening my cloak around myself.

"What are you doing out this late?" one of them calls, his loud voice echoes down the alley.
I take a breath and answer back, turning round to face them, "I was just coming back after visiting my mother. She's very sick." I cry, forcing tears to run down my cheeks. My comment is met with silence as the five guards now group together in a uniform stance, looking to each other with knowing looks. One of them finally speaks, but his tone seems skeptical as he says, "You shouldn't be out in the streets this late, miss. It's not safe."
I nod my head to him, "I know. I'm sorry. I just needed to see my mother."

The taller guard steps forward, "Let us escort you then."
My brain rattles through every option I could take. But all of them fall flat. If they escort me, where would I go? Not back to the Sparrows' base, that's for sure. If I try to walk away, they could follow me. And worst of all, they have all seen my face. Rhea Fellow's face. Marik Lightfall would hear of this encounter, I am certain.

"No that's okay, but thank you, I can handle myself walking back." I say to them, backing up with each word. But the looks on their faces reveal their distrust, as the hand of one guard hovers by his gun.

"We will escort you," the tall one replies, his tone is stern as he speaks.

"Or we could have some fun..." the guard with a horribly sparse beard starts to say with a slimy smile; the others collectively laugh but, before he comes any closer, my decision is made. At first, I was going to let them go, but he just crossed an unforgivable line. And his friends are less than innocent. They will have to die.

I let the darkness that simmers within me combust in an explosive act of pent-up violence. Swiftly, I slice my knife across his throat. Before he even hits the floor, I spring out and launch myself at the guard closest to him, stabbing him in the neck. Whirling on the ball of my foot, I do the same to the other standing next to him — thanks to their proximity and the element of surprise. Without a sound, they drop to the floor in a unified crash. The guards don't anticipate me; they don't expect that a girl in the dark could be carrying a knife. Or could be trained to kill.

The remaining two fumble at their sides for their guns, the shock evident on their faces. One forgoes his gun and advances on me with his fist raised, I block and stab at his arm, wounding him whilst I whirl on the other kicking his gun straight out of his hand. He catches my side with a strong blow that makes my eyes water. His grip tugs at my dress, ripping it and lurching me forward. Blinking away the stumble I hold onto his arm, twirling my body up so my legs wrap tightly around his neck, pulling him to the ground with me. His breathing tightly constricted, unable to move from his position, I raise my free hand and end his life with a fatal stab wound to the neck. Freeing myself from the dead weight of the guard, I rise to face the final man, covered in his dead comrade's blood. I must look like death personified standing before him, deadly and vicious in a blood-soaked gown. Not what any of them ever expected.

"What the fuck —" the last guard starts to shout, trying to alert the sleeping city, his gun pointed directly at me. But I sense his shock and slowness of movements at the scene in front of him, for the heinous act I have just committed. He doesn't finish his sentence as my knife flies and strikes him in the head with one fast motion. He falls to his knees with wide eyes as the life drains from his body in an instant.

I take my eyes from the scene, from the bodies strewn at my feet, and I breathe in deeply.

Shit.

I take another shaky breath, wiping the blood from my knife on one of the guards' uniforms, then place it back into its sheath. For the Sparrows, their safety, and for mine as well, this had to be done.

I run from the fallen guards, leaving no trace of me behind as I sprint back to the Sparrows' nest.

Chapter Thirty-Three

"Out all night again little bird? I was beginning to think the worst," Eris says, amusement clear in his tone. But I was in no mood for games. I cross my arms, clenching my jaw as I stare at him. I don't mention the guards I slaughtered, or that Eris now has a mess on his hands.

"One of my Sparrows has the camera; the broadcast goes live in two days' time," he says. Unless I am mistaken, his tone seems happy? An emotion I have never once seen or heard throughout the whole time I've known him.

"I thought this would look good on you," he says, holding up a silver bracelet encrusted with tiny black onyx stones between his large fingers. The metal swings back and forth while I stare at it for a moment. Ignoring his attempt to condition me, by always rewarding my *achievements,* I roll my eyes and speak.

"I found out more information." My tone is flat and expression harsh as I try to keep my anger at bay. Eris nods and leans back in his chair, waiting for me to relay what I heard.

I take a seat opposite him, picking up the lighter on his desk, inspecting it, toying with him. "Lightfall got drunk... started blabbing." Eris smirks, rolling his eyes, "A fool."

"He has no idea where the people are. He even asked me if I was keeping them down in the fields," I let out a short laugh at the memory and carry on. "He told Odessa Lightfall about a bogus patrol they are setting up; they are going to execute some guards to claim that the Penury people acted out in violence. But what was most peculiar was their talk of a deception that could put the city into anarchy," I pause, searching Eris' face for a response. His features remain neutral.

"They have no solution to our food shortage," I announce. "Altaras' gates have never been opened. They have lied to us this whole time." My voice is loud as the frustration builds; I expect the same reaction from Eris, for him to stand up and throw something. Shout maybe. But he remains calm, his features settled, unaffected by the information that will change our lives. Which suddenly makes me realise...

"You knew?" I breathe. My face contorts as I stare at him with disgust.

How can he sit here and lie to us. Withhold vital information from us... his Sparrows?

"Of course, I knew. I'm the leader of the rebellion, it's my job to know everything," he says calmly, like I'm stupid enough to even doubt his knowledge.

"Why?" I spit, standing up from my chair and letting it crash behind me. "Why the lies? Why did you never tell us?" I shout, tossing his paperweight across the room.

Eris crosses his arms in front of him, waiting a moment before replying. I bang my fist on his desk, leaning close as I shout in his face, "Explain."

"If everyone knew then conflict would break out..."

"Why not tell me! You made me go into this mission blind!" I shout. "Do you wish to see the Consulate destroyed? A war would be the perfect outcome so why not tell everyone!" I spit the words out, fury hot on my lips. He lets loose a deep laugh and shakes his head. As if I'm a child that knows nothing.

"Yes, I want that, but if Altaras knew, they would riot in the street. They have no guns. No weapons. They would be fighting an army blind. That can't happen, little bird. This needs to happen my way. The way it has been planned for longer than you have been around."

I wince, his words cutting deep inside of me. There's truth in his explanation, but that does not account for all the lies.

"Why lie to me? To us?" I ask as I look around the room, unable to face him. My palms are planted firmly on his desk, "Do any of them know? The Sparrows?"

"Vera. That's all."

"You are a lying piece of shit," I spit, "you..." but I don't finish my sentence as he launches himself at me with speed, grabbing hold of my arm with one hand, as his other connects with my jaw. My head ricochets, snapping my senses as I try to lurch back. But with my arm in his vice, he strikes my stomach with another blow.

The ringing in my ears is loud and my vision turns blurry. He relaxes his fist and takes a step back, releasing my arm from his grip, his face a ball of fury. Head spinning, mouth dry, I bite my cheek, distracting myself with the pain before I do something I might regret.

"You forget your allegiance, little bird."

Cracking my neck and rolling my shoulders, I stand upright. Composed. I walk over to the door, turning to say one last thing before I storm out of his office. The one thing I know he will hate. For he loves the hold he has over me, and I would have done anything he asked.

"You're dead to me," I snarl, staring him down. For a split second he looks less threatening. I have information that can ruin his whole operation. I will be his downfall. I glare at him, my tone intimidating yet provoking as I speak my final words to him.

"You're going to wish you didn't train me so well. That's the last time I drop my guard and let you hit me without retaliation." Slamming the door so hard on my way out, I'm sure the whole of Altaras hears me.

As I storm down the corridor, chaos erupts within Eris' office. I hear a door opening and I'm sure it's him hot on my trail to punish me for that last remark. But I was wrong. Instead, Axon calls out, making me stop in my tracks.

"I thought you were dead… again."

The rage in me dies down. It softens for Axon, but I keep stalking down the hallway, nonetheless.

Over my shoulder, I remark, "I told you I'm hard to kill."

Opening the door to my room, Axon follows me and closes it behind him. Again, I choose not to mention the patrol, they can deal with that mess themselves.

"This isn't funny, Birdie. You could have been killed. Everyone needs to be on high alert after what happened." His tone is heavy and out of breath.

I look up to him, the worry clearly etched into his features. "I'm always on high alert. I was fine, just stayed the night again that's all. I avoided all guards on the way back."

He nods his head in understanding, but then his face falters. His arm gently reaches up to grip my chin, to turn my jaw that I conveniently hid from him. A dark red welt present already. He sucks in a breath, "That bastard."

"It's not like he hasn't hit me before."

"I hate that you let…"

"Axon, don't," I snap, pulling away from him. I retreat from him, backing towards the mattress. I sit down and take a breath. "Do not tell me that I *let* this happen. That I *willingly* let him do this to me," I seethe.

"I know you can kick his ass better than anyone in this place. You choose not to. Just stop fighting with him all the time and then you won't get the repercussions. Just do as he says. The plan is working!"

I ball my fists. He thinks I should be an obedient little soldier, just like him.

"How dare you throw that in my face. Like you don't do the same? You would throw yourself in front of a bullet for him, even though he treats *you* like a piece of shit." I move to escape his proximity, but Axon's words follow.

"I don't goad him into throwing a punch though," he retorts flatly.

I shake my head with a vicious laugh, "I keep my sanity by provoking him. I will not let myself be a coward. He might not hit you, but he has you firmly under his thumb nevertheless," I look him dead in the eyes as I speak, "I will never again look weak in front of him."

"Your face says otherwise Birdie." A desperate stab to protect his ego.

"Fuck you," I hiss, unclipping the crescent necklace from around my neck and gripping it as I speak, "your loyalty to him makes you look like a fool."

I drop the necklace and crush it under my foot with a crunch.

"Get out." I order. My tone is harsh but voice quieter now.

Axon starts to interject but I make him stop. "I said get out, Axon. I need to clear my head. Just go make sure Lila is okay." Without another protest, he nods; his jet-black hair falls onto his face, and he exits my room, closing the door softly on the way out. It upsets me to hurt him, to see him continuously try to be there for me despite my constant dismissal. But I *can't* give him what he wants from me, those feelings just don't exist.

Pulling on my suit, I fasten my dagger to my thigh. Without another word to Eris or the Sparrows, I grab a few more knives and pistols from the armoury and sheathe the weapons at my hips. It's still dark outside as I leave the base; the wind is fresh and cool. Nature is calming; the guards are nowhere to be seen. After everything, the Citadel should be on high alert, to have patrols constantly walking the city in search of the fugitive people, for us. But they must be scared. Unsure of how to handle this.

It doesn't take me long to get there, I know the route like the back of my hand. I sprint down the cobbles, dodging the streetlights and any cameras dotted along my path. I have never run so fast, and the wind is on my side. I fly like a bird in flight, rounding the corner to the place that has haunted me for so long. I just need to be in its presence, even the familiarity of it will give me some sort of peace.

At that very moment, the bile that reaches my throat comes out as I double over and retch on the floor. Steadying myself on a nearby wall, I bury the tears that threaten to come. I want to kill him. I want to gut him and put a bullet in him for what he's done.

For the house that I was told burned to the ground, stands tall and just how I left it.
My *home.*

Chapter Thirty-Four

There's a glow of light in my parents' window. The bile burns my throat once more as I take another deep breath. It's now that I find out the truth. From *their* mouths. I use the stonework of my home to expertly scale the building, to reach up to the wooden ledge and slide the window open. I haul myself up and through without making a sound. Once I'm on the floor and my eyes adjust, I hold a knife in my hand for protection and scan the room, only to be faced with my mother and father, bolt upright in bed. A look of shock on their features.

"Elyria?" my mother cries out, her voice cracking. "Elyria, I know it's you," she says as tears threaten to spill, "You look —" but she can't finish her words, can't face what I've become.

I lower my knife and sheathe it. I regulate my breathing before I speak, otherwise the tears will come and won't ever stop.

"Lila is safe, I wanted to let you know." I say, my voice barely above a whisper. My parents sigh with relief, hugging each other tightly as my mother weeps.

I clear my throat; I still have things to say.

"What is the colour of the wall?"

The question is directed to my father as he pries himself from my mother, mouth agape. He says nothing for a few moments, so I press, asking the question again, "What is the colour of the wall, Father?" My voice doesn't waver, my tone is stern and hard. I can see from the dim candlelight that colour has drained from his face, but I keep looking at him. "Don't make me ask again."

It was all a *lie*. Everything is a *lie.* He's never seen the gold wall with its vines, or the inscriptions carved on it. If he had, he would know instantly. He never brought me flowers from outside of the wall or the girls jewellery from his travels. Our lives have been a lie and a trick.

He looks to the ground. "Don't be silly. It's brick, Elyria, like any wall."

And that was when I heard it — the sound of my own heart breaking. I couldn't contain my sob as it wrenched out of me. I hit the floor on my knees and start to cry, forgetting the pain Eris instilled in me for letting the tears out. Why does everyone lie to me? I have been kept in the dark time and time again. I can't take this *anymore*. I expect it from Altaras, from Marik Lightfall, from Eris even. But my own family? A sob escapes my lips again as I cover my hand with my mouth. I hear movement as the bed shifts, my mother crouching on the floor next to me. Her hands hover around my body, unable to touch me — from fear or shock, I do not know. And then she hugs me. She wraps her tiny arms around my body and engulfs me in an embrace. I cry more, my body shaking with the sobs as I feel her tears on my head as she cries with me. "I'm sorry, we're sorry," she repeats, over and over until there are no more tears left in me.

We stay like that on the floor for a short while before I shake her off me. Her warmth leaves my body; I make to stand but she ushers me to sit once more, her on the bed and me in the chair opposite. My father walks over to me, but I flinch away from his touch; he decides to retreat instead — a wise move. He stands by the door.

"There's something else you must know," she says, her crimson eyes searching mine for any recollection of the daughter she once had. "I knew you were with him from the moment I realised you weren't coming back."

The air has been taken from my lungs. More deception. My fists clench the sides of the chair so tight that with a hard squeeze, I could almost snap it. My mouth is so dry, I can't form words to speak, but she carries on. Her head is bowed as she talks creating a halo of black hair around her. My father then walks over, placing a hand on her shoulder.

"I can still taste the dirt in my mouth some days," she says, her voice cracking. Her eyes brim with tears as she looks up to meet my stare. "Sometimes I wake up in the night and check my nails for mud stuck there. I scrub at my hands in the bathroom repeatedly. Always sleeping with the lights on."

The guilt of what she is confessing is clear in her eyes. It only takes a moment for the realisation to snap into place; for her eyes tell me everything before she even speaks, the lie she's kept hidden from me this whole time.

"It was my fourth birthday. I remember my mother crying as I was taken away, put on a wagon, and dropped amongst the trees. There was a man with me; he was young back then, around twenty years old. He kept telling me not to cry, even though I wanted to go home to my mother so badly. He told me to follow him and not to look back. He crouched down and parted a bush to reveal a hole. I didn't want to, but I followed him down, even though it was such a tight gap. I followed Eris' movements. I was there for hours, crawling and then waiting, both of us in silence. It was so dark. So claustrophobic. Little bugs and worms were all over my skin," she stops talking, wiping her eyes gently on her sleeve. Shock grips my tongue in a vice. My brain is a mess of thoughts and feelings.

"Eris finally started moving again, then it was only a few more minutes of crawling. Then, the light hit my eyes. It was still night-time but the brightness of being above ground was harsh. I remember Eris pulling me out by the wrists once he left the tunnel; we were among more trees, it was like we were back where we started. He told me I needed to be quiet, that there was a man waiting for us to take us home. I was so relieved. Finally, the torture was over, and I could go home to mother and father." She was looking at her nails now, flexing her fingers, unable to face me. "The man was there. He was tall and cloaked, I couldn't see his face because it was so dark. We all ran, Eris had to hold me up as my legs were so numb from crawling. I remember the pain so vividly. We stopped and the man said our house was just up ahead. There were some houses I could see in the distance, so we went further, but I didn't recognise the road or the houses. I was confused and starting to panic. Eris kept repeating himself, telling me to stop crying. 'Don't cry, don't cry. We don't cry here. We listen and do what is asked of us.' I was so confused, but then a door opened, and a woman was there. It wasn't my mother. The man went inside and so did Eris, pulling me along. He took me up the steps and into the house. The lights were off. It was still dark in there, and I could only just about see her face. She crouched down to me and her words still haunt me, even now. I will never forget them — it changed my life."
She's crying now, but I don't want her to stop talking, even though the bubbling fury in my bones makes me wish she never opened her mouth.

"'Ariadne Nightingale, it's nice to meet you,' she said. 'This is probably very scary for you, but you've been so brave. This is your new home. You're coming to live with us; you're in Altaras now and everything's going to be okay.

Chapter Thirty-Five

Complete shock paralyses my body, rendering me useless for words. I take in a few shallow breaths, looking her in the eyes frantically searching for something — *anything* to say.

You're in Altaras now.

"You lived in Penury, didn't you?"

She nods her head, black hair falling across her shoulders.

"So, your parents... you grew up on the other side of the wall?" I run my hands through my hair and rise from the chair. I'm pacing the room now, adrenaline coursing through my body. "You lived out there?" I point out the window, my heart rate rapidly increasing as my chest tightens. My breathing is rapid — short, shallow breaths.

"Yes. I was born in Penury. Born to parents I vaguely remember," she studies my every movement. "My parents sold me to the Sparrows, to the mission is what I was told. It's the longest spy work anyone has ever completed. Thirty-five years I've been here, working with them — or *for* them, for most of it."

The revelation is like a punch to the gut, my insides contorting and compressing against each other. Nightingale eyes, the eyes of a Penurian bloodline. It takes all the strength in me to ask questions, to keep her talking.

"You knew he took me," I whisper. The hurt is clear across my face as tears slip from my eyes, "You knew and didn't come for me."

My mother softly cries, her hand reaching for my own, but I pull away as I seethe at her, "You're a Sparrow and you did *nothing* to free me."

"Elyria, rebel born: your name means 'a beautiful fire.' Just like the fire in your eyes. You are the strongest of us all..."

"Just answer the question!" I demand.

"I knew he got to you, but there was nothing I could do. We both know how Eris works. You would have known too much about the rebellion, and he would never have let me take you back." Her voice is pleading with me.

"Think of your siblings, Elyria, they needed their mother alive, not to risk getting caught by the Consulate trying to rescue you," my father interrupts.

My eyes shoot him daggers. Wrath spits freely from my lips, "Are you forgetting I was the one who saved Lila? I risked my life, broke her out and saved her from death!" My voice is loud as I defend myself, but I tame it. The last thing I need is to wake my sleeping siblings. "Yet what of me? I was starved, locked in isolation for days. I was kicked. Punched. Beaten so hard I would pass out, then regain consciousness to take another kick or a slap. I was left in freezing cold water for hours, till my body almost shut down. I shut my *own* hand in a door just so that he wouldn't break it first."

My father retreats from my words, from the attack. My mother puts her head in her hands.

"I wasn't allowed to cry, or he would burn me with his lighter or cigarette — whichever was closest." The memory makes me throw my head back with a short laugh. Everything I went through... they knew. "I'm guessing I don't really need to give you the details of Eris' techniques, Mother.

I'm assuming he did the same things to you?" The venom is hot on my tongue.

Looking down on her crumpled body, hoping my words wound her. She is the only one I can take my anger out on.

"You didn't come for me," I breathe, taking a deep inhale as I say the last words, "No one came to save me."

"In some ways, yes, I endured some of that treatment," she says, finally looking up at me. Her eyes are puffy and rimmed red. "I hated to think what he was doing to you. But he swore to me that you would be safe. I had hope you would become even stronger than I knew you already were. You always have been a fighter, Elyria, I knew he wouldn't break you." She goes for my hand, but I lunge away from her, back towards the open window. She left me on my own because she *knew* I was strong? *Bullshit.*

"You spoke to him? Why did you stop being a Sparrow? What did you even achieve if we're still here, if people are still being treated like this? You never changed a thing!" I yell, "You did nothing for the cause!"

Mother's eyes are wide — wild, like I've never seen.

"I've done more for this cause than you'll ever know," she says angrily. Hurt flashes across her face. "I have a lot to tell you, but for now, it is best left unknown."

I stare her down, my eyes hostile and unforgiving but she keeps talking, "Remember Elyria, *'Allegiance is our core foundation, our oath for all we do'.* Don't forget who you're working with."

I think back to the puzzles she made us do, the repetitiveness of the riddles each morning, making our brains work quickly, shaping us into problem solvers — skills I have now used. I remember the times we watched the briefings together, how her fists would slightly clench, and her eyes would never leave the screen. She never uttered a word in favour of the

Consulate or the Commanders. She never missed a briefing, *not one*. But accusation fills my brain. Why has she not done more? How could she sit back and watch every single day? "Tell me this one thing," I spit. This lie is the last of it. The final piece to the puzzle that is my past, and hers. The last thing that will make this whole mess make sense.

"Is the dreamland real? Is the dream girl you?"

Her face softens, like the anger has lifted. Only sadness replaces it now. My father goes to sit next to her on the bed, wrapped his arm tightly around her.

"Yes, it's all real. I am the dream girl."

Before I throw up, not wanting to hear the rest of what she has to say, I swing my leg out of the window. My father clutches onto my mother as she cries, but they don't try to stop me, they let me go. *Again.*

I cast myself out, launching to the ground in one swift motion. Hitting the earth with a thud. The long jump makes me stumble but I regain my footing, and sprint down the alley. Away from the lies.

She lied this whole time. Everything she's ever told us about herself has been based on a lie, or an exaggeration of the truth. My whole life has been masked beneath this cloud of deception. From both mother and father. I can't trust *anyone.*

How could they do this to me... to us? The story of the dreamland would soothe us to sleep as children, would make us calm. But mother was just recalling a memory. A memory from *outside* of the wall. I clutch my stomach as it tenses, suddenly feeling lightheaded. Before I pass out, I duck into an alley, hiding behind a large set of bins. I crouch low against a wall, my mind racing.

My father has never been outside the walls. He's never even *seen* the wall. His charade of travels and trade with other lands never happened. Everything he has told me — and my family — it's all a lie.

My mother was a spy sold from Penury. She's a *Sparrow.* How could I not have seen this, or figured this out?

I clutch at my head before it can burst, a headache racked with the memories, recalling all the conversations of my childhood as the deceit floods to the surface. I curl over and vomit on the floor, then tuck my head into my knees.

I sit like this for a while; I sit until my legs hurt and my tears have dried. The people of Altaras are about to start their day, my cover of nightfall has gone but the city is enclosed in a swirling mass of clouds. The air is gloomy, dark, and thick. Suffocating. I don't know how to act, or what to do. Stretching up, I crack my neck and flex my fists. My cloak clings tight to my body as I pull up my hood and exit the alley, checking for any signs of guards. I deem the route clear as I start walking, weaving in and out of side streets. I pass cafes with the doors wide open; people exit with their bags as they hug their hoods close to their heads to protect themselves from the weather.

Through my dazed state, I make it to the place that Eris won't expect me to go. Jade gardens. Jude.
Although today, its beauty is downcast by the greyness, mist swirls above it. It's still early, Jude may not be awake yet. But I sit and wait under the oak tree.

I will wait all day if I need to.

As the hours pass, no one enters the gates of the gardens. He's not coming. But I sit and I wait, for I have nowhere else to go. The air turns to ice as the mist wraps itself around me, but I'm grateful the rain has not come. My body remains dry, wrapped tightly in my cloak. I sit. And I wait.

Another hour passes, then another. And nightfall is again upon us. But I wait.

And as if my prayers are answered, through the mist, I see Jude Lightfall. He walks through the gates as I stand, my legs numb from the position I have been in for hours. His expression is unreadable as he comes closer, however, his guards flank him and stand by the entrance to the gardens.

"Hello," I say, clearing my throat.

"What happened?" he asks; his body is close to mine. Concerned, he studies my face as I realise he sees the bruise Eris left me. He takes my face into his hand and runs a finger over the welt. "Did your father do this? For not returning last night?"

I shake my head and pull out of his grasp. Eris — a *father of sorts.* I repress the sudden urge to laugh.

"Jude —" I start, but I don't know what to say. The words are lost, drying aimlessly on my tongue.

Jude's eyes soften as he looks at me, *pleading* for me to explain. "Rhea, please, what's going on?" Stepping towards me again, warmth radiates from his body as he closes in, curling his arms around me tightly. Instinctively, I bury my face in his chest as my head tells me to stop, to back away from him. But my soul tells me to stay. To bury myself deeper.

Jude's lips are on my forehead as he tangles his fingers lightly in my hair, tugging gently so I look up to him, "What's happened?" he whispers, "You're confusing me."

My heart beats frantically, my breathing unsteady. The warnings in my brain tell me to stop. Not to lose focus. But I shove the thoughts so far down until they are barely whispers in my mind. Our eyes don't break contact, his deep brown gaze pouring into my soul, trying to break my every being.

Sucking in a breath, I go to open my mouth to speak but my words are silenced as Jude's lips crash to mine. He holds the back of my head, our lips desperate and fighting for dominance. I stretch my hand up and hold the back of his neck, my fingers intertwine in his soft hair as he, again, tugs at my own to gain further access with his tongue. I reach up on my toes to get closer to him. I *need* to be closer. To be engulfed by him.

My mind races as the kiss deepens. A moan escapes his mouth as he whispers against my lips, "All I need is you."

I smile amidst the kiss.

"All I want is you."

I pull away, gasping for air. "Jude..." He tries to come to me again but I back away and place an outstretched palm against his hard stomach. Tears start to well in my eyes, threatening to fall, but I suck in a breath, "Please listen first." I let out, looking up to face him again. Shame rattles through me, boiling low in my stomach. I decide to tell just one truth — one that may not hurt him as much as the others.

"There is so much I need to tell you. But first, your father has lied to us... to all of Altaras," I say, my eyes glued to his as I speak. "The patrols. The trades. All of it are lies."

"What are you talking about?" His brows furrow in confusion. Either he has no idea or he's a better liar than I would have guessed.

"Altaras' gates have never been opened, Jude. No one has *ever* left this city." My tone is hard now as the truth comes out, the fury reviving in my body. Anger for the deception Altaras has put its people through. Realisation washes over him as my words set in. He had no idea either. He's been lied too, the same as me. Jude runs a hand through his blond hair.

"Is this true?" He comes closer to me, placing his hands on my shoulders and giving me a gentle squeeze. "How do you know this?"

I stretch the truth as much as I can; the less he knows of the Sparrows, the safer he will be.

"It doesn't matter how I know; it matters what we do with this information," I say as I grasp his arm. "We need to do something about it. The food shortages, groups of people disappearing to be killed... people will start to figure this out, but the Consulate will just try to hide it with more lies!"

I witness the gravity of this revelation sink in as I continue, "People will die. From starvation, or by a bullet. Both by your father's hand."

Jude inhales a breath, his jaw set. "I can't speak to my father. I don't know what to say, Rhea. I don't know what to do with this information."

I nod my head in understanding. "It's a lot to take in, I know."

Jude releases a short breath, as his mind ticks on. After a few moments, he answers, "I can get us in to the briefing room in the Unity Building. We can tell the city, Rhea."

I think through his plan. I could sneak into the briefing, but what's to say they wouldn't shut the cameras off as soon as I start speaking?

"We need more time to think about what we're going to do." He decides, bringing his hand up to caress my head, "We have time."

I smile up at him, knowing in my gut that trusting him is the right thing to do. We need people on our side to help us. Doing this alone would be foolish.

"I may know someone that can help us. Meet me tomorrow on the corner outside Fernhurst's bakery, we can talk then."

"Okay."

Jude levels his head with my own as he whispers, a gleam in his eyes, "Whatever you say, I will do it." I bite my cheek to stop from smiling as my worry disappears beneath his gaze. Slowly — ever so slowly — hope replaces it.

"Don't be late," I say and close the distance between us with a quick peck on his lips. But we stay interlocked, lips warm against the cold air as we both savour the sensation of the other.

"I will always be early for you."

I nod my head and close my eyes, our foreheads resting against each other. Jude's breath is hot against my face, his closeness radiating warmth against the autumn breeze.

"Tomorrow morning," I say as I finally open my eyes and pull away.

He nods his head and lets me out of his arms, returning to his normal composure, jaw tight as I walk away from him, leaving to find Xannu. To ask her for help — help to finally end this.

~

A bell announces my arrival; she looks up from behind the counter, her eyes — covered in red powder — go wide when she sees who's entered.

"Elyria, what are you doing here?" she gasps, walking slowly to me. Her eyes are wild, analyzing me, scoping me out.

"I didn't know where else to go," I say, my voice slow.

She ushers me to the back of the boutique, putting her arm around me, "Eris is going to have a fit if he finds out."

"I don't care what Eris does," I say firmly, "He can kill me for all I care, I'm done." I sit on a box, my shoulders dropping from the weight of tonight's revelations. "Sit tight Elyria, take a breath and let me shut up the shop, I have one order to send out and then I'm done."

"Ok, tell me everything, what's happened?" as she returns, pulling her silky black hair into a ponytail and stands in front of me, hands on her hips. "Speak, Elyria."

I sigh. "He lied, my parents lied. I have been kept in the dark my whole life." Xannu waits for me to explain; she really is a girl of few words. "Eris never told you that he's been outside of the wall?" I wait for her to answer. But her expression says it all.

No.

"What are you talking about?"

"Eris, he lived in Penury, or went to Penury often. Could still be making trips there, I don't know." I say as I relay the information to her, "He took my mother from Penury, she is... or *was* a Sparrow."

Xannu sucks in a short breath, her eyes showing she is clearly taken back. "He told you this?"

"She did. I went to my home. He told me it burned to the ground, but that was a lie. My mother knew I had been taken by him. Recruited to become a Sparrow." I take in a breath, "Altaras never makes trips outside of the gate. It's all a lie, Xannu. The commanders tricked us all into believing they leave to trade and God knows what else, but they never have!" My voice rises as the truth comes out, the anger a blazing storm refusing to settle. "They hide the guards and merchants, everyone that pretends to leave the gates. My father would be hidden underground for weeks — months, even — to keep up the act that they were beyond the wall. This deception has been going on for years. No one has *ever* left Altaras."

Xannu turns around, her hands now folded in front of her midnight blue dress, but she doesn't face me, "I didn't know. Not any of it."

"We need to tell the city; I have a plan." I grip onto her arm, trying to make her understand, to believe me. But her next words take me aback. I release her arm as the words leave her lips. For they have never left her lips before, "I'm so sorry, Elyria."

Her tone is off, confusion rattles through me. *Why won't she face me*?

I hear a drum of footsteps. *No, it can't be...*

"What's going on, Xannu?"

She turns around, tears brimming in her eyes. "He made me, I had too."

My response dies in my throat as a sea of red guards pour through the front and back of the shop, cornering me like a mouse. Their boots are heavy, but their shouts are louder. Guns aimed at my head. Quickly, I pull the knife and gun from their sheaths, aiming them at the men which now fill the room as I back into the wall behind me.

"Why?" I whisper. A tear trickles from my eye.

"On your knees, girl," a guard shouts. "Put down the weapons."

I look to Xannu, silently begging her for this to end, for an explanation. This cannot be happening. She looks back to me with sorrow in her eyes, an expression I have never seen there before.

"Now!" another guard shouts; I hear the click of the safety button release on his gun.

'I'm so sorry,' she mouths, but I'm past caring. I begin to fire rounds onto the nearest guards and throw my knife, striking one of them square in the head; Xannu ducks, seeking cover behind the counter. A few bodies slump to the ground with a heavy thud, but none of them fire back at me.

Then, a pain in my shoulder knocks me square to the ground. The blinding agony clouds my senses; I'm rooted to the floor as a volt of electricity courses through my body. Paralyzing me.

This is it, I think. *This is how I die.*

Then, the world turns black.

Chapter Thirty-Six

Blinding pain jolts me awake. I clutch at my shoulder in agony, my fingertips grazing the area to find no blood. No hole in my suit.

"You killed so many of my men," a voice says. The pain in my shoulder settles and I open my eyes, only to be surrounded by darkness. That voice, the one that I hear in my nightmares — but who's face does it belong to?

"I trained hard to hit a target," I groan, trying to sit up against the cold concrete. My head pounds as I try to search for the voice.

"You're in no position to make jokes, girl." the man spits the last word like an insult, but I laugh deeply, my voice scratchy. I know the voice to whom I'm speaking with. I've heard it every time the briefing flashes on the screen, ever since I was a little girl.

"No, but my humour maintains my sanity."

"Tell us about the rebel group; we may let you live." After a few moments, I spit my words at him, "Showing sympathy or mercy is not in your nature, Mr. Lightfall."

"You have one last chance girl," he sneers, his voice now raised, ignited with rage. But this is the moment; I will be killed if I speak, or if I keep my mouth shut, so I say the only thing I wish to say to Marik Lightfall. My last and final words to him.

"Fuck *you.*"

"Very well, Miss Nightingale."

My blood runs cold. Nightingale. He knows my *name.* My hands shoot up to my eyes. The contacts have gone. The footsteps of Marik Lightfall grow quieter as he walks away. Leaving me in the darkness. My senses are disorientated, but my eyes have slightly adjusted, I can make the outline of my hands and feet, but that is all. Eris locking me in the dark cell for days as 'training' may have paid off. And whilst my mind won't kill me in this place, starvation might.

I relive my past training of this situation: keep my mind sharp and senses awake. I cross my legs and close my eyes, inhaling and exhaling in slow controlled breaths. I begin to meditate. A coping technique taught to captive prisoners — a method to instill focus.

After what feels like hours, a voice alerts me from my trance.

"Stand up! Back against the wall!" This is not the voice of Marik Lightfall, but instead of someone I do not recognise. "Now!"

But I stay fixed where I am, resting my arms above my head, my outstretched legs crossed at the ankles. My suit has been checked and emptied of weapons, likely removed when I was unconscious. That's okay, though. I still have my hands.

"Get up," the man says, clearly tiring of my disobedience.

My pearly white teeth flash in a devilish grin, "Only if you ask nicely."

As the door opens, my body is shocked by the sudden exposure to the light as it blinds my vision. An obvious ploy to distract the senses. I cover my eyes with my hand and squint to see the figure blocking the exit. I blink. And blink again until I see the long pole held in his grip.

"We can do this the easy way or the hard way," he says, smashing the metal against the wall with a loud *clang.* I don't reply, but jump up on all fours, poised to fight this man to the death. I charge, aiming for the weak spot behind the knees, but he has the upper hand of perfect sight, hitting my stomach with the pole. I jut to the side, not relenting as I go again. This time, my aim is for the pole, and I manage to grip it tightly in my grasp, yanking hard to distract, whilst my leg comes up and kicks him in the neck. He doesn't expect the force, but I don't expect the bolt of electricity that shoots from the pole, zapping me to the floor. The sensation paralyses and contorts my body, now remembering the pain which brought me to my knees at Xannu's boutique.

My vision is clear, but my body is useless. The man reaches over, electrocuting my side again. I cry out in pain, screaming with the agony of it. Never have I felt excruciating pain like this before. The man hits me with a final bolt of power before my body shakes to a stop. I can't feel my legs or move my arms as he bends down and binds my wrists. His breath reeks of blood, alcohol, and raw meats as he spits in my face, zapping me one last time. My next cry is a low sound filled with pain as tears leak from my eyes. Then, his boot comes down on my head, and the lights go out.

~

Ice cold water soaks my body, reviving my sleeping form. I reach to wipe my face, but my arms resist as I remember my hands are bound. Somehow, I manage to rise to a kneel, coughing and spluttering as I blink the murky water from my eyes, clearing my vision to reveal what's in front of me.

The Commanders.

Sitting in the chairs are the ten that I have seen every morning for as long as I can remember. As I look to each one, death and hatred seep out of me. I spit at the floor in front of me, a grimace set on my face as I set my eyes on one man.

"How charming," a voice says, but I stay silent. Just staring up at him.

"Elyria Nightingale," Idris Amal announces my name, standing as he talks. His words are aimed at me, but also his fellow Commanders. The use of my name makes me shudder, but I will not allow them to break me. "You are charged with the murder of four Altaras guards. You are charged with conspiracy against Altaras. You are charged with the attempt to overthrow the Consulate. You are charged with espionage. You are charged with the attempt of inciting rebellion against Altaras," he lists the crimes off one by one whilst I grind my teeth, my jaw tight with anger. "Due to the nature of the offences, you are deemed a significant threat to us, your crimes are... *unforgivable*," he turns his head to the left, "Mr Lightfall will be overseeing your... questioning."

Marik Lightfall stands, his white hair almost transparent as the artificial white light beams down on us, "We are going to get to know each other *very* well, little rat."

Without responding, I continue to glare at him, dead in the eyes.

"We hope you cooperate," Idris Amal says, just as something hard smacks me on the back of the head, rendering me unconscious again.

I count three days. Three days, so far, locked in this cell. The only way to track the time is by the single occasion each day where one of the guards opens my cell window to chuck me a slice of stale bread. I never touch it, the hard lumps remaining on the floor. The smell of mildew and dried blood fills the room, it permeates the walls in a lasting stench, a reminder of all that's happened here.

On the third day, I am summoned. The door to my cell bursts open; I'm greeted by two guards standing at the exit.

"Easy way, or the —"

But I don't let him finish as I shoot up and run for them, using my shoulder to barge the speaker in the stomach as I encircle the other by the neck. I wiggle my restraints. Fearless determination courses through my body as I use the loop of the binding to swing myself up, hauling my body weight so I land behind his back. I pull down hard on my wrists to strangle him with the leverage. The first guard now stands as the shock of being winded wears off — he charges. Mustering my depleted strength, I pull again with my wrists, sending the guard falling back as he grapples at his throat. I roll away just in time for the other guard to join us as he jumps over the fallen body which lays coughing and wheezing on the ground. I'm too quick for him, too nimble as I sprint as fast as my legs will carry me down the hallway. Shouts echo behind me as I run. This dark underground bunker is much like the Sparrows nest. But, as I turn the corner, luck evades me as I skid into a large, *red* chest. As we collide, he wraps his big strong arms around me, tightening his death grip.

I kick and thrash, trying to get free, but he's strong, using his power to bind my arms and shoulders in a vice grip. The previous guards reach us, their grimaces clear as one of them spits in my face.

One places a gloved hand to his neck; the dark red marks evident from where I had caught his neck earlier, "You fucking little bitch."

His face reddens with embarrassment that I was able to swipe at him.

"Always the hard way," I say with a sarcastic smile, but again my head smacks into the wall and the blackness comes once more.

I wake to another dump of water, the ice-cold liquid burning my skin. My head throbs and I want to groan — to cry out, but I save my reaction. I refuse to show pain as I see Marik Lightfall sitting before me.

My legs and arms are bound to a metal chair, the bindings chafe my flesh as I tug at them hard. The room is different from the one I was in before as a white light shines down on us; one shines from behind him too, the light making it impossible to see past him.

"You keep giving my guards a hard time, little rat." Marik says coldly; his arms are folded in front of him. He's dressed in a dark suit with a red tie.

"They should be trained better," my voice is scratchy, throat burning, as I get the words out.

"Quite a mouth on you, Elyria, were you always this vicious?" Leaning forward to meet my eyes, his smell is pungent, reeking of heavy musk and alcohol. I turn my nose up at him, sitting straighter in my chair, even though the movement makes my head throb. Marik Lightfall takes in a short breath, clearly frustrated. He likes people doing what they are told.

"I was a blind fool to let you in my home," he seethes, to which I smirk in response.

He stands up from his chair, walking to the back of the room; I squint, but see nothing except artificial light.

I laugh deeply, spitting the words from my lips, "You were the drunken fool spilling Altaras' secrets at the dinner table, Mr. Lightfall. As a Commander, I expected better of you."
He clenches his jaw, the memory resurfacing as he shouts again, "Tell me about the rebel group you work for!"
I shut my mouth.

"If you give us something we can use, we'll go easy on you... not that you deserve it."
My silence answers his questions as he walks off out of sight. I would rather die than give them up, I would rather die than be a traitor, even if they betrayed me. Marik Lightfall enters my vision again, this time holding a gun in his hand. I chuckle, but it's not a humorous laugh. No. It's the laugh of a girl who now stares at death.

"You won't kill me here," I say confidently. "You want to make a spectacle of my death. Doing it down here with no show is not your style, *Marik.*"
He walks over to me but stops behind his chair, gripping the top. "You're quite right, Miss Nightingale. I won't kill you here. But I can still inflict pain."
As he says this, he aims his gun to my chest. I expect the gun to fire, to be impaled by the bullet. I await the click of the trigger, but the noise is replaced by the sound of the door as it opens. Footsteps falter behind me. I'm compelled to turn to the noise and see what's happening, but my eyes are trained on Marik Lightfall. As the footsteps draw closer, a small smile appears on his lips. A whimpering sound can be heard from behind me: a soft whine and dragging feet. My heart stops, though I refuse to look in its direction. Then, the bodies come into view and my insides churn. A guard is pushing someone forward. Their arms are shackled, concealed in a white tunic with a brown sackcloth over their head. Forcing the person to

sit before me in the empty chair. But I already know who it is in front of me. Her auburn hair flashes at the bottom of the bag.

My fists clench as my jaw tightens. I'm going to *kill* him.

"Elyria, unfortunately your family have disappeared, gone into hiding before we could get to them, but have you met Miss Lacewood?" he says, his voice gloating and full of self-satisfaction.

The guard removes the bag that covers Clover Lacewood's head. I hold in my vomit as I look at her small frame. Her bruised face and tear-stained eyes. She doesn't look malnourished, so I assume she hasn't been here longer than a day or two. Clover shudders against the light and frantically looks around before her eyes settle on me. Instantly, her gaze softens with relief.

"Elyria!" she squeaks, the sob ripping through her as she shakes, eyes searching my face to make sure it's me. "Oh my god, it really is you."

My eyes well with tears but I blink them away, "I'm so sorry, Clover," I whisper, "I'm so sorry he is doing this to you." Our eyes meet and I know she's frightened. "I saw you at the full moon ball, I saw you happy, I thought you would be safe," I hold in a sob, "It's going to be okay," I wish I could go to her, to hold her hand — promise to keep her safe. But I can't promise her a lie.

"I thought you were dead," she sobs, her body shifts in attempt to reach me, but the bindings restrict her movements, "I thought you were captured at the gates. You disappeared." Tears stream down her face as she whispers, "Your family wouldn't speak to me, I thought it was my fault."

I try to hold it in, but a tear escapes my eyes, "I'm so sorry."

"Tell us about the rebels," Marik says from behind Clover. His voice is powerful and loud as he speaks. "Tell us, or she will get hurt."

Clover doubles over, her sobs forcing me to close my eyes. I'm going to *kill* this man.

"Any information will spare her life," he grimaces, "are they all rooks? We gave them that nickname generations ago, scrabbling in the dirt for worms." Marik laughs. "A large group of rooks symbolizes bad fortune. If they gather it is seen as bad luck on the way, they lived up to their name, didn't they?" Marik shakes his head with disgust.

By saving her, I kill them. By killing her, I save them. I can't make this decision. How can I pick one over the other? My mouth goes dry as I inhale, opening my eyes to face those before me. Marik remains standing behind her, his gun raised to her back, before he begins a steady walk round in a circle, pausing to stand behind me. Gun still raised. I do not turn to face him. I look straight at Clover, her body shaking as she cries.

"Just kill me." I say, my voice rising to a shout, "Kill me over her."

Clover straightens, her body still shaking as her eyes flick to me, "Don't tell them any..."

But before she can finish, Marik Lightfall puts a bullet in her head.

Her blood splatters my face, coursing down her chest. She goes rigid as she jolts back in her chair. I hear nothing except the drumming of my heart in my ears. My mind flashes to all the memories we shared together as children. The fun times and love we shared, never to be felt again. Going to the wall, holding onto each other when elite children would ignore us, the tight squeeze on my arm when she was nervous, her excited squeal in a curious moment and the endless optimism that shone in her eyes, her shrieks of delight when she saw me in the hallway. I choke down a sob. We should have never gone to the gate. This is all because of me, my friendship has caused her death. My disregard of her vulnerability has killed her. I was too caught up with the Sparrows to realise what danger she was in by being associated with me. There is only one thing that settles my mind, that calms my hatred for myself, I can only avenge her, my sweet, innocent Clover.

"I'm going to kill you!" I scream, thrashing in my chair as I bare my teeth in a feral growl.

Clover is dead. I killed her.

I fall forward, my head between my knees. My anger stops the tears from coming — I can't cry. I will not break in front of these men, yet the rage builds as a loud scream escapes my lips.

"That's a shame to have poor Clover Lacewood's death on your conscience. You had the power to save her but chose those traitors instead." His voice is behind me, taunting. "She is dead because of *you*."

My body shakes as I sit up. I open my eyes to face her crumpled, lifeless body. Blood soaks the floor around her. It's everywhere.

I killed her.

I repress the bile rising in my throat, my stomach continuing to churn as my fury escalates.

"I will kill you, Lightfall." I spit, "I will kill you for that."

He laughs, the sound deep and merciless. "I don't think your chances of killing me are very high, little rat. You forget that I stand, and you kneel."

I say nothing as I look at her body: sweet, innocent, and pure. Now dead because of me. My teeth grind as I curse his name. Not that I believe in a higher power, but still, I blindly pray for him to die a thousand times, I pray he will die by my hands.

"Take her back to her cell!" he shouts to one of the guards. As they haul me up, I don't fight this time; I let them escort me back to my cell in peace.

Back in the dark hole of my cell, I'm finally alone. I allow the tears to fall, and they do so, silently. My body trembles as I hold my knees close to my chest, and I cry.

Clover is dead because of me.

Sweet, innocent, gentle Clover. The girl who would sit with me in class when no other child would. Who joined me on our missions to see the gate. I left her in the dark to protect her, but ultimately my friendship with her got her killed.

If Marik Lightfall can kill the child of an elite, he has the power to do whatever he wants — to whoever he wants.

And he *must* be stopped.

Chapter Thirty-Seven

The next days are torture, literally and figuratively. I am hauled out of my cell repeatedly, beaten more times than I can count. Every night, I wake screaming; my throat is raw from the nightmares I suffer. Even in sleep, I don't escape the torture. I'm trapped by visions of beatings: faces swim before me — Eris, Red Face, Marik Lightfall, and even Axon. All throw the punches to deliver my pain. Sometimes, Axon holds me firmly in his grip whilst Eris delivers the blows and I struggle to get free, his grip tight on my arms as I try to fight back, no escape from the horror. And then I wake.

My body is bloodied but dragged to the same room in which Clover was killed. They strap me to the table and the guards, most often Red Face, take pleasure in using an array of torture techniques on me. Shocked, beaten, burned. Seared with a branding iron, a permanent reminder of this hell on my skin. Days spent slipping in and out of consciousness, more often out than in.

I don't know what my body looks like now, its appearance unknown to me as each act of violence is met with closed eyes or screams of pain. I can't bear to look at the damage. I will not show weakness. I will not cry. Red Face likes to get close to me; spits at my face, his putrid breath reeking of disgusting foods, weapon of choice curled in his grip. He shouts at me to talk, to tell him everything I know. But I say nothing — I stay silent even as the poker sizzles my skin, burning the flesh raw. The pain is blinding as once again my body surrenders to darkness. I'm holding out for as long as I can until they decide their torment is wasted on me. Until they end this suffering for good.

On the final day of my failure to cooperate, Marik Lightfall waits for me. I don't look up from the floor, but I know its him standing next to Red Face. Today, my legs can barely hold my weight so the two guards drag my body to the steel table instead. I suck in a painful gasp as the metal burns against my raw back, as Red Face straps down my limbs.

I try not to wince as his ruddy, meaty fingers rub against my skin, securing me to the table. He inclines my head towards his. "You deserve this, you bitch".

I spit in his face, the action causing him to recoil as he wipes the mucus from his eyes.

The punch that follows makes my vision blur as iron fills my mouth, the metal tang common to me now. I lick my lips, baring my teeth in a bloody menacing grin as the laugh sets low in my throat.

"Fuck you," I spit towards him once more, the blood splatters his clothes. Staring up blankly to the ceiling, the row of blinding lights above makes my eyes wince. I don't turn my head to face them now; I accept the pain that's about to come.

"I have heard you are still unwilling to give up any information, Miss Nightingale," Marik Lightfall says as he walks to the table. I can smell the alcohol on his breath as he gets closer, along with the stench of my own blood and burnt flesh. "And still, you stay silent."

He taps his finger on the metal above my head. "If silence is your last wish, we can make this happen."

I stay still, even though every instinct in my body wants me to jerk away from him, repulsed by his presence. He moves from the table, and mutters under his breath to Red Face, who then heads towards me. He uses his stubby fingers to lock my head in place; I don't thrash, I don't scream. I don't cry. But my body seizes as I see the device in Marik Lightfall's hand. Hideous metal spikes encircling a collar — I close my eyes. *Please, no.*

"I will kill you." The words are whispered. The sound isn't my own anymore, my voice is unrecognizable. Defeated.

"No, I don't think you will."

I suppress the smile that tugs at my lips, knowing just the thing that will set him off. My final attempt to shatter his ego. If these are my last few words, I want him to squirm in the knowledge that he was so wrong about me. I want him to know how much he underestimated me. I want Marik Lightfall to know that it was me who killed his men.

"Do you remember last year, Marik?" I say, locking eyes with him, "Do you remember the whispers of the killings in the middle of the night? The question of who was doing this? How were they disappearing without a trace? You had no clues, nothing to direct you to the killer, all of you lost and misdirected. I want you to know that the *Night Slayer* who picked off your friends one by one whilst they slept — that was me."

My lips curl in a bloody smile as I watch the realisation settle on his face. Disbelief contorts his features, whilst Red Face swears. I would smile — laugh even — at Marik's shock that a girl assassinated his commanders and elite men in their beds, but there's no time for laughing. Not as Marik flares his nostrils, hastily placing the device tight around my neck. The barbs pierce my skin as he adjusts it, placing the muzzle over my mouth. The pain is unbearable. A groan gurgles low in my throat, my legs and arms now thrashing as the spikes dig in deeper, drawing blood as it trails down my neck matting my white hair.

"I will sleep soundly at night knowing your end is coming, *Night Slayer*," he spits my title as he steps away. The muzzle is fully bolted in place at the back of my head; I'm unable to suppress the tears as they now fall freely in uneven rasps, unable to open my mouth and panic restricting the air entering my nose.

"Take her back to her cell."

My limbs are unbolted from the table, Red Face sits me up yet the burden of the metal weights me back down. He binds my hands in front of me but, again, I do not fight. I am done fighting now. The two guards pick me off the table and drag me back to my cell as they whisper, "The Night Slayer, Lady Death, killer of our Consulate men. Finally going to die."

I cry from the pain, the sound muffled by the metal gag lodged between my teeth.

The metal is heavy in my mouth, my breathing uncontrolled and sporadic. I'm hyperventilating — my fear — losing control.

The spikes pierce into the skin of my neck, sharp metal drawing blood every time I move. If I try to open my mouth, the metal tightens around my head, and the barbs penetrate deeper. I want to scream but the pain of moving my lips clouds my brain.

I'm ready to die, I think, *I want to die now*. The thought repeats over and over in my brain like a song.

The tears are hot on my cheeks as I cry out. The contraption is so heavy I can only sit upright, the wall bearing some of its weight. I stay in that position for hours as the blood trickles down my neck, rivulets down my chest and back, sticky against my fingers.

~

I wake from my trance as the small hatch opens, allowing an influx of light to illuminate the room. I don't need to look down to know my bound hands are covered in blood, and the tears still stream down my face. They burn hotter and my body shakes, protesting the barbed muzzle, as Jude's face comes into the light. His eyes are bloodshot, as if he hasn't slept in days, his face prickled with a stubble that shows he hasn't shaved in a while either. He knows. I make a sound, a cry mixed with a moan as the metal contracts.

"Please don't move," Jude whispers, as if it pains him to say comforting words to me, "it will be worse if you move." His eyes are closed, head bowed to the ground. His hair falls in waves, concealing his gaze from me. I cry harder, wanting to open my mouth, to say everything that's running through my mind.

"Elyria," he whispers my name so quietly it's like a sin on his lips. Rhea is gone, and she will never be back, I have done this to him, manipulated him so that the memories he shared with Rhea no longer hold true. "Tell me it's not true. Tell me he's lying."

Then, his eyes meet mine. They're full of pain; he can't bear to look at me as he closes them again in a tight squeeze. *I lied. I'm sorry.* A bang fills the room as he punches the other side of the cell. I moan in response, the tears mixing with the drying blood on my neck. *Forgive me.*

"I always wondered where you went, how you disappeared into thin air... *Starlight girl*," he trails off, recalling the name he labelled me with all that time ago. "You killed people. With your bare hands." He doesn't bother to hide his disgust.

I'm sorry, I want to say. *It was the only way*. I'm a monster, just as much as them, and Jude will never forgive me.

But his voice softens as I make a muffled sound at the back of my throat, "Stop moving, you're making it worse." He closes his eyes and rests his forehead against the door. "Just listen."

I blink my tears away, trying to calm my breathing, but it won't settle.

"I know the truth. You spied on me. You used me. It was all a lie."

I want to stop breathing. I want to scream and tell him it wasn't all a lie. *Not all of it.* But all I can do is look at him. Plead at him with my eyes. *Forgive me.*

"You lied to me." His voice is so quiet, his words only meant for me. "I thought we had something." A small sigh escapes his lips, "I look like a damn fool."

I want to go to him, to hold him, to reveal everything. I wish I could speak. To explain myself to him. This is my punishment. To be silenced when I wish to do the one thing a spy should never do — tell the truth.

"Elyria," he says, finally looking to me. His sad dark eyes meet my own in a silent conversation. "I know why they chose you. My adoration for you was clear as day, all that time ago. An idiot could see the desire I had for you."

Had.

"And even as Rhea, I still wound up under your spell."

He bangs his fist hard against the cell door, "Was it all a trick?"

I shake my head *no* despite the vicious pain it causes, as fresh blood starts to drip once more. I need to show him how wrong he is.

"I will never trust you again." His voice cracks as the words get out.

You can't. I want to say. *Don't trust me. Don't let me break you. I'm so sorry.*

I moan into my tears, my body not having the strength to stand. To go to him.

He looks to me one last time. Hurt, pain and anger are clear on his face. His eyes look almost black. He composes himself with a flare of his nostrils and a crack of his neck.

"You're worse than him, Elyria. You're dead to me," he says finally, slamming the window closed. The room is, once again, submerged in darkness.

I cry for all the pain I've caused. And for Jude who hates me, who will likely never forgive me.

Chapter Thirty-Eight

I sit with the muzzle for what seems like an eternity; hours or days, I can't remember. My mind is a blur now. I don't sleep for the pain is too intense; I sit upright for hours on end. My mind returns to that dark hole, the space it cannot escape from. *Please kill me. Take me to death.* I think over again. *I think I'm ready now.* To prevent insanity from completely overtaking me, I focus on a memory. The deep rumble of his voice, the melodic sound of each word that escapes his lips. I hope I hear him again. I hope I hear Jude's voice again.

Finally, the cell door opens. Not looking up, one of the guards clears his throat. "Lightfall wants this over your head. Don't move."

I don't respond while the guard places a sack over my head, his movement pressing the metal barbs further into my skin. The pain intensifies.

Counting our steps, I know they take me further than my torture room. Suddenly, the air is no longer thick, but cool and light as it filters through the sack's material. Fresh air fills my nose. It's cold and sharp against my back, whipping the linen fabric against my now scabbed burns. I wince at the feeling. The air changes again, and I assume we're back inside. We reach the destination as one guard lets go of my arm. My body stays upright with the other guard's support; he lowers me to the ground and I kneel, my shoulders slumping from the weight of the metal and, also, from the exhaustion.

The boom of Idris Amal's voice startles me, as the reality of what is happening finally sinks in. "Hello citizens of Altaras," he says, addressing the city. The briefing. Everyone is watching me. Just like they watched Jakk. "What you see here before you is a traitor."

He pauses for dramatic effect, his voice loud and stern, "It has come to our attention that we have a rebel among us." My breath hitches. He's mentioned the rebellion. Why would he do that?

"Any act of conspiracy against the beautiful city of Altaras will never be tolerated in these walls. We make it our sole mission to protect the innocent people and remove the vermin that threaten to harm our sanctuary."

The sound of his words bellow, ringing in my ears, my body becoming rigid as he speaks. This is it. I am about to meet my end — finally find peace. My suffering will be over. I exhale a shaky breath as I hear footsteps approaching me. This time, it is Marik Lightfall's voice I hear.

"Anyone detected of harbouring fugitives from this *rebellion* group, or suspected of any involvement, will suffer the same fate," he says the word rebellion like its poison on his tongue, "Elyria Nightingale and her father have been found guilty of these crimes, so will be sentenced to death."

My heart stops. *My family.*

The material sack is roughly lifted from my head, and I hold in a scream as I see the petrified faces before me. My father's hands and mouth are bound and gagged as he kneels to my left. His eyes are panicked as he sets his sights on me, on my muzzle and blood-soaked tunic. He lunges to my side, but the guard pulls him back. A groan escapes his lips, muffled by the gag locking his teeth apart.

"Father is first," Lightfall announces.

My eyes don't leave my father's gaze as Marik walks behind us. He is so close, if I could only outstretch my arm, we could touch. His light eyes are nothing like my own as he stares back at me.

In my father's gaze, I understand the silent words he tells me. *I'm sorry,* he says. I hope my eyes convey my forgiveness. Sickness continues to build in my stomach, worry plastered all over his face. Then, quick and easy like taking a breath, the gun goes off and my father slumps to the floor. My father is dead. The man that brought me flowers to paint on my birthday. That man I yearned would return home when my family needed him most. I'll never hear his loud voice in the kitchen again or how he teases Lila about boys and dotes on my mother. His boots will never be by the door again. After all the lies, he just wanted to protect me from the truth.

His body crumples, blood spills around him. I close my eyes, shutting the image out. *Please kill me. Let this end now.*

"And now for the little rat," Marik Lightfall says in my ear.

With all the strength I have left in my body, I throw my head back. The pain is excruciating, yet the metal connects with his face as he staggers back in shock. *Fuck you,* I want to scream, but all that emerges from my throat is the shrill, hysterical shriek of an animal. My last act of hatred towards him.

"You little bitch," he shouts. I can't see the effect the headbutt caused, but I hope I broke his nose. I close my eyes, ready for the bullet to lodge into my brain.

But it doesn't come.

Instead, I hear commotion behind me. Lightfall shouts a word, but he doesn't finish — his voice is suddenly incoherent; I want to turn to look, but the pain is too much.

My confusion doesn't last, as one of the guards crosses my path, gun in hand. But as I look up, I notice his bright blue eyes. Those eyes do not belong to any guard. No. *Axon.*

Is this real? Is Axon here or is this one of Red Faces tricks? Is this a vision I have conjured to put my mind at peace before death?

"You're okay now, Birdie. You're okay," he says into my ear.

I want to sob as his body engulfs my own, his arms scooping me up as I let out a sigh of relief. As Axon moves from the stage, Marik Lightfall kneels, his arms raised as a guard points a gun to his head.

What's happening? I want to ask. *Am I dreaming?*

"Let's get this off you," Axon says, his voice a whisper as my body trembles in his arms. If this is in fact a dream, I have never felt safer.

Shots blast from behind us, the sound unbearable to my ears as they're consumed by a shrill ring. Axon begins to run now, the movement making my body scream in protest.

"Fuck," he shouts, as he starts to pant, his breathing hoarse and rapid. "They weren't supposed to shoot yet. Fuck. Don't worry Birdie, you're gonna be okay."

My mind rattles against the blur of my vision as Axon keeps running. He reaches a door which opens with the ease of one hand; I close my eyes and wait for this nightmare to be over. The cold air bristles against my skin, signaling to me we made it outside.

"Just a little further, then we'll get this off you." His breathing is laboured but he runs a while longer, then skids to a halt. "Here we go birdie. Just a little pinch, then it's off. Okay?" he says gently as he settles me to the ground. The grass is wet and prickles against the cuts and burnt skin ravaging my body. A twang of metal snaps as my wrists are freed from behind my back, my fingers tremble violently as I reach up to touch the collar. My throat makes an unhuman sound as I scream, the metal pinching and tightening as force is applied to the back.

"I'm so sorry Elyria," a voice says, but my mind remains distracted with the throbbing pain that rips through my body. The scream builds again, crying out low in my throat.

"Just a bit longer, its coming." A hand is on my shoulder, but it doesn't distract me. "Almost got it."

My body shakes. Then, the metal makes a loud snap, and the collar is released from my neck. I shudder as the collar falls to the ground; the barbs no longer impale my skin as the muzzle is lifted. Tears stream down my face as I finally open my mouth to let in some air.

I sink to the ground and sob; another scream exits my lips. Covering my head with my hands, I shake uncontrollably on the ground.

"You're okay Birdie, it's off, it's off." Axon repeats, his body so close to my own. "Thank you, Lightfall."

I try to look behind me, my breathing rapid and eyes wild. My body goes rigid at the name, but my breathing instantly calms as I see who stands there. Jude. There with a large pair of bolt cutters, his hands covered in my blood.

He cut it off. He freed me.

We look to each other, his eyes so dark in this light, his head cloaked with a hood. *I'm sorry,* I want to say. I would shout it if

I could. That's all I wish him to know — how desperately sorry I am. But the words don't leave my lips. His face is unreadable as he drops the cutters from his hands to the floor. He says nothing.

"We have to get out of here, they won't wait much longer," Axon says, "Can you stand Birdie?" I want to shake my head no, but my silence is answer enough. As he picks me up, I wince into his chest. "Let's get you somewhere safe."

I look behind us, the dropped bolt cutters resting next to the heap of metal. The muzzle gleams in the moonlight as we leave them behind.

Chapter Thirty-Nine

The pain distracts me from thinking of my dead father. *Dead.* His body slumped to the ground as soon as the shot when off. I wince as Axon tightens his grip around me, running with me in his arms as I try to gather our surroundings, but my mind remains foggy and dizzy with fatigue. After a while of running, Axon slows to a stop, there's some murmurings and a door opens. My mind clouds as I try to put voices to faces, trying desperately to understand my surroundings. The house is dark, a few dimly lit candles illuminate the rooms. Axon, who still carries me, places me gently onto a sofa. The material is rough; I cringe at the feel of it against my skin.

"Do you have a sheet or something?" Axon says. "We need medical supplies as well."

A soft voice answers his question; I can almost decipher a soft 'yes' before footsteps leave the room.

"She hasn't eaten," another voice says. I look up and my eyes connect with a tall frame standing by the fireplace, his arms crossed in front of him, refusing to look in my direction.

"I'll go find something," Axon stands from his crouched position then hesitantly leaves the two of us. I want to sit up. But the pain is so intense, I cry out at the movement.

"Stop, just stay down," the voice speaks again. *Jude* speaks again from across the room. Tears brim my eyes as I look up to the ceiling, my mind starts to settle as my thoughts no longer seem so scrambled.

"I'm sorry," the words crack against my dry throat and cracked swollen lips, hoarse from all the screaming. I will not cry. I will be strong now.

"Don't lie Elyria," he says, his voice raised. I suck in a breath. "I got you out and now we're even."

I keep my eyes to the ceiling, unable to face him as he continues.

"We don't owe each other anything anymore."

Even? "I'm —" what I'm about to say is interrupted by Axon's return. He kneels before me, setting a bowl beside him. His eyes look pained as he studies me.

"Soup will be best. I'll do it slow, okay?" He tries to sit me up and I wince at the pain against my spine. Once my back rests upright, he brings the spoon to my lips; my mouth trembles as I open it, the liquid is warm and smooth down my throat. I can only manage a few mouthfuls before sickness rises in my stomach.

"She's going to be sick," Jude's tone is short as he stands behind Axon. But he's right, it's not long until I retch the soup onto the floor beside us.

"Great, thanks Birdie." Axon stands up, amused.

"Sorry," I manage to say, twisting to face the person now entering the room.

"A sheet and I've got some alcohol, bandages, needle, and thread. I thought some aloe might help?" the voice suggests, her tone high as she speaks.

"Thanks, Tissa. Lightfall, will you clean Elyria's wounds whilst I clear this up?" Axon asks. Tissa. Tissa is here.

"Can't she do it?" Jude nods to Tissa who stands beside him, then turns to exit the room. A tear rolls down my face watching him leave.

Axon gently puts his arm under my knees as he lifts me up, placing the sheet beneath me. I bite my cheeks so hard against the pain, I'm sure they bleed too. He kneels on one leg, laying the bandages on his thigh. In silence, I watch as he doses a bandage in liquid, then holds it close to my neck. The smell is so strong I want to vomit again.

"It's okay, I've gone through worse," I let out, and close my eyes.

The alcohol burns through my open wounds and the pain festers. I suck in a breath and clench my fists so tight my nails draw blood. Axon carries on, cleaning the holes around my neck as he travels down each arm, wiping away the dried blood and disinfecting each gash.

"Do you have any on your stomach?" he whispers. I nod my head in response.

"I'm going to take this off, okay?" He pulls at my blood-soaked linen shirt. In pain with the stretch, I raise my arms to help him lift the top over my head. Discarding the shirt into a pile on the floor, I'm left in my undergarments. Axon's eyes rake over my body, so I squeeze mine shut. He wipes the alcohol over a long cut across my stomach, then starts working his way up my legs, focusing attentively on each wound.

"I need to do the stitches, alright?"

Axon picks up the needle and thread, "Just a pinch," and I brace myself for the pain.

It takes a while for Axon to stitch each gash; the one at my stomach the most painful, bringing tears to my eyes as I cry out. Again, darkness dulls the pain and when I come to it has settled to a hum as he finishes the last stitches, covering each wound with a bandage. His arms bear my bodyweight as he props me up against the armrest of the sofa, my back facing him. I hear another voice suck in a breath, then footsteps leave the room, a sharp slam of a door echoes in the distance.

"That bad?" I let out, forcing the amusement in my voice.

"No, he's just being dramatic," Axon says, but I know he's lying.

I rest my head against the sofa, the cooling sensation of the aloe soothing my burning hot skin. I sigh in relief and close my eyes; somehow, my brain switches off and I fall asleep.

Chapter Forty

I wake with a blood curdling scream, my mind still swimming with the nightmares of the cell, of being back in that awful place, in the darkness. Gradually, my breathing slows as I gulp down the breaths, realizing I'm no longer there. It's only a nightmare. I was rescued and now I'm in Tissa's home; the warm red light from her stained-glass windows throws a subtle glow around the room. Jude sits in the chair opposite me, his eyes trained on my body. He startles and sits upright in his chair once he sees my eyes are open, watching his movements — oblivious to me waking in a fright.

"Some of these are old," he blurts out, his jaw clenched. It's a statement, rather than a question as his eyes trail over the many faded scars dotted among the bright new blisters and wounds — and fresh stitches. His gaze continues to rake up and down my body, studying me intently.

I nod my head and whisper, "Yeah they are."

My voice is still croaky.

"Who did that to you?"

My eyes meet his. They look almost black.

"It doesn't matter,"

"You don't need to keep lying, Elyria," he snaps, but then regains his composure as he scoffs, once again repeating my true name. "Elyria."

I shift to sit up slightly, this new tone of anger seems strange coming out of Jude's mouth, directed at me. "It doesn't matter because that was my training, Jude," I say flatly; his face looks pained as I try to console him, "It was in the past."

He furrows his brows, his tone sharp as he repeats my words, "Ah yes... *training*."

I let the comment slide, my body too exhausted to fight with him. Jude gets up from his chair, only to return moments later with a lukewarm drink.

"That girl, Tissa I think her name is... she said when you wake you should drink this." He holds out the cup, but my hand shakes violently as I reach to grab it. Jude sighs, clenching his jaw as he sits back in his chair and holds the warm mug to my lips. I look to him, his eyes a mixture of so many emotions, but I can't seem to think straight to place them.

I take a small sip as warm chai coats my tongue and soothes my throat. I could cry again but with relief.

"How did you — Axon?" I mutter my words, nodding my head towards my friend's sleeping body. "I thought you would let me rot in that dungeon after you found out."

Jude shakes his head, letting out a short exhale as his nostrils flare.

"That's the difference between me and you, Elyria. I could never live with myself if I left you to suffer," Jude moves his attention to Axon as he flexes his hands. "He wasn't hard to find. Practically tackled me in the street asking for information."

My heart tightens. To think Axon would risk exposing himself for me. To get answers. I need to know what happened — why would Axon risk this? Why rescue me at all if Eris himself gave me up to the Commanders?

"I am sorry for deceiving you," I whisper, "I know... I know that won't mean much, but I'm sorry I caused you pain."

The apology is tight in my throat. The words scarcely leave my lips, yet Jude deserves to hear it, "I'm sorry for that. But I'm not sorry for the reason I did it. For the people of Altaras. We need to be freed and it was the only way."

Jude curls his lip, hands bracing on the armrests of the chair. I can see the veins of his arms as he tenses, his body radiating anger. "I'm just another pawn in your game — you blew up the Citadel for fuck sake!"

"No. You weren't a pawn. If there was another way, I would have done it. Yes, we blew up the Citadel, but we did it to rescue those people and I would happily do it again if it meant the same outcome."

"You're being naïve, Elyria, if you think manipulating and using me was the only way to start a revolution," he sneers. The look contorts his handsome face, making his features harsh and sharp. The blow hits. I hate being wrong.

"I was following orders. It was *his* plan." I hiss.

Jude pauses a moment — his anger settling as his black eyes lighten. His next words are spoken softly, his eyes finally resting on my own.

"Was any of it real?" My heart pains, tightening at his words. I open my mouth to speak but the sound of Axon clearing his throat cuts me off.

"Good to see you're awake, Birdie," he says, stretching and rising from his chair. I'm not sure how long he's been awake but, by the look on his face, I'm sure he's heard most of our conversation.

"Tell me what happened." My eyes dart between the boys in front of me, their expressions flat. "From the beginning, tell me."

I shift so my legs are planted on the floor, ignoring the screaming of my muscles and tight skin. I lean over, my burns exposed as I focus my attention on Axon. He clears his throat again and folds his arms over his chest.

"Eris has a plan."

His name makes my blood boil.

"He told us that having you captured was a good diversion," Axon continues. My torture was a *good diversion.* I hope Eris isn't dead so I can slit his throat myself. "Not all of us agreed, Birdie. As for Xannu... she was just following orders. She didn't want to give you to them."

Pain enters his eyes as he talks of his sister's betrayal to me, but I had a long time in my cell to think about it. And, in some twisted way, I forgive her. I understand. I accept the loyalty she has for him; she would do anything Eris asked — even if that meant handing me over. That loyalty wound its way deep into my veins too. All the people I have killed by his orders. The lives I've taken from his command.

"Tissa managed to get the information about the briefing — where and when they planned to execute you." He nods his head towards Jude. "And Lightfall over here got us into the Unity Building. We had Sparrows from all over the city in on it. We knew when to strike and how to get you out," His face softens as he walks back over to my side, crouching down and placing a hand on my shoulder, "your father was never meant to be there. We didn't know. I'm so sorry, Elyria."

The mention of my father makes my chest hurt. I focus my attention to the ground, slamming out the visions of his crumpled body on the floor. His pained expression just before he was shot in the head. Axon's hand tightens his grip. "We had another Sparrow with me disguised as a guard. He held a gun to Marik Lightfall's head so that we could get you out." My gaze darts to Jude, whose eyes are distant, muscles tense.

Would he be okay hearing of his father's death? Is Marik Lightfall even dead?

"Tissa watched the briefing live. She said after the Sparrow put a gun to Lightfall's head, the screen went black. They switched us off. Shots were fired but we don't know who is dead or who is alive... "

I stare at Axon, "And that was Eris's big plan? It all goes to shit?" My tone is harsh, furious even — I don't mean to argue with Axon, but he's the closest I can get to Eris. "And Lila, is she safe?" I blurt, my heart pounding at the thought of Eris harming her because of me.

Axon glances over to Jude before he speaks — wary of revealing something? I can't put my finger on it, but Jude already knows of my real family. He knew the moment he researched my true name, all that time ago.

"They are all safe."

All. My shoulders relax and I sigh, "Good."

A slight cough interrupts our conversation as Tissa stands in the doorway. Dressed in bright orange silk nightclothes, she's wearing the same colours she would in the nest — our canary. It pleases me that her home is just as warm and bright as she is, thankful Eris hasn't blown out her spark.

"Does anyone want any tea?" she asks. Tissa has one of those voices that flutters around the room like a song, so light and delicate.

I smile and nod my head, "Tea would be great. Thank you Tissa."

Jude and Axon nod in agreement too as Tissa scuttles out to the kitchen.

"Why are we here?" I ask Axon, "What are we going to do now?"

I'm overwhelmed by all the questions rattling in my brain, I just want to make sense of all of this.

"Tissa said we could use her home as a safe location if things went bad. No-one would expect her to take such a risk. We were all supposed to meet somewhere else… but I don't know how safe it is yet, you just have to sit tight whilst I find out some more information." Axon stands and walks over to the door and grabs his cloak. He's leaving – right now. He looks to me once more, but his eyes are holding something back, like he wishes to tell me something, but he only smiles, "Get some rest Birdie, you deserve it," and shuts the door behind him.

Chapter Forty-One

An awkward silence lingers between us for the next few hours whilst we wait on Axon to return. Jude is deep in thought, silent, refusing to look in my direction, whilst Tissa nervously sips her chai and spins the silver ring around her finger. The myrrh incense lit in the corner of the room compels me to close my eyes, thankful that I'm no longer inhaling the stench of dried blood or mildew from the cell.

"I'm sorry this happened to you, Elyria." Tissa finally says, "I can't even imagine what you've gone through..." She's unsure of how to console me; Tissa and I have never had much of a friendship due to her scarce visits to the nest, and apart from our gender, the similarities die there. Her soft spoken and harmless nature is the opposite to my quick tongue and tendency for violence. Opposites like Lila and Gia, now I think about it.

I nod my head in understanding and thanks, but it feels surreal to thank someone apologizing for my torture.

"How long was I even in there?" I ask, "I lost track of the days." My brows furrow as my mind tries to piece together the fragments of the last few weeks.

Her doe eyes soften as she says, "A little over a month."

The air is sucked out of me. *A month?* I was tortured for more than a month? My mind is swimming as my breathing intensifies. How did I lose so much time? I thought I was only there for a few weeks — two at most? How could it be longer?

"I don't remember it being that long," I whisper as my lips and hands tremble. I was in that cell for so much longer than my mind allowed me to think. Perhaps that was a blessing? A warm, fragile hand closes around my own, squeezing. Tissa smiles but it does not reach the sorrow in her gaze, "It's okay that your mind is in a bit of a muddle right now. Your safe, just hold on to that."

I'm safe. I'm out. I'm alive, I think to myself. Tears brim my eyes, but the tears don't come. I will shed no more tears for *them*. This version of myself is no longer an option. I must move on for my own sanity and strength. Nodding to her words, my lips tremble as I open my mouth to speak, but the words don't follow, and I can only mime the *thank you*. I blink back the tears to stop them from falling and a squeeze of my hand tells me she understands my pain.

"You need to eat something. I have some olives and cheese, how about that?" she suggests. I nod my head and she scurries to the kitchen to prepare it.

I turn as sudden movement catches my attention; Jude is walking to me intently and I tense, holding my breath. But he's not angry as he kneels, our foreheads so close, we're almost touching. He does something I don't expect. I take in the warmth his body radiates and savour the smell of him — he smells like freshly cut grass, of rain, of the flowers that grow in his mother's green house. I close my eyes, breathing it all in.

Jude places his forehead against my own, the touch sending shivers down my spine as he whispers in a low stern voice, "Do not let this break you. Don't let *them* break you. Do you understand me, Elyria?"

A single tear sneaks through my closed eyelids.

"You will not be broken," he says finally, his tone resolute with those final words, forehead still pressed against my own. Even after all I have done to him, a fragment of him still cares for me. And I don't understand why.

He removes his head, straightening up and walks away, but my eyes are still firmly closed as I tell myself...

I will not be broken. I repeat. *I will not be broken.*

~

The sound of the door opening jolts me awake; I try to sit upright as Axon enters, my teeth grit through the screaming of my muscles. His breathing is shallow and rapid.

"What happened?"

Axon stays by the door as he answers, "It all happened so quickly after we fled. The Sparrows overthrew the guards at the Unity building. The city's power fell right when the Commanders had guns to their heads... anything to protect the elite bloodline." His eyes meet mine. "Eris plans to execute Marik Lightfall tonight at a live screening."

My heart races. The city is no longer under control of the Consulate. This should be a time to rejoice and for happiness as Eris' plan finally falls into place. This feeling, however, is replaced by anger. I was just *expendable.* As was Jakk, and Clover, my father, all innocent of any crime and killed because of the web Eris has created. I look to Jude, his face stonelike as he lets out the words, "He deserves it."

He deserves worse.

Axon starts to speak again, "He's taking over. We did it. Everything is as we wished it to be. What our fathers died for!" His voice is surprisingly upbeat at the mention of his dead father, reminding me of my own. But I don't feel the same joy and hope that Axon exudes. Only doubt. Does Axon know Eris lived in Penury — that he likely continues to visit? Will the gates finally open now he has the power? I keep the information quiet, for now. I don't know whether I can fully trust this plan yet.

"We leave in an hour. He wants us present." He changes his tone, it sounds almost apologetic when he says, "He wants Jude there as well. A united front."

I want to be sick again. The thought of Jude witnessing his father's death – no matter how despicable he is, it's a sight I wish for no one.

"No. He's not going," I snap, my voice suddenly raised.

"Birdie —"

"No. He's not going. And that's final."

Jude clears his throat, "It's fine, I can go." I start to protest, but he stops me with a raised hand. "I decided my fate when I cut off your muzzle. I'm in this now."

And with that, the decision is made. We will go to the Citadel — to the Unity building where Eris will execute Marik Lightfall, and the city will be in the hands of the rebels.

Axon half drags, half carries me to Tissa's bathroom to let me clean and prepare for the *event.* Finally, I'm left by myself for the first time in days. Turning to the mirror, I'm unprepared for the reflection. I've not seen myself in weeks. A hollow, painfully thin girl looks back at me. I reach up and touch the bandage around my neck, my fingers shaking as I prod the skin at my sunken cheeks and the blue bags under my eyes. My lips are swollen, cracked with blood, my skin has lost its glow; amongst the bandages, a mess of red and purple welts, and yellowing bruises scatter my body. I squeeze my eyes shut for a moment, my body shivering.

You will not be broken; I say to myself. *You will not be broken.*

I look to my hair and bite my lip in frustration; it's sticking out in all directions — the icy white it once was now crusts with my own blood, a nest gathering at the back of my head. I have no idea where to start. The porcelain bathtub beside me is not an option; I shake my head as flashbacks return of being covered in water: electrocuted and suffocated. My head is heavy in my hands as I try and regain focus. *Breathe. You're safe. You will not be broken. Breathe.*

There's a knock at the door, Tissa peeks her head round, looking as timid as ever.

"I thought you might need some help?" She steps into the room and quietly closes the door behind her.

I nod my head, flashing a forced smile. "Thank you."

Tissa finds the washcloth near my hand; without so much of a word or question, she runs the tap and dampens the cloth beneath it, bringing it up to my face as she says, "You're safe." Over and over, she says this as she wipes the cloth across my skin.

I don't allow myself to cry. I just listen to the words and beg silently that they are true.

Tissa clears my face and hair of blood, wiping it away with her delicate fingers; she smiles once she reaches my hair, "I have an idea," She departs from the bathroom, only to return moments later carrying a few amber apothecary bottles filled with liquid.

"You may not want to do it, but it might make you feel a little more like yourself." she says hopefully, her doe eyes shining, "We were pretty much the same colour anyway."

I nod my head, this time with a genuine smile on my lips. Tissa gets to work, combing out the matted hair, and applying the liquid from roots to ends. Her tender hands soothe the panic of being touched — there's no hurt in her actions, no sharp infliction of pain. Calmness overcomes me as she runs perfumed oils through the strands, stroking me like a wounded child.

I need this — to allow myself this brief sanctuary— to escape for a moment, to help me heal and accept everything that has been done to me. I close my eyes and let the feelings come, breathing through them as they rush over me like a wave. I mourn for my father, for my mother and my siblings, wherever they may be. I let the emotions consume me for these few moments. And then, I block them out, fortifying the wall in my mind in the same way I did when I first arrived at the Sparrows' base. There is no other choice but to keep my feelings at bay, to protect myself by blocking the emotions and shutting them away.

I will be weak no longer.

It takes a while, but the results are something a little like magic.

"Thank you Tissa," I sigh, looking at my reflection. Crimson eyes filled with a little hope stare back. Whilst my face is still bruised, and neck still bandaged, dark raven hair falls around my shoulders in glossy soft curls just like before.

"Much better," she sings, evidently pleased with her work.

She's right, I do feel better, more than when I first looked at myself.

"Axon gave me this before I came up," She quickly leaves the room, returning with black leather material clasped in her

hands. "Xannu made it for you, since we knew your other was probably gone..."
She holds out the new Sparrow suit in her arms, and my heart twists at the mention of Xannu. But I must forgive her; she was following orders, it wasn't personal.
Tissa helps me into my suit, the material scraping along my bandages and stitches; I curse at her whilst doing so. It's looser than before, yet once I regain my muscle, it will fit like a glove. This one is different to my other; not a full bodysuit, leather trousers and a jacket with a sash of material hanging from the belt at my waist, accentuating my figure in all the right places. The boning of the corset cleverly disguises the long delicate knives; no one would know they were there, the handles shaped to the curve of the bustline. The arms have the same secret pockets, but the beauty of the armour is much more exquisite than before. This one is made to make a statement — a show.

My white bandages peak out from the neckline of the suit, so Tissa quickly returns with a black silk fabric and wraps it loosely around my neck. The ends drape over the back of my shoulders which she fastens with gold brooches. She hands me a selection of her own earrings, which I choose from, and Tissa then places them in my ears, trailing the array of gold studs and hoops down each ear. A guard had removed mine in the cell — any metal is a potential weapon he said, and he was not wrong — I would have made use of anything to hand. The earrings make me think of Xannu again; how, on more than one occasion, we pierced each other's ears — thinking the more we had, the fiercer it made us look.

"You look beautiful," Tissa smiles, once we're done. I want to roll my eyes but think better of it. She helps me down the stairs, despite my groans and curses.

My body will heal. *This will get easier.*

A low laugh erupts from Axon as he sets his eyes on me, "You look menacing. Glad to have you back, Birdie." Having heard the compliment before, the memory of Seven, Xannu and I heading to the Citadel returns. *Menacing.* This time, I do roll my eyes and flip him the finger which makes him chuckle more, baring his white teeth in a grin. Jude only stares, his jaw tightly clenched as his muscles flex under the tunic. He turns his head away.

"Okay, it's time to go." Axon says, breaking the tension.

"Can't keep his highness waiting," I reply, the fire returning to my voice.

Chapter Forty-Two

We walk straight past the Citadel gates. Not a single guard stands in their original postings; there are no patrols or citizens of Altaras wandering the streets. A ghost town. They must be cowering in their homes, frightened, waiting for someone to give them orders, to tell them what to do. Axon reveals that the guards are being kept underground, that everyone not on our side is locked away with guns to their heads. To me, this sounds just like what the Consulate would have done. We are no better than them.

Eris wants us in the Unity Building; he will have everything ready for our arrival.
But a low, burning sense of distrust sits in my gut. The little trust I had for Eris is gone, replaced only with caution. Jude trails behind us as we walk in, head down. I don't know what's going through his head, but it can't be good.

The Unity building comes into view with its huge dome and arcade of stone columns which wrap around the front of the building; a grand stone archway is hard to miss in the centre of the Citadel. Axon leads us up the expanse of white marble steps that reach the entrance, weaving us through the extravagant foyer and to the centre stage of the hall, where I was bound and gagged by that metal device. The memory sends a shiver down my spine, as does the firm hand placed at the small of my back, urging me to walk on.
I don't need to look up. I know the feel of Jude's touch without even looking in his direction — engrained in my veins. There on the podium, where the Commanders normally sit, Eris

takes their place high above the ground. His legs are splayed out in front of him like he's never been more comfortable, dark hair tied back showing the growth of his facial hair. He appears older, a more ominous look about him, and his eyes are directed solely on me, a wicked smile on his lips as we stand below him. I stare up at him, hatred coursing through my body; this man sent me to near death, and I will never forgive him. I'm not the forgiving type.

Eris narrows his eyes on me, trying to work out my reaction, decipher the thoughts swimming in my head. But I mask the anger, my face showing no emotion as I look at him. He finally clears his throat and bellows down to us, "I'm so glad to see your alive, little bird." His smile returns as he lounges further back into the chair, his legs now resting on the low wall in front of him. "And I see you obeyed my command and brought your friend," He nods in the direction of Jude. "I hope they didn't go too rough on you, but your appearance seems intact, bar the few bruises on your face." Axon straightens beside me waiting for me to react, to bite back. But I don't. I just stare.

"Oh, don't give me that look... You look less pretty when you scowl," He rolls his eyes and waves his hand in the air. "The Commanders will be executed for their crimes, for capturing you as well. You will have your revenge, little bird. In just ten minutes, their blood will pool at your feet. All will be corrected in this city."

From beside me, Jude begins to speak, to ask the question on our minds. "What of the food and the water shortage?" He's strong — powerful even — as he talks.
Eris chuckles and lights a cigarette from his jacket pocket, the smoke swirls around him, "That is no longer an issue." He

talks as though Jude's question was irrelevant, like the problem means nothing to him.

"What do you mean? How has this been solved?" Jude quizzes, his tone apprehensive. But Eris stays silent and looks to Axon with a nod of his head. Once more, I am left in the dark, but this time I don't question him. I only stand and watch as Eris's plan falls into place.

Axon clears his throat, his jaw set as he speaks, "It's time. We need to get into our places."

Confusion crosses Jude's perfect features as we follow Axon to stand across the stage; Eris is sat on the platform to our left, the camera faces him to our right. A Sparrow, one I have never seen before, stands behind the camera and signals a thumbs up to Eris, to which he rises. The camera rolls.

His voice booms as he begins to speak, he will captivate everyone listening at home with his presence, sat in the seats of their old Commanders. Speaking with authority and power.

"People of Altaras, this is not your normal briefing. I know that you are used to the Commanders who sit here, but I now take their place." He pauses for dramatic effect. The action, this whole performance makes my blood turn cold. Eris then carries on the show, "The Commanders of our beautiful city have lied to us since the day they were appointed. They have tricked and manipulated you all, using violence and fear to maintain their power and control. But this stands no longer!"

His voice is calm as he speaks, showing the people that he is not a barbaric man shouting to inflict command — unlike his true self — but a calm, organised leader facing the facts.

"We are the rebellion. The Sparrows. And we stand to fight injustice."

Dumah, Seven and two unknown Sparrow's file onto the stage; with them are the figures of the Commanders, bound and gagged. My eyes immediately land on Marik Lightfall — his eyes wild, knowing he's about to die. Jude stiffens beside me. Unconsciously, my hand searches for his, but I think better of it, drawing my hand back instantly.

"The Commanders have taken your mothers, fathers, wives, and husbands. Even your innocent children have been killed for the sake of preserving their lies. They will be executed for their crimes. The city now belongs to me," Eris says, looking down on the now kneeling Commanders. Idris Amal shakes as he bows his head, ready for the blow.

I look to Eris. His plot to overthrow them has worked — they *kneel* before him. But I'm not stupid or naïve enough to think this is it; I know he has something else up his sleeve. There's a bigger picture with Eris, there always is.

"Let their reign end!" he shouts, raising his arms to the air as the Sparrows fire a bullet in the back of each Commander, their bodies thumping to the ground in a repetitive *thunk*. Except one Commander still kneels.

"Jude Lightfall," Eris roars, "Give the final blow." Jude looks up from the ground, his eyes wide as he stares back at Eris. Axon moves from behind me, and shoves Jude forward with his hand. I whirl on Axon, my teeth bared as I seethe.

"What the fuck are you doing?"

Axon's bright blue eyes look back at me, "Orders, Birdie."

I look to Jude his dark eyes burn into mine, the words fall from my lips in a rush to stop him, "Don't..."

But Axon intervenes, pushing Jude forward to the centre of the stage. My minds rushes to fathom out the scene that unfolds before me as Axon forces a pistol into Jude's hand. Jude towers over Axon as he looks at him in their standoff, his eyes are narrowed, his body tense whilst Eris sits above, delight flashing in his eyes.

"Jude Lightfall has pledged his allegiance to the Sparrows. To the rebellion. And he has offered to end all our suffering with the final bullet."

The wicked smile returns to Eris' face. Axon steps closer to Jude, muttering something incoherent. As he walks away, he points a gun aimed directly at Jude's head. It confirms what I suspected. Either Jude kills his own father, or they both die. I release the gun from my holster and point it forward at Eris's head whilst he laughs. I sneer, my finger on the trigger, but what stops me from firing the bullet, from killing Eris, is Axon diverting his aim from Jude to me.

We stand there, for what seems like an eternity. I'm looking down the barrel of his gun to those angular blue eyes I no longer recognise, as he does the same. Our weapons pointed but we wait in deadlock. I wait because I will never be the first one to pull the trigger, but I realise in this moment that I am a fool for trusting him. How long has he known of Eris's plan? Was he a part of the plan to have me captured by the Consulate?

"I'm disappointed in myself, Axon. I'm disappointed that I allowed myself to trust you when I've known all along that all you are, and all you ever will be, is Eris' little bitch."

Axon's face flashes with the smallest glimmer of hurt, but still, he aims the gun at my head now with a stone-cold expression, waiting for me to lower mine. Taking a breath, I know Eris will never let us leave alive if we don't cooperate. That, if Axon doesn't put a bullet in my brain, Eris will. Or another one of his minions. So slowly and regrettably, I lower my gun and divert my eyes to Eris, who only watches us from his platform in glee.

Looking to the man knelt before his son, Marik watches me with deep disdain, acknowledging my presence. I speak with calmness, a voice of icy death, a numbness to the world, "I have hated you in life, and I will hate you in death. The innocent souls you took will feast upon you for eternity. Your suffering will never end Marik. I'll see you in hell."

The ring of the shot catches me off guard as Marik Lightfall falls to the ground, the blood soaking his ice white hair in a pool of deep red. I hear the laughter that leaves Eris's lips, Jude's face is set like stone as the drift of smoke rises from the end of his gun. The gun he just used to shoot his father.

"You surprise me, Lightfall. I didn't think you had it in you." Eris gloats as Jude looks up to him, finally diverting his eyes from his father's lifeless body.
In a deep low voice that sends shivers through my whole body, he murmurs, "Don't call me that."

"Very well. Pet names are only for my sweet girl," he says with a sinister smile in my direction. I want to vomit, to launch myself at him and rip his eyes out. Jude looks as though he wants to do the same as his fists clench, tucking the gun into his waistband.

"Little bird, step forward please."
Axon beckons me forward as Eris's eyes refuse to leave mine. But my feet remain planted firmly on the ground.

"One of my best, brightest and most cunning Sparrows was tortured beyond your wildest nightmares. To those who harm a Sparrow the worst of luck will follow, for they are known to carry away the souls of the dead. If you encounter a Sparrow, take it as a sign that your path is likely to shift soon!" he shouts to the camera. "My daughter was captured and taken from me. Her pain was inflicted by so many, yet she will have her revenge. Revenge on one perpetrator in particular."

My stomach twists at the reference of me being his daughter; I should laugh in his face. I could never be, not with his twisted mind. A father should never raise his hand to his daughter — my father would've never done such a thing. A daughter should not be turned into a monster, for her father's own sadistic gain. A Sparrow enters the stage, dragging a bloodied guard behind him. My teeth grind to the point where they might snap as Red Face slumps to his knees in the growing pool of the Commanders' blood. My eyes find Eris again, who merely nods down at Red Face. He knows what I want. In his sick game, he gives me this one ounce of privilege — something I wished for after every beating, after every burn to my skin, after every gob of spit in my face. So, I take it.

I cover my face with the scarf that Tissa had wound round my neck, the fabric flowing behind me as I walk forward, crimson eyes blazing, focused. Completely aware that the camera now tracks my every move, I stalk onto the stage, full of confidence and determination. I stand behind Red Face; his body is stiff as I bend down to his ear, whispering so only he can hear my words. The stench of him is rancid, urging me to recoil. I stay, *this is for me.*

"I will sleep soundly at night, knowing I was the one to end your life," The words drip from my lips in a deadly lull. "I told you I would kill you. And I always keep my promises."

I drag my dagger across his neck as slowly as my hand will allow. Poetic justice — I think that's what they call it. He maimed my neck, so I slice his. In my eyes, a gleam of satisfaction enters, finding peace in the violence.

I don't wait to hear him gag on his own blood, or the sound of his body as it hits the ground. I leave the stage, as my performance is over, returning next to Jude who only stares at me with dark eyes. He probably thinks I'm a monster — and maybe he's right.

The camera is off. The briefing finally over as Eris starts to clap: a slow, long applause, laughing as he does.

Chapter Forty-Three

That was a masterpiece. I couldn't have thought that up even if I tried. Not the girl in the woods anymore, are you Elyria? You, little bird, know how to steal a show," he chuckles.

My body is rigid as he walks down from the platform to the stage. He steps over bodies, red footprints trailing in his path. Eris... he's been planning this for longer than I have even been a Sparrow, his web of deception runs so deep. Did he have a part to play in Jakks death? The small Sparrow boy killed for a crime that was so unlike him, so out of character. Had Eris set him up? Ordered him to carry out an act that would set off a spark for the rebellion?

"This is all a game to you, isn't it?" I snap, stepping forward to meet him, "You relish in this newfound power, the new title of having this city under your finger, whilst we do *your* dirty work. You had me captured and tortured, all for this big show. Was Jakk sent to his death as well?"

"Jakk's death was needed to start the flame," his voice teeters on amusement now, relishing that he had us tricked for so long. My eyes flash to Axon who stands rigid — he didn't know.

"I knew you could handle it. You're the only one I could trust who would stay alive till the end."

I roll my eyes. Is that his version of a compliment? To say I was the only Sparrow that could last prolonged torture? My hand instinctively hovers over the gun at my hip.

Eris' lip curls, "I never wanted this city, little bird. Have you not been paying close enough attention?" he questions me like a child as my stomach knots. But, somehow, the pieces quickly fit together, my mind slotting the puzzle to completion. Eris has been planning this rebellion for longer than I have been alive. My mother's confession of how she was once a Penurian living her earliest years on the other side of the wall. Eris' determination to have me join his rebel group, his band of Sparrows. I have Penurian blood running through me, my mother once a Sparrow alongside Eris… this has all been for one thing. It's been in front of my face the whole time, but I was just too blind to see it. I look to his leather cord necklace, with the three *Sparrow* feathers attached. *His family.*

Penury.

The liberation of his people, the vengeance for his homeland.

I stare at him, the disgust clear on my face as I spit between gritted teeth. "You're just as bad as them. No one will ever see you as a leader."

I understand his plan now, the speech and performance were all for show. I know what he's going to do because I know that mind of his better than anyone here. Eris' brows raise with a knowing look, for he knows I've figured it out. He bends down, his voice low so only I can hear, "A city that thrives on power always needs a sacrifice," He then regains his normal stature to speak, "I will see you again, little bird. You know you will never be able to fly too far from me. We are made from the same fire you and I."

We are nothing alike. We share nothing other than spilled blood and time. He may have been playing with fire, but I was made from it.

"Fate will not be kind to you Eris, it will not be as forgiving as I am being now. The next time I see you, you will die."

I roll my shoulders and leave him standing in a sea of blood. He knows I have just spared his life, yet still calls after me with one final remark, "And it will be a bloody fight. You underestimate me always, little bird."

And he's right. That was my biggest mistake: underestimating him.

Moving past Axon, my eyes remain straight ahead as I barge his shoulder, his body jerking from the action. I know he is aware of Eris' plan — his true, whole plan — that's why he was gone for so long at Tissa's; he was reporting back to Eris, finalising everything. He lied and kept me in the dark, just as much as Eris did. I can no longer trust him.

"Birdie, I didn't want to keep you from knowing his plan," He tries to take my arm, but I shrug him off. "Stay? For me?"

"You point a gun to my face, then ask me to stay? You're out of your damn mind!" I laugh with a twisted tone, "Freeing me from one torment only to deliver me to another."

Axon only shakes his head, "Come with us Birdie, you'll be safe with us."

My face goes slack as I shake my head, my lip curling. "I will never be safe with either of you." I tense as I let the last question leave my lips, "Did you lie about knowing my father was going to be there with me?"

Axon only looks to the ground; his actions tell me all I need to know.

I let the words fall out of my chest, for he finally needs to hear them, "You remind me of my pain. Every time I look at you, I see the trauma I endured, the beatings and the tortures he had me suffer and made *you* inflict upon me. I don't want to remember that every time I look at your eyes, your face."

I keep my chin up, staring deep into his bright blue eyes, "I don't look at you and feel comfort. No, I now feel sick to my stomach. I feel anger."

His shoulders slump as I deliver the final blow, "You can't be the one to save me from my nightmares, when you're in them."

I don't look back at Axon or Eris as they watch me leave. Dumah and Seven look to their feet, unable to watch. *Traitors. Tissa is better off without him.*

Footsteps behind me turn out to be Jude as he runs to catch up. Does Jude not see that I am a monster? A devil that just sliced a man's throat with a smile? But I don't ask, and we don't say anything as we walk. We're silent, leaving that place behind us, escaping the horrors we inflicted.

"I won't offer my condolences. But I'm sorry you pulled the trigger," I say finally, once we're a far enough distance away.

He cracks his neck before he speaks, "I don't expect you too, knowing what he put you through."

I nod my head, jaw set. "Eris. He's planning something deadly," I admit, "Do you trust your mother? Do you know where she is?" I ask, keeping my gaze focused ahead.

"I don't know where she is," he says, shaking his head. His tone is firm but laced with emotion.

I take a deep breath, "I trust Tissa. We'll go to her, then I will explain."

Jude only nods his head, as his towering body blindly follows my own. I don't know how long we have but I know we need to hurry. I hope in my heart I'm right about Tissa.

We run to Tissa's, breaking a sweat as my body begs me to slow down, to stop pushing so hard. Knocking on her door, it quickly swings open as though she's expecting us. She's standing, her face shell shocked.

"Oh my," she says, opening the door wider for us to enter, "I saw everything... that was... he played the footage you took of the rescue. He showed the city images of the captured people."

"I know," I say, walking further into her living room, but I stop dead when I see Xannu standing near the fireplace — her hair slicked back, eyelids covered in red powder. The faint fading yellow tinge to her cheekbone, *Eris*.

Zirk sits in the chair next to her, his expression full of worry and panic, whilst an unknown man with light skin and long blond hair sits in the chair beside him, their hands clasped together in a tight hold. I notice the gold band they both wear on their ring finger and raise an eyebrow, smiling at them both.

"Got married while I was gone, Zirk?"

He squeezes the man's hand, "I've been married to Nikolai for a long time. I just never told you all."

"Some secrets are worth protecting," Nikolai says with a half-smile. One of his eyes is glazed over with a cloudy sheen; my first thought that maybe he has lost full sight, but soon enough his left eye focuses on me as he speaks again. "Zirk has told me so much about you, Elyria. He's very fond of you."

"We're glad you're safe, Elyria," Zirk says, his statement etched with sorrow. At least Zirk has always been an ally.

Xannu shifts in her seat.

My shoulders tense immediately, guard back up as I cross my arms in front of me.

"I should kill you," I spit.

"You have every right to," she replies, standing, "I was a coward and I fell into his trap."

I let out an exhale, my fight is not with Xannu. With a roll of my neck and flex of my fingers, I breathe. "I guess I was under his spell too."

And I speak the truth. I do forgive her; she was following the orders of a man who sold us a dream. A man who taught us to defend ourselves, whilst throwing the punches, who gave me gifts to redeem his abusive behaviour. She nods her head in silent thanks, but I continue, "He has a bigger plan than this."

Xannu nods her head, "Once you told me he lived in Penury, I started to figure it out as well."

"What plan?" Jude's question is directed at me, "If you want me on your side, you're going to have to start telling me what's going on, Elyria."

I look to him, and my eyes soften a fraction, but then I carefully return my guard as I reply, "He's going to burn Altaras to the ground, and he does not care who burns with it."

Tissa puts her hands over her mouth to cover her gasp. I look to Xannu who only nods her head in agreement.

"He's been telling us this whole time. Feeding us bits of his true plan beneath the façade of getting close enough to you to kill your father. Things he's said to all of us, and to me alone. It was in plain sight," I say. "I don't know how much time we have, but it won't be long. We need to get out of here or we'll burn inside this place."

Jude nods in understanding as Tissa sits down, bracing her head in her hands for a moment of thought, then springs up in a moment of hope.

"The gates! We can go through the gates!" she says triumphantly.

But I know that's not an option. Eris could be there. I doubt he'll let us leave without a fight and, even if he does have access to opening the gates, the gates have never been opened. I'm sure he will try it, but...

"I have an idea." Xannu clears her throat, "but you won't like it."

"Spit it out then."

"While you were gone, I was curious about the water shortages. I searched the maps for how Eris has been coming and going from Penury so often, and how he has remained undetected in his movements."

I think back to my mother's story, how she came to Altaras through a dark underground tunnel. The Penurians probably knew of or made multiple entry points after all these years.

I hold in a breath as Xannu voices the realisation aloud, "He knew so much about the wells."

My eyes light up, "He's been traveling through the water system."

Xannu nods her head, "Yes sort of. Zirk found these amongst Eris' things," She unfurls two maps onto the table. We cram around to look as Zirk points to the west wall, unremarkable on the original map but dots penciled on the second from a later discovery. "There's a sewer tunnel here. That's our way out."

"Sewer," Tissa wrinkles her nose.

The thought draws a low chuckle from my throat as I shake my head, "That bastard has been swimming in shit."

"Will we all be able to get down there? How big is the tunnel?" Jude questions with furrowed brows.

"Hopefully big enough." Zirk answers.

My attention turns to him — the man who trained me to fight. To survive. Seeing him here among us is like a weight lifted from my shoulders, the relief of his allegiance to us washes over me — he defected from Eris, as did the other Sparrows in this room.

Xannu carries on, "We can get as many civilians as possible to the sewers; we can make our escape before the city blows."

Tissa looks confused as she speaks.

"But why does he want to burn the city? It doesn't make sense."

I divert my eyes to look at her sweet innocent face, her scared doe eyes burning into my own. "Eris is from Penury; he has been a spy for them his whole life. We know he has ulterior motives to take the city down because Altaras locked the Penurians out. For centuries, they have been branded savages and thieves. And he wants revenge for his people." I whisper the words my mother once said, her words of warning: *"Allegiance is our core foundation, our oath for all we do."* He was talking of Penury — not the Sparrows. The memory of his speech to the rescued fifty resurfaces. '*We are the future of this city*'. He wasn't talking about the Sparrows — no. Penurians are the future.

"But he got his revenge on the Commanders?" Tissa cries.

I respond quickly with a sternness to my voice. "He is a *vengeful* man. All those weeks ago he spoke to me of power and sacrifice. This is his path to power. His true allegiance to Penury shown by sacrificing Altaras. The place that kept them out when we had so much, and their children starved. He cares nothing for the people of Altaras."

Tissa swallows a lump at the back of her throat, and in the smallest whisper she says, "Dumah?"

My insides tense at the mention of her lover. Of her confidante that has chosen to side with Eris, over what is right. As well as her.

I decide to not shout about his deceit or his allegiance to a monster. I choose to comfort her in her time of pain, like she did for me. "You'll see him again." I say, reaching and holding her shoulder, "Your love will always find you, even if you think it's lost."

Tissa nods at my words, her eyes closing as she steadies her breathing.

"Go get changed, we leave now. Bring only what is essential." Xannu orders.

We all nod our heads and start to search the house, packing things of use in a bag for each, but it's hard to pack for the unknown. I angle my head to Xannu as she stacks cans of food into her pack, "Axon isn't coming, you know that right? You're okay with that?"

Xannu's eyes close for a heartbeat, then says, "My loyalty to Axon died when he sided with Eris. He may be my brother, but I will not forgive him for that."

Jude stands rigid as Tissa walks to him, passing him some clothes, "Dumah kept a spare set here, they will keep you warm."

He nods his head and places the tunics, trousers and spare cloak in his pack, his face blank. I wonder what he thinks of this. Of me. The girl no longer wearing pretty dresses or standing amongst his mother's gardens. I wonder what has become of Odessa Lightfall.

I turn my attention to Xannu.
"My family?" I ask. A simple question that hopes for so much in the response.
She smiles — it's a small smile, but light flashes in her eyes. "Axon got Lila out. She was with your mother the last I heard."
This brings my heart rate down a nudge, comfort to my ears. At least Axon did *one* thing right. My mother can protect them now.

"Weapons," Xannu announces, handing out daggers, guns, and grappling hooks for us all. "I don't think Eris will miss these since he has a whole Altaras armoury to raid," She passes me a set of throwing knives. "You might need these, though." She winks, hoping to restore our bond and I send a wry smile right back at her, placing the cool metal within my suit's compartments.
Then the blast goes off, tossing our bodies to the ground.

Chapter Forty-Four

The shake rattles the house, knocking cups and books from the tables. We brace ourselves on all fours, but the explosion does not wrap us in fire. It's far enough away for us to only feel its effect. Israfil really is ringing the bells of judgement with his bombs.

"We need to leave!" I shout, racing out the door as the others follow.

Xannu barks an order, "Get as many people as possible to follow, now!"

Smoke rises near us, the bomb having gone off in the direction of the Citadel. Tissa, Xannu, Zirk, Nikolai, and even Jude, banging on doors as people start to shout and scream after hearing the blast. The wise follow us in our attempt to flee but others, resistant to reason, stay. Children carried by their parents, the older dragging behind as they follow us blindly. We pull them out of their homes, shouting at as many as we can to listen to us — to any elite, medi, or rook we find, to hurry and leave everything behind. We don't have the luxury of time on our side.

But people resist. Some lock their doors and refuse our cries. They are fearful of the unknown and would rather burn than save themselves.

My body screams at me to stop. It needs to rest. It's tired and needs to heal, but I shove the pain down and ignore it, my adrenaline taking over. Luckily, Tissa's house is closer to the west wall than the Sparrow base, otherwise we wouldn't make it in time.

Tissa has tears streaming down her face as she begs people to follow us — a shy little bird out of her comfort zone, panicking and pleading with people in a desperate attempt to save them. Jude shocks me, his actions full of decisive, strong command, omitting a presence that makes people listen to him instantly, voicing orders sternly and full of confidence. His emotions are shoved behind a wall, focused on the task at hand.

The vibrations of the next bomb hits me first, the sound, and then the heat. I'm thrown to my back as the blast knocks me over. I hear nothing except the ring in my ears as I look around me. A building is on fire, its windows blown out as it burns bright from the inside. Orange flames lick the sky as it engulfs the home. The roaring fire swiftly travels to the house beside it, trapping more buildings in its deadly grasp.

Two arms come under my shoulder blades, hoisting me up. I blink the dizziness away, turning to face a man I have never seen before. He hastily helps me to my feet and ushers me forward to safety with crazed eyes, urging me forward. *Run*, his unspoken words say. The man turns on his heel and sprints towards others who have fallen.

Steadying myself, I watch the mess Eris has caused — the destruction inflicted upon this city.

I'm out of breath by the time we reach the west wall. My legs burn and my stitches are likely open and bleeding. My muscles beg me to stop, but my mind refuses. I'm nowhere near as quick or stealthy as I run. I stumble and am slow to catch my breath. My injuries make this so much harder than it should be. I curse Marik and Red Face for creating this setback, for making me weaker in this moment when I need all the strength and fighting power I can muster.

Another blast goes off in the centre of the city and again the fire catches and begins to spread amongst the homes. The screams of Altaras' people start to get louder against the sound of roaring flames.

"Xannu, where do we go?" I scream to her. Zirk is close behind, his eyes dart around the trees — looking for something. Xannu's frantic, watching the explosions, her mouth open in shock.

"Xannu, focus!" I snap, my adrenaline getting the better of me. We need to move quickly. There is no time to watch and mourn yet.

Xannu jerks her head away from the red city and looks around. We stand before the thick tree line, the golden wall standing just beyond but out of sight. The crowd of people gather, crying and panicked as they frantically look to us for guidance.

"There's a bunker around here in the trees, it should be directly across from the west point of the wall," Zirk shouts, dashing into the trees with Xannu hot on his heels.

Another bomb goes off and the crowd collectively shudder, gripping each other with closed eyes and shaking bodies. The flames start to rise from all directions, everywhere we look the city is burning. Altaras is burning. Fire comes closer to us with every passing moment. I look to Jude who carries a small girl in his arms; she cowers into his neck as he soothes her, rubbing her back with his hand. His mouth moves as if consoling her; I divert my eyes from them, focusing on the tree line, waiting for Xannu and Zirk to return. After a few moments, Xannu bounds out of the foliage with a shout, waving her hand for us to follow.

There, deep amidst the undergrowth, stands a concrete slab with an iron door. The entrance hidden by whoever had used it last; piles of leaves and branches are pushed to the side, uncovered by Zirk who stands next to it with folded arms. Zirk unbolts the metal door by its sliding bar. The iron door, heavily rusted, scrapes across to reveal a ladder plunging deep underground. They look to me expectantly and I quickly understand what they are asking of me. Who's going to be the first to venture down? Who's going to take the risk? They know I can out-climb both of them, even in my current state.

"Ladies first," I say to them both with a wink, "I'm so sick of being underground," I groan. Quickly, I swing my legs over, planting my feet firmly on the metal steps. Before I make my descent, a wailing mother rushes forward, holding her child in her arms.

"Please. *Please* take her for me. I can't carry her and climb," she screams.

I don't need to think twice; I look at the sweet innocent girl clinging to her mother's chest and hold out my arms.

"Quickly, pass her to me," I order, beckoning her forward.

The blond-haired toddler is thrust into my chest; the weight of her makes my burned, bruised, *cut* skin scream in agony. Her mother wails and puts a shaking hand on my shoulder, stroking her child's hair with the other. Her gratitude is shown as she nods her thanks. My eyes meet hers, and with a quick nod, I descend. The girl clings to me as we go.

"It's fine, you're safe. Just hold on tight. Mummy is just going to follow us down, okay?" I coo as she buries her head into my neck. The action brings tears to my eyes as her small frame presses against the wound that circles around my neck, the reminder of the collar once etched into my skin.

The climb down is quicker than expected, but slowly the light fades and we are swallowed by darkness. I climb further and further away from the light, finally stepping on the floor with a splash. My boots are soaked in thick grimy water. My cloak trails behind me as we wade forward towards a silver speck at the end of the sewer tunnel. Other than that, it's pitch back. I feel around with my free arm, fumbling for walls or anything in front of me.

"Shit," Xannu mutters behind me, her feet now also splashing in the knee-high water.

"Literally," I grumble.

"It's okay, we're going to find somewhere safe. It's all going to be fine," I tell the girl, holding her tight against me. Telling her for her sake, but also mine. Being plunged into darkness once more makes my stomach churn, reliving the fear of being back in that cell. But I can hear the people following me — their cries and splashes as they hit the ground, plunged into darkness too. I'm not alone here.

Wading forward, the light becomes brighter with every step and my eyes begin to adjust. I can finally see my hand in front of me, and the light turns out to be a hole where water rushes out, cascading over a lip in the distance. But our progress is halted by a heavy iron grille. I feel around the bars — there must be a way to get past this.

I hoist the girl higher so that the sewage doesn't touch her, and crouch to feel the bars beneath the water. Thankfully, my hands strike gold and reveal the bars cut away, leaving a hole undetectable above the water, but big enough so that an individual can easily get through. In and out. I scowl at the thought of Eris and how easy it was for him to sneak in and out of the city, and how stupid the Consulate could be for not securing their city or knowing that their waterways were breeched.

"Xannu take her," I say, passing the child over. She takes the toddler with an outstretched arm, although a whimpering boy is attached to her hip. Xannu's eyes flash with sadness and despair as the children hang tightly to her body.

I put a hand on her shoulder and squeeze. "I will kill him," I say to Xannu, "I will kill him for what he's done to us." With a grimace, I turn away and crouch. Holding my breath, I sink under the murky water, propelling myself by grasping onto the metal grate. Through the hole and out the other side. Spitting and wiping the sludge from my face and hair, I try not to retch. If my wounds aren't already infected, I'm sure they will be now. I'm kneeling, shoulder deep in wastewater with my hands through the hole.

"Don't be frightened, it's just a little wet and smelly but then you'll be out the other side like me," I smile to the children; the boy is half submerged in grimy water, but the girl waits in Xannu's arms: their faces pale, tears streaming down their cheeks. "Hold your breath for me, like a good girl, like you're waiting to blow out a candle on your birthday cake."

The little girl stares at me and holds a breath. Quickly, Xannu kneels before she can open her mouth, pushing her down, her little hands flailing to find my own. I grip them, holding onto her as I pull her under and though the bars.

"All done. Safe now," I say to her once she resurfaces. The girl splutters, clawing at her face with chubby hands. I wipe away some of the grime, but she doesn't make a sound, not even one tear.

Xannu and I repeat the action, passing the children through, as some of the adults join my side to help hold them above the water. We have just under one hundred civilians in the tunnel — *not nearly enough.*

"Tissa, don't look so frightened. If these babies can do it, you can." I assure her, smiling and winking though the grate. She settles her nerves and crouches, her bright yellow dress floating upwards as she submerges. Her nose wrinkles in disgust as she surfaces next to me.

Xannu passes a couple of our packs through the bars, some small enough not to get wet. Then, she pulls herself through and follows the group that have started to walk to the opening. But I hang back. We are not complete. My panic rises.

"Jude?" I call out. He didn't pass me, and I can't see him in the darkness. "Jude!" I shout again. My hands grip the metal as I try to search the darkness for any sign of him. A few seconds later, I hear splashing as Jude's tall muscular build appears as he wades quickly towards me. My heart rate slows now he's in view, tension relaxing. His face looks worried as he searches mine, voicing his concern.

"What's wrong? What's happened?"

"I… I just couldn't find you," I say, my voice trembling. "I was..." But the words don't seem to leave my lips. *I was worried*, I want to say.

Jude bends low, feeling for the bars. Then with a deep breath, he dunks beneath the water, reappearing on my side of the tunnel.

"I wanted to go back for more people, but the fires… they're at the tree line. I couldn't get through. It's too late." It pains him to say it. This Jude is so different to the arrogant boy I first met. It's unimaginable that this pure, kind soul was inside him all along. And I ruined him.

"We did as much as we could, Jude. You did what you could." My eyes search his.

I want to say more to ease his pain, but I'm afraid he will not want to hear any words coming out of my mouth. Jude's eyes stay locked on mine, and for a fraction of a second, they soften.

"Let's go," he breathes, wiping the murky water from his face. It clings to the tips of his blond hair, the darker strands plastered against his forehead.

I lead the way, wading through the water to catch up with the rest of the group.

Jude and I find everyone gathered at the edge of the hole, the water rushing at their feet. The bright light beams though the opening; I go to shield my eyes, but lower my hand.

"What is everyone looking at?" I ask, pushing my way to the front as Jude follows closely behind.

"Elyria, come see," Xannu says, wide eyed and mouth gaping. Her hand finds my own, interlacing our fingers. As I stand between her and Tissa, I follow their gaze. I stumble back, only to knock into the hard muscle that is Jude. Regaining my footing, I stare — my mouth open. I'm making this up in my head, I say to myself. I must be.

Blinking again, the scene is still before me, I gaze upon the snowy peaks of the grey mountains, the tips touching the clouds as if in greeting. They cascade down into the valley below, filled with trees so dense, so green, you would get lost in seconds. The hills roll in the distance. Streams flow down into ravines from all directions. I squint my eyes to see better, but the same image, the same wonderful view remains unchanged. Like a painting, like something dreamed. The air is fresh through my nose; it's cool and warm all at once, stroking my skin. Little gusts of breeze fly through my hair and I close my eyes to take it in.

I can't believe this is real. We've been kept from this our whole lives.

My mother was born in this beautiful land. My ancestors lived on this soil, they smelt the same air as this, looked at the same mountains. How could my mother forget this place, how could she not fight to return to this haven?

The sounds of people weeping snap me from my trance, from the thoughts rushing at me. Everyone is looking at the view, crying and hugging each other as they stare into the distance. To the outside.

"But they said Penury was a waste land?" a woman's voice gasps.

"How can this be?" another cries.

Because they lie. They all lie.

I don't know what I expected to see — perhaps a desolate area of sand, or dead trees stationed by dried up lakes — not this luscious vibrant valley filled with healthy, thriving earth. I clear my throat before I speak.

"I don't think the Consulate even knew it was here. They were always told Penury was a wasteland. I guess after so many years they started to believe their own lies," I squeeze Tissa and Xannu's hands, all of us unable to take our eyes off the beauty before us.

Zirk adds, his voice soft as he talks, "Maybe it was wasteland, but just grew back after all these years."

"Maybe it did," I say under my breath.

We don't have time to stand and admire; I don't know what Eris has planned. None of us do. It could be more bombs, or even demolishing the wall. The next steps are uncertain, so we must move. And fast. The water rushes to a pool in the ground below. As I peer over the edge, it falls almost fifty feet, plummeting into a rocky lagoon. Stepping around the lip of the tunnel, I discover a small ledge which holds another metal ladder, sturdy. It's covered in vines and foliage to hide its presence.

"We need to get out of here," I say to everyone, "Eris could have more plans for the destruction of this city, so we need to move quickly."

Xannu looks to me, then to the ladder, terror on her face, "The children?" she questions. "They won't be able to climb down safely; it's such a huge drop."

We both look at all the small bodies carried by the adults.

I survey the group. We must have about twenty children among us; some of them are capable of climbing, but toddlers hang from their parents' hips.

"We'll carry as many as we can," I say to her, to which she nods her head, but the worry remains clear on her face.

I position myself with the valley to my back and the group to my front, raising my voice so that everyone can hear me. My voice echoes in the tunnel as the words leave my mouth.

"That ladder is just like the one we've all just climbed down. It will be a little more slippery from the waterfall, so everyone needs to take it slow and grip tightly. Don't panic and we'll all be okay."

I hold out my arm for someone to pass me a child — the same blond toddler is pushed into my arms.

"Hello again, little one," A small smile softens my face, "You're going to be the first Altaras girl on new soil." I say to her. She looks back at me with big wide eyes, "Just hold me as tightly as you did before, okay?"

The girl grips her arms around my neck, her little legs squeezing my middle — right where I can feel my stitches pulling and tearing as I make the second descent today. The metal bars are slippery and cold beneath my grip as water splashes over me; I flinch, suppressing the fear that now comes with water cascading over my face, pushing my torture to the back of my mind. This is no time to be scared, I say to myself. You must be strong for them. Show them how unbreakable you are.

The climb is easier than I expect as the girl weighs next to nothing. Above, the others join me on the ladder as they start their climb down. With an arm looped around the step, and the girl tightly wrapped around my chest, I turn my head to look at the view behind me. The vast stretches of evergreen forest and grey mountains in the distance, I smile up at the sky as the fresh air whips around me in greeting. The silk fabrics around my neck flutter behind me, dancing in the wind. The heat from the winter sun beams down on us, drying our hair and warming our faces. I can even hear bird song against the rush of the waterfall as they call to each other, swooping above the trees in flight. The sky is limitless to them. They fly free.

Chapter Forty-Five

The rocky ground is just one step below us as I look out to my surroundings. The bottom of the waterfall creates a sewage lagoon, rolling down the hill in a small stream. Thick forest is all around us, spreading out in all directions as I rotate my head. It's so dense, I'm not sure what direction to take, or what our next step is.

As promised, I look to the little girl, hooking my arm around the step and holding her close with the other "Ready?" I ask. Her bright blue eyes are answer enough.

She unhooks her legs and releases her clasped hands so that I can place her down onto the ground; she stands on wobbly legs but looks around with wide eyes.

Right here, right now, this little girl won't understand or appreciate the significance of this moment, but one day she will.

I step down, reaching for her outstretched hand as we survey our surroundings. One by one, the people of Altaras finally plant their feet on new soil, staring in awe and hope. Faces are uniformly tight with anxiety, but most look up at the huge golden wall now in view, glistening against the evening sun. Even from the other side, the golden wall shines, highlighting its intricate patterns. It stretches so high, causing a crick in the neck yet, even then, you are unable to glimpse the top. People murmur and point, gaping at the cage, blocking out the sounds of the explosions, the roaring flames, and the screams.

Zirk, Nikolai, Xannu, Tissa and Jude stand to the side of the gathered crowd, scanning ahead for any signs of danger. The stronger of the group climb back up to carry the remaining children down waiting patiently above. It was a tedious task, a necessity for their safety.

With everyone safely down and awaiting instructions, Zirk begins to speak. "We should head west," He points in that direction, "the water seems to be heading that way, downhill. It's our best option. We must find a clean water source."

I nod my head and wring out my soaking hair, throwing it over my shoulder as I speak.

"West it is. Xannu, can you stay at the back and make sure everyone is staying together? We'll take the lead."

"Of course," she says with a nod of her head, sheathing her pistol back into the holster at her hip. She turns to leave and informs the group to follow us.

We trudge for what seems like hours, going deeper and deeper into the forest as we search for water. Wildflowers litter our path, carpets of them growing lusciously amongst the trees. Children are being carried whilst others limp, dragging their exhausted bodies forward over rocks and fallen branches. The terrain is unlike anything they have ever experienced before. The journey is mostly silent as we all survey our surroundings in awe; the canopy of trees makes it hard to see the sky, but I know from the chill in the air that it now nears nightfall, the darkness slowly creeping in. The scatter of bugs and animals keep us alert, for we are in their territory now. We walk blindly amongst them.

Zirk shouts from up ahead, finally alerting us of a discovery; him and Nikolai both wave their arms in the air, beckoning us over. As we emerge from the pine trees, the canopy opens, revealing the night sky. The frenzy of stars reflects off the still water in the huge lake; the night in all directions, sparkling and casting a glow around us. As we file around, we gape at the scene. My feet have a mind of their own as they walk forward out of the tree line and into the water's edge. My boots submerge. Crouching down, cool liquid touches my fingertips as I create patterns with each movement, making ripples in the glass-like water. I pick a pebble from the bottom and rub its smooth surface between my thumb and forefinger, closing my eyes to the sounds of crickets. The ripples could be fish swimming alongside me; I relish in the sound of nature.

Still knelt at the lake's edge, I turn to the group who watch me intently. Even the Sparrows that are here wait for me to act. To say something. It has now dawned on me that, in the mess of all of this, they watch me. They study my moves and what I'll do next. Unconsciously perhaps, I have taken the lead and they follow. In this moment, they wait for me to tell them what to do.

The men and women of Altaras look to me, worry clear on their faces. They look for guidance — to tell them they are safe. I look at Xannu, and she responds with a slight nod of her head, urging me to go on like she shares the thoughts circling in my head. Fear can make even the strongest of us need comfort. Words to ease our panic.

So, I stand, facing them, the water still at my ankles, and I call out. My voice is strong, ignoring the lump that forms in my throat as I speak, "I'm so sorry we couldn't save more." I raise my chin higher, looking to Xannu again. Maybe she's thinking of Briar, wondering if she made it out, or of Seven, who took the side of Eris. I look to Tissa with tears in her eyes for Dumah. The friends who may now be our enemies.

"I'm so sorry this has happened," I swallow the lump, "I give you my word that I will never rest until justice is served. I will protect you all with my life; I *swear* that I will fight for us to the end. We should stay here until we know more and figure out what's next." I look to my Sparrows and to Jude who looks back at me, waiting for me to continue. Tissa's glassy eyes meet mine.

"We won't be able to go back. But for now, we're safe, we have all this land to explore," I smile to them. "To move on, we must be strong and not dwell in the past. This is a new beginning. We have been blessed. We are free from tyranny. We can live a better life."

Over the next few hours, the group starts to settle; we manage to get a fire started, placed in the middle of the bank between the tree line and the water's edge. Our people now sit by it to stay warm — some sleep but others only stare into the flames, lost in the thought of their destroyed homes. The thought of loved ones that did not make it out alive.

Tissa sleeps near the fire, the blanket she had packed is now washed and dried, resting over two sleeping children close to her side. Xannu sits gazing into the flames, her legs crossed under her as she flares her nostrils, looking at the embers as they rise into the night sky. Zirk and Nikolai sit close together talking in hushed voices.

Jude sits by the water's edge on a rock facing the mountain; his blond hair shines like ice under the moonlight as his back faces me, his black tunic now dry and rolled at the sleeves. Slowly, my body takes over my mind, as I go to sit next to him on the cold surface of the rock. My feet stretch out in front of me, and I cross them at the ankles, leaning back on my arms. The smell of Jude — of cut crass, rain and earth — it mingles with the smell of pine trees and of the wildflowers next to us. I breathe it all in, consumed by it.

"I understand if you think I'm a monster," I admit, breaking the silence. My face is now trained on his eyes that slowly drift to mine.

Jude picks up a stone and throws it into the lake with a splash as ripples appear.

"I don't think you're a monster," he says, his voice low as he speaks. "At first, I was angry that you faked everything. After all, I was captivated by you. By your beauty — your mind. But after I found out, I realised you did it for the sake of everyone else. The way you protected those people, I saw the fire in your eyes, the passion that burns inside you to do what's right." Jude swallows, then continues, "I must put my anger aside and think *why* you manipulated me. I was the easiest target, and it was for the greater good."

My jaw clenches, I'm unable to look at him now. "Don't say that," I whisper, "it wasn't all pretense."

I take a breath as the truth finally comes out, as I finally allow myself to share the emotions I kept hidden for so long. "You gave me the time to breathe. To be free. To avert my mind from Eris' abuse, allowing me to be above ground after so long kept away. Jude, you gave me peace in those few moments away from it all. That day we spent in your mother's greenhouse, I wanted to tell you everything. I was scared; I was *trapped* by him, bound by his authority." I pause as the words roll off my tongue, my eyes falling to the ground. The truth he needs to hear spills out of my mouth, "It was real. It was real for me."

I bite my lip, still staring at the stones. We have both lost our homes, our family. Our fathers are dead, and possibly our mothers. I have killed people. Slit someone's throat in front of him.

I broke his trust.

I would not be surprised if he doesn't believe my confession now. But still, his actions over the past few weeks are all I can think about; he continues to be by my side. He *chose* to escape with us rather than stay behind with Eris. And, after everything, he followed me. Rather than taking the safe option to be with them.

"Why did you follow me? You could have stayed with them, with Eris," I ask.

Jude takes a while to answer as we sit in silence.

The muscles in his shoulders tense as he speaks, "When I saw you in that cell. What they did to your body, your mind. The aftermath of what you had gone though. Something broke inside of me. It changed me," His lip curls, like the memory is physically painful, the anger bubbling inside of him threatening to break out. "I should hate you, but that is not a possibility. Hate, and you, will never align in my mind. But I can't trust you Elyria, you've burned that trust to the ground."

His words cut deeper than anything I have felt before. My mouth turns dry as I close my eyes. *What did I expect?* For him to forgive me after everything I did to him?

His deep brown eyes shine with flecks of gold under the moonlight as I finally look to him. Our gaze burns with something — I can't even begin to understand it. Jude shifts to lean back on his arms, our hands so close I could graze him with my fingertips, if either of us move an inch.

I could never hate him either. Our lives have been bonded with blood and memories.

Jude looks back out to the water. The trust Jude has for me may never be restored.

After all the betrayals I have faced, losing Jude would rip me apart entirely.

But that's a chance I'm willing to take because I feel it in my bones, my soul calling for him. Even if he does not feel that same tug, my soul pines for Jude Lightfall.

"I promise to you, I will never lie to you again. I swear it on my blood and breath," I say, looking out at the cascading ripples in the water, that slowly still to create the mirror of the night sky once more. All I can do is to try and make him forgive me, make him believe my words are sincere, to tell him my truth with as much conviction as my heart possesses. Giving him a tiny shred of hope that he can trust me; all I have left for him to take. Even if we are too far over the edge, too deep in the lies.

In the corner of my eye, the hint of a roguish smile appears on his lips; he cracks his neck and smiles, "Did I mention that you look better brunette?"

A slight smile tugs on my lips as I playfully push his side with my shoulder. His words send warmth rushing though me, against the ice in my veins and the anger that festers away. He calms me like the ripples in the lake, like the soft sound of the wind.

As we sit alone staring at the water, the stars shine above us, the moon glows in the distance. We don't speak another word, only admiring the view. Sometimes, silence is the only conversation you need.

~

I search for the tallest tree I can find and begin to climb it. Using what little strength I have left, I haul myself up despite my aches and wounds screaming at me to stop. To rest. But I resist and keep climbing. The bark cuts my hands and twigs scratch at me but, I reach the top of the tree, holding onto the trunk to swing my legs around a thick branch. The needles of the tree part so that I can see into the distance. I finally see over its edge: the gold wall and the flames that roar beyond it. Fire dances across the sky, the embers rising like shooting stars. Thick, black smoke clouds above like a blanket. If I close my eyes, I can almost hear the screams, but the roar of the flames engulfs the sounds.

All I can do is watch the city I despise crash and burn, because of me...

The buildings collapse as Altaras falls, the ring of burning tree line flickers off the golden wall. Even in the dark, you can see the glistening of the metal as it glows against the flames. So many people are dead. So many people we could not save. Innocent lives taken only for vengeance and spite. He did this for Penury and the cost was bigger than anyone could realise. But tears don't fall, and they don't threaten to break, for only rage boils and fills my stomach, rising to burn bright in my eyes, igniting me from the inside. Emotions of sadness and pain are locked, bolted, and sealed shut — never to emerge. As I stare into the flames of Altaras, anger pulses through my veins, like a switch turned on. I'm ready. No longer will I be at anyone's mercy. If I cannot be better than him, I will be so much worse.

The need for retribution burns in me. It's much stronger than Eris' ever will be.

I'm not the girl underground in the Sparrows' nest or a captive locked in a cell by the Consulate or even confined by the walls of Altaras. I'm a bird, stretching my wings, flying into the unknown world without anyone to report to. No one to take orders from. Not as a Sparrow or even a Nightingale, but a bird of prey ready to sink my talons into Eris. The puppet master throughout all of this, who had everyone under his thumb.

Not me. Not anymore. No longer will I participate in his game. No one can hurt you if you take that power away.

I climb down the tree, back to the camp of people we saved: the hundred people who made it out alive. I sit across from the fire, next to Xannu who rests her head on my shoulder. An action we have never shared before, but I smile at the newness of it, and the warmth it brings. I spin my dagger between my fingers, feeling its cool metal against my fingertips as Jude sits on the other side of our makeshift camp, watching my every move from behind the fire. He angles his head, face illuminated by the light, casting a warm glow across his features. We stare at each other through the flames and the rising embers.

The true enemy is one we never saw coming. Over and over in my head, I repeat the new mantra that will keep me going. Spur me on. It will keep me strong, keep me from breaking.

You will not be broken. You are safe. Eris will die. I will become his wrath.

I think of all the ways I could kill him, all the ways he could suffer. Because now I am on the hunt, now I am a bird of prey.

Epilogue

The sound of footsteps thrashing through the trees wakes me as I steady my gaze into the glowing fire, keeping us all warm. Everyone is asleep now as dusk is upon us.

Branches snap and the rustling of leaves draws closer. In an instant, I jump to my feet, my throwing knives clasped in my hands as Xannu joins me with her gun raised, aimed at the tree's edge. Our eyes are deadly, focused on our intruder.

But as the figure emerges from the trees, I lower my knives as the air is ripped out of my lungs. Signaling for Xannu to lower her pistol, she hesitantly follows my command.

Ragged breaths escape her lips, and her eyes are bloodshot as she sets them on me. My mother opens her mouth to give us her message.

"Elyria, you need to prepare. He's coming. He's coming for you all."

Acknowledgments

Firstly, I would like to thank you, the person reading my beautiful, harrowing story. I poured my whole heart and soul into City of Birds at a time when I needed an outlet to express all the emotions, pain and struggles I was facing at that time. Writing helped me when I needed it most. So, thank you for deciding to read Elyria's journey, and mine because we are so intertwined, it means more to me that anyone will ever comprehend. Books help us in more ways that we think. Thank you to Harry, my love, my biggest supporter, the one who listens and never rushes me - you know me better than I know myself, I couldn't have done this without you. To my family and friends, thank you for waiting patiently in my process, I hope you're happy and enjoy. Eden Northover, my editor, you were the first person to ever read City of birds, you gave me the confidence as a first-time writer and helped me so much in bringing this to life. Irene Martinez for making a beautiful cover. Daniel Fernandez for the amazing Unity Building illustration. Harry for the illustration of Elyria (inspired by another unknown artist) Lastly thank you Chiara and Laura for being the most positive, supportive, uplifting friends - being on this writer journey with you both is life changing. Eda, Maya P, Anna k, Naomi, Lance, Hayley and all my author/reader friends, supporters and followers, I never could have done this without your constant friendship, advice, our long in depth talks about WIPs, the worlds we've built, and where our characters are going next. Most importantly your support. City of Birds was made for all of you as well as myself - I hope you can resonate with the characters, laugh, cry, get angry at them, I hope you found yourself in some of them - They are for you.

I hope you all continue this journey with me, Elyria and all the characters in City of Birds - our story has only just begun.

Thank you

~ E x

About the Author

Elisha Reids was born and raised in the South of England and completed a degree in HR with Psychology in 2021. She however realized that her calling in life is writing, putting her dreams and thoughts to paper. Elisha harbors a love of strong character development, creative world building, jaw dropping plot twists – and of course romance! As a passionate advocate for mental health and wellbeing, Elisha is always open about her own struggles, and tries to depict this in her characters in a way that is raw and honest, but also supportive to those who may resonate.

Follow me on @elishasreads tiktok

Follow me on @elishareids Instagram

Add City of Birds to your Goodreads! Don't forget to leave a review x

Printed in Great Britain
by Amazon

36396389R00189